Groggy was an understatement was the first thought as he climbed through the fog that was his mind, and tried to wake up. He vaguely remembered coming to earlier, and thinking the most ridiculous things, ever. He paused for a second, not even breathing, as he assessed his condition. His head was still pounding, but slightly less this time. He exhaled in relief. Maybe he was going to live after all. Whoever had found him, he owed them a big…

He froze as he tried to touch his head and see how bad the injury was. He heard chains and his hand could not move any further. Chains. He clenched his hand and felt cold metal on his wrist. Eyes wide open, he jerked his head up, almost screaming with the pain to look at his hand. Following the chain attached to the cuff on his wrist he saw it was very securely attached to a cement post. He was shackled. Shackled! *What the holy fuck is going on?* Head snapping in the other direction, he found that arm in the same state. *Someone is going to get their ass beat!* Leaning forward he went to stand up and found out he could only lean about six inches forward before the chain ran out…

On. The. Collar. Around. His. Neck.

Also by Jacqueline Paige

ANIMAL SENSES
1 *Heart*
2 *Scent*
3 *Passion*

MAGIC SEASONS ROMANCE
1 *Beltane Magic*
2 *Solstice Heat*
3 *Harvest Dreams*
4 *Autumn Dance*
5 *Winter Mist*

Dreams
Three steamy stories that started with a dream

Curses
Two tales of curses.

After the Silence
Volume 1 Bree

SINGLE TITLES
Solitary Witchling
Salvation
Café Serenity

<u>Writing As: J. Risk</u>

THE ALTEREALM SERIES
1 *The Huntress*
2 *The Seer*
3 *The Empath*
4 *The Witch*
5 *The Chronos*
6 *The Warrior*
7 *The Telepath*
8 *The Healer*
9 *The Kinetic* (coming soon)

PASSION

Animal Senses Book 3

Jacqueline Paige

Published by FRP
Copyright © 2019, 2020 Roxane Kerr
Edited by Gaele L. Hince
Cover art by: Off the Wall Creations

Excerpts from *Salvation* by Jacqueline Paige and *The Huntress Book 1 in the Alterealm Series* by J. Risk copyright ©2016, 2019 Roxane Kerr

ISBN (paperback): 978-1-7774387-3-9
ISBN (digital): 978-1-7774387-2-2

When *Heart* was first published I had a trilogy in mind. After writing the second book, I knew there were too many wonderful, intriguing characters to stop at three stories.

The trilogy has been reworked to become the *Animal Senses Series*.

Find a comfortable corner and hang on… this is going to be quite the ride. I hope you enjoy reading it as much as I do writing it!

Jacqueline

Prologue

Calum paused when the voicemail came on. Devin was probably busy with his mate, again. He grinned, "Guess your busy with… royal mating… *stuff*." He chuckled, "I'm at the bottom of some mountain, in the middle of the back-country nowhere—even more than your camp *nowhere* kind of deal. I've tracked my missing clan members to here." He glanced up the incline to the dense, foliage-covered mountain. "I'll let you know when I find out more." He hung up and sighed. Maybe being away right now was a good thing. With Devin newly mated and Kelsey coming home to Gage… it was going to be messy with a whole lot of *true-mate* issues that Calum didn't have, couldn't relate to, and hoped he'd never have to go through himself. His responsibilities with the alliance didn't leave him time for those distractions.

Turning off his phone, he stuffed it into the waterproof bag and sealed it, then jammed it into his pack. Normally he didn't take his phone with him, but this was an unknown area and knowing he'd have it, just in case, made him feel better. The challenge would be not to lose his pack, as he'd been known to do occasionally.

The small village he'd stopped at had warned him away from coming here, despite confirming they'd seen the men from his clan in the photos he'd shown. They'd said there was bad *juju* on this mountain, and few ever came down off it. Calum wasn't sure about the juju garbage, but if there was even a small chance of the males from his clan being on this mountain, he was going up to find them.

That little village was on the strange side. The way the people watched him gave him the creeps. He wondered if they could smell an outside shifter in their territory, but he picked up no scents that led him to believe there were any shifters among them. He may be paranoid, and they could only be watchful of strangers. With the missing males from his clan, and Tomas' association taking females from other clans, he was allowed to suspect everyone of nefarious intentions. If anyone had a problem with his suspicious nature, they could eat dirt as far as he was concerned.

It had taken him over an hour to get this far up with his car. He was definitely considering getting a truck when he got back. His car hadn't been much good for off-roading. He looked around the area he'd parked. It may have, at one time, been a parking area or rest stop, but it was long deserted, overgrown and ignored. If anyone managed to get up here on the not-really-a-road trail he'd taken, they were more than welcome to break into his car. Locking it, he tucked the keys behind the front tire's rim. He'd learned a long time ago to never take keys on trips into the great wilderness. Losing your clothes or pack was almost always a certainty, losing your keys left you trapped.

He looked back down the way he'd come again before turning toward the incline. "This should be fun." He sighed and started climbing.

His senses were on overload, so many scents, all familiar, but not, at the same time. He took his time moving through the thick vegetation, checking for anything that might set off his animal instincts. His cat was already on full alert, which wasn't necessarily unusual, but it made him more aware of what was around him, and a little jittery as well. As soon as he found something to follow, he'd shift and let his animal side take over the tracking.

He walked along a flat area, happy for the break from the upward climb, watching for somewhere he could stow his pack so it wouldn't be found, not that he anticipated this being a high traffic area, he just couldn't take it with him. Nothing said 'not a normal wild animal' like a big black cat carrying a pack around his neck. He chuckled at that thought.

A few times his cat moved against his skin, telling him to hurry up. He wasn't sure if it was the new area to explore, or if he sensed something, but it wasn't like he was drawing this out like a holiday or anything.

When he finally found a spot he'd be able to locate again, he stripped down and stuffed his clothes in the pack. For half a heartbeat, he thought about pinging his location to Devin, just in case, but doubted there would be any signal here.

Shifting, he stretched to his full length and then wasted no time getting moving. This was more like it, four paws meant for this terrain carried him faster than inflexible boots and man-length strides ever would.

When he cleared the dense growth, he paused and scented the area around him. There was a faint smell that tasted familiar, but it was too difficult to tell where it was coming from. He crept through the plush leaves along the ground, trying to see if he could pick it up again. At least one of the missing men had been this way, but not recently enough to be able to pinpoint their every step. The growth here was like it was at Devin's camp, but on steroids. The leaves a deeper green, the trees were twice as thick and taller. All this made staying out of sight easy, but seeing what was around him more difficult.

As soon as he located the members of his clan, he was going to find out what had led them here. They had enough area to run and roam, that was a hell of a lot closer to home. There was no reason to come this far and trek up this stunning chunk of dirt. If it turned out to be for some stupid hormone-enticed reason… he was going to smack them in the head. With a large paw. A few times, at least. He had enough going on right now with Devin learning the ropes to lead the Alliance, he didn't need to be traipsing around some damn mountain looking for stray cats.

Stopping, he sniffed the air. There was… Crouching low, he tried to identify the scents. A nervous twitch moved over his coat, something was off. He inhaled and took more time trying to analyze what he was smelling. Slowing his breathing, he listened. Ears flat, alarms going off in his head, he looked around him. With years of carefully honed animal intuition, he knew he needed to get the hell out of here. Now.

Spinning back in the direction he'd just come from, he paused for a heartbeat and realized he was too late.

Chapter One

Shaelan stood with her arms crossed, looking out the large bay window. From this viewpoint atop the ridge, she could see down into the whole village. This view alone should make the position of the village healer a coveted job. With the scenery and quiet space, who wouldn't want this?

The job wasn't popular though, then again to live in this house and hold that position, you had to start training and learning early in life. From around eight years old, the lessons started. With the remote location of the settlement, you had to learn every plant, animal, and mineral, on the mountain then utilize all you could. Accessing modern medicines was virtually impossible. They had some brought up in the regular supply runs, but those took a week, sometimes two, depending on the season. Knowing how to deal with any situation using what was at hand was of the utmost importance.

Shaelan had known this was for her, even when she was a child. While her friends were playing hide and seek, she was studying the plants on the ground. It felt like a calling, even then. She'd gone against her father's wishes and climbed the hill to the medicine woman's home and knocked on the door to ask for training. Since then, she hadn't thought of anything but healing.

Her mother supported her, when not in sight of her father. Honestly, Shae could never recall any tender moments with the man. He looked at her with... disappointment? Loathing? Something, she wasn't sure what, she always saw it in his eyes. Billie, her best friend, said it was because Shae wasn't a boy. So, essentially it was nothing that was her fault.

Turning back to the window, she watched—what was his name again? Morris... she watched him come up the path to get Nona-Eve, their healer, medicine woman and Shaelan's mentor. He was one of the guards at their prison. A place Shae had never been, but knew when she took over it would be on her list of responsibilities. Something she was both looking forward to and dreading at the same time. Nona-Eve was, she had no idea how old, but when she retired, Shae would be *the* medicine woman in the village.

You weren't just the healer of the people, but all of nature as well. Helping the animals in the area also helped the environment the people needed to live in. Shae took her responsibilities very seriously. She planned on being the best medicine woman in the history of the village.

It had taken her a year to persuade the village council and her father, the head of it, to let her go off the mountain and attend one of the schools there. That had never been done before. Very few left this village for the 'outside' world. She'd been so shocked when they had finally agreed to let her go, she hadn't even paused to find out where they were sending her.

Once settled into a small house, in a town not much bigger than the village, she was then transported to and from the campus. The couple she stayed with were quiet and kept to themselves. In the two years she was there, she could probably count the conversations she had with them on both hands and have fingers left over. A man, she still knew nothing about, lived over their garage and took her to school each day. It wasn't what Shae had intended when she got down off the mountain for schooling, but she took advantage of the two years without her father's cold or indifferent glances.

In that time, she'd taken as many courses as she could that might help her to be a better healer, as many as her brain and body could cope with. Sucking up the knowledge while she had the chance. She wanted to help her people and change things. Nothing drastic, just enough to make their lives easier. She'd taken courses on plants and medicines, but also on agriculture to help their crops and maybe bring a few new methods and techniques to help her people thrive.

She also used the time to soak up as much as she could about life outside the village, finding any and every excuse possible for her escort to take her to malls, libraries, and other public gathering places. Within reason of course. She couldn't justify needing to go to a club or party, not that she was sure she would have, but anywhere else she could manage to finagle she did. Once she came home and took over as the healer, she knew that's where she'd be until the day her last breath left her body.

Society off the mountain had been so different, and at times, absolutely terrifying. The horrible things people did to each other almost had Shaelan coming home early more than once. It may have been one of the first confirmations that she'd had that proved the life of the village, in such segregation from the rest of the population, was a good thing.

The knock on the door had her heaving out a long sigh before turning to go open it. She pulled the door open and gave Morris a brief empty smile.

"Is Nona-Eve available?"

Stepping back and motioning for him to enter, she nodded. "I'll go get her."

Going quickly to Nona's bedroom, she opened the door and peeked in. Nona sat on the chair by her window. "Oh. I wasn't sure if you were still sleeping."

"Heh, I could only wish for such things, child. I'm awake with the dawn each day whether my body is rested or not." She got up slowly and straightened with care. "The curse of this life, dawn is the only quiet moment you can ever find, so you learn to take advantage of it." She motioned to the door. "Who's out there?"

"Morris?" She still wasn't sure of his name. "One of the guards."

"Tall and gangly-looking one with a twitchy eye?" Nona cringed one eye to exaggerate what she said.

Shae grinned, "Yes, that's him."

"Morris," Nona said solemnly and walked by her. "You should come with me. Grab my bag and make sure there's disinfectant and bandages in it."

Shae nodded and went to grab it. Checking the bag, she made sure it was well stocked, then rushed out to the waiting area.

"She has to find out someday, unless you all plan for her to do this job blindfolded." Nona told the guard with a clipped tone as she struggled to put her jacket on.

Morris gave Shaelan a skeptical glance and then looked back to Nona. "You're sure I don't need to check with…"

Nona paused in what she was doing and waved in an annoyed way toward the door. "Yes. Go."

Shae went over and helped her get her other arm in her jacket, pulling her long grey braid out of the way so it wouldn't get snagged again.

"Should just cut it off and shave my head, be simpler." She grumbled and went out the open door.

Shaking her head, Shae followed and pulled the door closed. Nona's brusque personality was one of the things she loved most about her.

Morris was halfway down the path ahead of them before Nona reached the first small landing area on the stairs.

"Elevator would be a great idea too, don't suppose you found out how to build one while you were gone learning?"

"No. I was more concerned with nature, not construction." Shae smiled at her.

"That's too bad." Nona walked a few more steps in silence then paused and looked at her. "I don't want you to be upset by what you might see, so I'm warning you now."

Shae nodded, a seriousness replacing the lighthearted banter they usually had when around each other.

"He'll be chained up, that's for our safety more than anything." She started walking again. "I didn't ask details, but it will most likely be from fighting, so cuts and welts are more than likely what we're dealing with in there. The odd time it's an illness or other complaint."

"Okay."

"Sometimes they'll sedate them, the real riled ones, before I get there."

Shae helped her down from the last step. "Oh, okay" She almost hoped they had this time, her nerves were strung tightly at the thought of finally finding out what was behind the prison walls. Billie and she would try to get a peek when they were teens, but most of the time Billie just wanted to flirt with the one guard that worked here.

She hadn't seen Billie since she'd returned, each time she'd gone to her house they had given her some excuse. Shae didn't know why, but once she got through catching up, she was going to find out. While she was away, Billie was one of the few she missed. No modern communication in the village was definitely one of the things Shae liked least.

As they approached the entrance to the prison, butterflies filled her stomach. When the solid wooden gate swung open, Shae took a deep breath and let it out, slowly. She'd followed Nona around for years, so she wasn't sure why her nerves were singing this time, perhaps it was finally seeing what it was like in here.

Another guard, Earl, opened the inner door and nodded to Nona. "Two for you today, Nona. A few stitches may be required for the one that got a little too close…" He paled and looked at Shaelan.

Nona mumbled something then waved him aside. "Nothing we're not used to." She took off her jacket and handed it to him. "And the other?"

He put the jacket on a chair by the door and started walking. "He was just brought in, we're sedating him now, hopefully it takes this time…"

Nona stopped and looked up at him, then shook her head and started moving again.

"He got a little banged up coming in…" he glanced at Shae nervously for a second, "maybe just give him the once-over."

What was the big deal about her being here? Sick or hurt was the same, whether you were in chains or not. Shae wondered if she'd know either of these men. She really hoped not. Staying quiet, she followed Nona into a room as Earl held the door open for them.

She wasn't sure what she expected, but it seemed darker than she'd imagined. Not just the lights, but the aura as well, and… *what* was that smell? It was like someone found a sale on the worst smelling incense and burned it all at once.

Nona took the bag from her. "It's stinkweed. Used to help cover up the other… less pleasant odors."

Shae didn't know what could be fouler than that weed, but she was sure she didn't want to find out. The room wasn't large, but it was empty. Cement floor, no windows… maybe this was just for medical purposes while Nona was here? She stopped suddenly when she noticed the man by the wall. With both arms in shackles, the chains secured to cement pillars. She'd thought 'in chains' had been Nona's phrase for handcuffs, not actual heavy chains.

Shaking it off, she went over and took the bag from her mentor's hand. The blood was running down the man's side right through a poorly patched-up wound. She knew the next steps for this, even if she was unsure of protocol.

"You'd think after thirty years, they'd put them on a table, or give me a stool." Nona mumbled.

"I've got it, Nona." She knelt beside the man and glanced at his face, or what she could see of it as it dropped toward his chest. They hadn't been kidding about sedating him. Placing her fingers on his jugular vein, she checked his pulse—more for her own peace of mind that he was just drugged.

He was alive, and his pulse was oddly strong for the amount of blood running down his side. She pulled off the gauze and tape quickly and leaned down trying to see around the hand that hung awkwardly in front of his chest. Glancing over her shoulder, she looked at Earl. "Could you hold his arm up, please?"

"Sure thing."

She heard the scuff of his boots on the cement floor. The chains rattled, and then the arm was yanked up above his head. Eyes wide, she looked up at the guard. "Maybe a little lower, so he doesn't bleed out before I get this closed up?"

"Oh." He lowered it down.

Nona chuckled from beside her. "You tell him, child."

She held clean gauze over the five-inch cut as she reached for the disinfectant in the bag.

"Always use the coarse stitching in here, child, in case they get rambunctious later on." Nona told her.

Shae nodded as she cleaned the area. She didn't know what he'd got a little too close to, but it was all the way through the flesh. He was lucky it hadn't hit bone. Later, when it wasn't her first time inside, she'd be talking to whomever was in charge about something sharp enough to do this to one of their inmates. She wasn't knowledgeable about law enforcement or custody guidelines, but common sense predicted you kept sharp objects from prisoners.

As she finished the last stich, the door behind her opened.

"Nona, one of the kids fell out of a tree, broke their wrist."

Nona tsked, "I'll be along shortly, Morris."

The door closed. Placing the tape over the stitches, Shae picked up the supplies. "I can go now and check on them."

Nona nodded, "that would save me trying to rush. I can give the other fella a once-over and then meet you there."

Chapter Two

Calum kept his head down and completely still while he assessed why his skull was pounding like someone had taken a hammer to it. If he'd fallen down the damn mountain, Devin and Gage would never let him live that down… ever.

Think. What is the last thing you remember? Damn, his head hurt. He breathed out slowly, his chest seemed okay. Hadn't he been in cat form? His mind was a swirling pool of sludge… aside from the pain, that was clear. *Focus.* He had shifted. *Oh, shit this is worse.* If he fell while in cat form… hell, he'd have to leave the country so they wouldn't heckle him for life. A cat *always* lands on its feet, the jokes would haunt him until his dying day.

He attempted to open his eyes. His eyelids were fluttering and straining like he was lifting weights with them, they were that heavy. Maybe he needed to start at the bottom first. He moved his right leg, then left. They seemed uninjured and oddly, not entirely attached to his body. He'd come back to that. His head though, he must have wacked it a good one. Deciding he should just lay right down and sort this through while he wasn't so lightheaded, he tried to lean to the side and met some resistance. Something was caught around his neck. To move either way he was going to choke himself. *Brilliant, I've fallen off a damn mountain and I'm strangling myself with vines as I'm slumped here and think of...*

Voices. He heard voices and just hoped they weren't only in his head... also that they weren't anyone he knew that would tell those two thankless bastards he'd grown up with... and couldn't live without, about the predicament he'd landed himself in.

Groggy was an understatement was the first thought as he climbed through the fog that was his mind, and tried to wake up. He vaguely remembered coming to earlier, and thinking the most ridiculous things, ever. He paused for a second, not even breathing, as he assessed his condition. His head was still pounding, but slightly less this time. He exhaled in relief. Maybe he was going to live after all. Whoever had found him, he owed them a big...

He froze as he tried to touch his head and see how bad the injury was. He heard chains and his hand could not move any further. Chains. He clenched his hand and felt cold metal on his wrist. Eyes wide open, he jerked his head up, almost screaming with the pain to look at his hand. Following the chain attached to the cuff on his wrist he saw it was very securely attached to a cement post. He was shackled. Shackled! *What the holy fuck is going on?* Head snapping in the other direction, he found that arm in the same state. *Someone is going to get their ass beat!* Leaning forward he went to stand up and found out he could only lean about six inches forward before the chain ran out...

On. The. Collar. Around. His. Neck.

Clenching his jaw, he inhaled and exhaled slowly through his nose while he tried to digest the fact he was chained up like a... hell, an animal didn't even get restrained this way. Giving his head a quick shake, he stared at the wall across from him as he concentrated on the last thing he'd done. He'd shifted and was looking for his missing clan mates, he caught a scent that made his fur stand on end and was going to hightail it to higher ground when... that was it, then he woke up with the headache from hell and chained to a god damned wall.

He jerked his arms forward, hard, a few times, testing the strength of the chain. Whatever they'd given him, he was either weak as a kitten or they were solidly attached to the wall. If he could partially shift, the cuffs might pop, but the cold metal collar, that felt damn heavy… *that* insured he couldn't shift anything at all. Even partially shifting required most, if not all, of his muscles to expand… he'd choke before he transformed all the way.

Dread hit him as he looked around the very solidly constructed room, with no window and only one door. Where the hell was he and why? Tipping his head carefully, he looked down to see he wore no shirt, but they'd at least put some sort of cotton pajama-like pants on him. That was a plus, he supposed, that he wasn't chained here butt naked.

He heard footsteps outside the door. Putting his head back down he watched through his thick bangs. When they came to check on him he could head butt them… then what, watch them fall on his legs? That wasn't going to work. The door flew open before he could formulate a better plan. He couldn't see anything but the boots they wore. *Damn.*

"He's out now."

"Yeah, finally after a double dose."

Three men stepped in the room.

"You gave him two tranqs?"

Holy shit. That explains the fog.

"Took two to bring him down, too."

The one walked closer.

"Strong son of a bitch."

"He was huge too, chief. If I had to guess, I'd say bigger than you are."

"Really?"

Calum fought to stay limp and appear unconscious. Carefully, he tried to inhale. *Bigger than you?* Were they shifters? He couldn't tell for sure, the drugs must have his senses messed up.

"And his coat was black?"

Someone chuckled, "as midnight."

"Well, that's… but his eyes are *green?*"

My eyes? What the hell do my eyes have to do with anything?

"Not just green, chief, but deep green like emeralds. Never seen a color like that before."

Chief grunted some sort of acknowledgement. "He's out now. Get Nona back down here to patch him up. I don't want him bleeding out before we can find a use for him."

Bleed out? I'm bleeding? It took patience he hadn't thought he possessed to remain still. He tried to take stock of his body and all it's parts, but he was still half numb from *four* god damned tranquilizers. Four. He was lucky he was breathing at all.

They left and closed the door behind them, loudly.

Jerking his head up, he tried to see where he was bleeding. Turning, he looked at his right arm and saw blood dripping under it, down his ribs, but couldn't see from where. His senses were wrecked if he couldn't smell blood dripping from his own body. And *what* the hell was that god-awful smell? Had they rolled him in garbage before they chained him up? He didn't know who Nona was, but hoped they got here soon to stitch him up. Not being able to shift meant the healing would be slow. After they stopped the bleeding, he was going to create some bleeding of his own. On their bodies.

When the door opened again, he had just enough time to slump forward without being seen doing it.

"He's still out. Poor bastard will probably nap for the next week." He could only see the one pair of boots. "You'll be fine here, won't you? I need to get over to the other side and check on the real criminals."

"You tell that Travis if he doesn't stop scrapping and getting locked up, his momma's gonna skin him alive."

Wait, that sounded like a woman. Tiny feet sticking out of a long skirt stopped beside the boots. *Damn.*

"Will do. Doubt it will matter, he's got troublemaker imprinted in his bones."

She chuckled softly.

"Are they planning to tell Shaelan?"

"Talked to her mother earlier, she's coming after dinner tonight to fill the poor child in. I'll be surprised if she doesn't already know some of it, she's an observant one."

The boots stepped back. "Just give a holler if you need me, I'll be back around in a few minutes."

"Will do, Earl."

Calum watched the boots leave and the woman came in and closed the door. She stood in front of it.

"You can stop faking now, he's gone."

He lifted his head slowly, with a flip of it, moved the hair from his eyes. Standing in front of him was a tiny, elderly woman with a long grey braid hung over one shoulder. Well, hell, he couldn't hurt her even if she stuck knives in him.

She stood there, a stern look on her face, clutching a brown bag. "He had no idea you were awake." She snorted, "personally, I'm surprised you're alive with the amount of tranquilizers they pumped into you." She looked him up and down. "Pleased you are though." She took a slow step in his direction. "Now, are you going to behave, or do I have to stick you with something to knock you out?"

He didn't want anymore drugs in his system. "I'm good."

She gave him an abrupt nod and walked over. "Let's see what damage you've done to yourself."

He gave her a hard look.

Tsking, she leaned down and looked at his shoulder. "Looks like you kept running after the first dart, you have a few gouges here, probably skidded to a stop..."

He jerked on the chain around his neck trying to see the back of his shoulder.

"Just settle down, it won't be permanent damage once I get it cleaned up and stitched together." She bent down and opened her bag. "Do you want me to numb it?"

He shook his head, then flinched when she poured something cold on it. Stung more than he cared for, so he grit his teeth as she dabbed at it a few times. "Why the fu…" Captive or not he still couldn't swear in front of the granny-doctor. Some fierce cat he was. "Why am I here?"

She was silent for a few moments. "That's a long explanation, I don't have time to explain before Earl comes back looking for me."

What the hell does that mean?

He winced as she put the needle into his skin and tugged on it.

"I imagine…" she pulled it through his skin again, "your rare green eyes will have bought you some time."

He hissed out a breath as she did it again. *Rare?*

"They're not sure whether to be afraid of you or what to do with you, yet, so that gives you a few days of peace."

Calum huffed out a breath after she tugged on it again. "So I have green eyes. What the f… hell does that have to do with anything?"

She made some sort of noise, he wasn't sure what it meant.

"Your clan all have eyes like yours?"

He heard scissors clicking and hoped that meant he was done with being stabbed. "Some."

"Mmm." Was her response. "Try not to rip those out. I'm going to check your head now, make sure there's no more holes."

He eyebrows went up at that. How bad did he look? Staying still, he let her run her fingers over his scalp. He tried inhaling with her this close, and thought he picked up the scent of cat, but couldn't be sure with that other stench filling his nostrils.

"You alpha of your clan? Your size is a good one."

He wasn't much in the mood for chit-chat, but wanted information and if she could provide it… "No. That would be my uncle."

She made another noise under her breath. "Alpha's family..." She tsked, "I know this is some kind of thing to wake up to, but just keep your head down, don't give them any more reason to shoot you with those damn darts." She paused on one spot that was tender but it didn't sting, so he hoped it wasn't serious. "Fools don't seem to understand every body has a limit, even a solid, fit one." She touched his shoulder and looked down his back. "Legs and backside okay?"

"They don't hurt." He wanted to growl, but manners had been ingrained in his very soul, so he clenched his teeth and said nothing.

"I'll come check that shoulder tomorrow." She bent down and cleaned up her supplies. When she moved back over to the door, she stopped and looked at him. "Be sure to eat and drink when they offer it, keep your strength up." Her dark, weary eyes implored him.

"Thanks." He half meant it at least.

She gave him a small smile. "I'll see if I can persuade them to give you more room to move."

He nodded to her, not sure if he should thank her for that or not.

When she left, he ran everything over in his mind that she had said. None of it helped him one bit. He still had no idea why the hell he was chained up here... wherever the hell *here* was. What his eye color had to do with any of it, he had no clue either. His brain was sluggish, he was tired, presumably from the drugs, and just wanted to wake up and find out he was sleeping under some tree somewhere having nightmares.

All he knew was when these drugs finally wore off and he could focus longer than a goldfish, he was getting some answers and getting the hell out of here. Somehow.

Chapter Three

Shaelan took the free time Nona had given her to walk around the village. A lot had changed while she was away, but in some ways, it would never change, she knew that. She loved her home, and most of the people in it—there was just something she couldn't put her finger on that made it feel out of sorts all the time. She couldn't see herself anywhere else, but didn't always want to be here either.

There were many new buildings she'd have to familiarize herself with. Wouldn't be good if the healer got lost when she was needed. She hadn't asked Nona what the head count was now, but she was guessing their little village was large enough to warrant the title of small town. However, to be a town, it would have to have a name, which to her knowledge it didn't. It was just 'the village'.

Despite being secluded, there was a store with basic items you'd find in any other store, only more rustic, without things like slushy machines and other fancy automations. They had power, so it was possible, just too frivolous. Their power came from wind and water, which wasn't always constant, so there were times of lights out early to let the storage systems recharge. The endless power she saw when she was away had been a marvel. So too was the shower, the water pressure was unlike anything she'd experienced, and if she could admit to missing one thing in that other place… that would be it.

Pausing, she glanced in the store window and watched a small boy giving his mother his best 'please' smile for some of the homemade candy. Almost every family here crafted items to contribute to the store, along with whatever was shipped onto the mountain.

Money for the collective fund for the village was also made by selling the wares to a broker on the other side of the mountain.

Shae had often wondered where the knowledge for all of this had come from, the power, water, even brokering items… If no one left the mountain, how did they know about wells and windmills… and everything else? They didn't have telephones or televisions, and sadly there was no internet up here, so how? It was just one more question that made her feel this place had secrets. Question was, did she want the answers or was ignorance the better route? She's pondered this frequently since being old enough to understand such things.

Stopping, she sat on a bench near the meeting hall, just to observe everyone. With her years of training, she'd been excluded from much, but was content with just watching people. It could be quite entertaining.

So many faces she recognized as she looked around. Since her return though, she had noticed so many that seemed… different, for lack of a better description. Many held wary expressions in their eyes, even with the fake smiles on their faces. She'd even seen fear and couldn't imagine a reason for it. She was going to have to catch up to her two gossiping aunts and see what she had missed in the last few years, maybe the fear was warranted and she should be aware.

She paused to watch a teacher go by with a six or so rambunctious middle school children. Had she and Billie been that excited at that age? Probably, maybe even worse. In Shae's mind the best age was around six or seven when everything was fresh and not serious.

Most of the children were like her, with dark complexions, and hair—actually for the most part the entire community was like that, the few with lighter hair and skin tone always stood out. She was sure there was a story there too.

During her pre-teen years, she'd had a crush on a boy with blue eyes and red hair… her father had put a stop to that, forbidding her to hang around with him. To this day, she still didn't understand why. His family was respectable, he wasn't a bad child, so why? Shae sighed, Billie may have been right in that her father was some sort of racist, or at the very least prejudiced against those that didn't fit the 'norm'. It wouldn't surprise her if it were the truth. He didn't even approve of his own daughter.

As if he'd somehow heard her thoughts, the door at the hall opened and out walked her father. With him was a man around Shae's age, that her father seemed to never be without since she'd come back. They were together each time she'd seen her father outside of the home he and her mother lived in. Maybe he was an assistant of some sort her father was training. He was many things in her mind, but she still respected the fact he oversaw the entire community.

They were in deep discussion over something that looked quite serious. It dawned on her then, they looked so much alike, Brock could have been his son… her brother. She cringed at the thought. Just her over-active imagination again, as Nona liked to call it. Brock was no different then she was with her dark hair and dark eyes, although there was something about him that made her skin crawl. He never had any emotion in his eyes, they were always cold when she'd seen him.

Getting up, she decided to go before they noticed her. She didn't get two feet before her father's voice boomed behind her.

"Shae."

Turning, she smiled as they walked to her. *Hey, Dad, hug?* Neither returned the smile. In fact, almost identical, cold expressions were on their faces.

"I heard someone fell out of a tree."

I'm great, dad, how are you? Had he even asked her that since she'd come home? "Yes, a few of the boys were climbing and one of them fell. His wrist is fractured, but not badly. It should heal without any issues." She tried not to react to the critical look he was giving her as he noted her wearing jeans and not a skirt like most of the women here.

"Good."

She stood there with a plastic smile on her face, hands clasped in front of her. Looking up into his eyes. Shae wasn't a short person at five foot eight, but her father still seemed to tower over her, adding to his menacing aura.

"I heard you were in the yards this morning. I don't want you going there unless Nona is unable."

What was with that place? Seriously. "It's part of my job." She tried to sound nonchalant and keep the snarky tone out of her voice. She'd learned the hard way years before that tone only got her back-handed, although she doubted he'd do it in front of someone. He continued to glare at her, she felt colder from his expression. "Nona wanted me to know my way around in there. Just in case." It was a reference to Nona's age. Actually, she and Nona had been using it for years to shut people up about Shae helping on calls. There was nothing physically wrong with Nona, thank the stars for that, but making people believe she could leave this world unannounced at any moment always distracted others long enough for Nona and Shae to get away with little things.

He gave her an abrupt nod. "Just don't go in there unescorted."

Why he thought she'd want to go hang out at the jail for any reason other then to administer medical attention, she couldn't even fathom. "Of course." She gave him her best I'm-a-dumb-obedient-girl smile hoping he'd dismiss her so she could go anywhere but here.

"Your mother and aunt are going up the hill to visit with Nona tonight, you need to be there." Without waiting for an acknowledgment, he turned and the two walked away.

Sure thing, Dad! I love you too. Heaving out a breath, she spun around to go back in the direction of Nona's. One thing was for sure, she never regretted the day she moved up on the ridge with Nona-Eve. She loved and missed her mother, but the cold aura that surrounded Shae whenever her father was near, she did not miss.

Shae closed the book and watched Nona-Eve fuss with a tray of cookies. She'd changed her mind three times so far about what to put out when her mother and aunt came to visit. Not used to seeing Nona be anything but calm and settled, she got up and went over. Taking the tray from her hands, she looked down at her. "You know Aunt Marilyn will eat anything you put in front of her. I'm sure this is fine."

Nona heaved out an uneven breath.

"Are you feeling okay?"

Nona groaned in a loud dramatic way. "Yes, just ghosts of the past chasing me tonight."

Shae had no idea what that meant, but the tender look her mentor gave her assured her she was all right. "Okay." She set the tray down. "I'm going to go unpack the boxes of supplies I brought back. They've been sitting there unopened for two weeks."

Nona waved a hand around. "They're fine where they are. Don't need to go mixing them up with everything else until I have a chance to go through my inventory. The print on those bottles is so damn small I almost need a magnifying glass to see them..."

Sighing, Shae leaned back against the counter edge. "If you need glasses, we can..."

"I don't want no damned things pinching my nose and making me look like a granny."

Shae curbed the urge to grin. "Nona-Eve, if you need me to sort through things and check expiration dates, I'd be happy to." She shrugged. "I noticed you were almost out of a few items on your shelves, so I'll do that and put the newer ones to the back."

Nona waved a hand, "Fine, fine." She walked over to the window. "Where are they?"

Shae walked over and looked out the window. "I'm sure they'll be here soon." She hadn't realized Nona looked so forward to social visits. "There's Aunt Marilyn going toward mom's now." There was no mistaking her aunt from this distance. She dyed her brush-cut hair odd colors and wore the most nauseating patterned clothes ever created. Tonight, her hair was pink and her outfit... well there was nothing pale about it. From this distance, it looked like fire engine red and bright orange was this evening's choice.

"Good. Good. I'll go put the kettle on." Nona moved into the kitchen.

Shae watched her, there was definitely something bothering her. Whatever ghosts were chasing her, she hoped it wasn't serious.

Aunt Marilyn was one of those people that talked endlessly, asked hundreds of questions, and never waited for answers. It was always amusing to visit with her. She was probably the most outlandish character in the village and the complete opposite of her sister, Louisa. Aunt Louisa was quiet, dressed conservatively and spoke in a soft voice.

She took a fresh tea into her mother and sat back down beside her. Shae loved her mother, she was the most caring soul in her life. Smiling at whatever Aunt Marilyn was boisterously laughing about, she hadn't been paying attention, she studied her mother. Her light brown hair was pulled back into a tight braid, making her mother's youthful face look even younger. Everything about her mom seemed young, until you looked into her amber eyes. All you could see when you looked into them was the kind of sadness that put a lump in your throat. Shae didn't know what could put such a forlorn look in her eyes, but it wouldn't surprise her if her father was somehow responsible. He didn't openly show her mother any affection, so Shae could only hope he at least did in private. Someone as kind and loving as her mother deserved to be cherished.

"You're not listening to a word I'm saying, Shaelan Kelani."

Shae cringed at the use of her middle name and looked over to her aunt. "I'm sorry, my mind just wandered."

"Heh, when mine does that I call it senility." Her aunt quipped.

Laughing, she glanced at Nona, she was very quiet. "Are you all right, Nona?"

Nona nodded slowly, "I'm fine, child. Nerves are just singing me songs."

She had no idea what that meant, but then realized both her mother and aunt were silent and watching her. Looking from one to the other, she exhaled slowly and carefully spoke. "What's going on?"

"A big pile of *crap* if you ask me," her aunt spat out, "your father should be here telling you. Its his fault."

Shae sat up straight and stared at her aunt.

"Most ridiculous thing I've ever heard, hiding a body's own heritage until it's almost too late to tell them…"

Raising a hand to quiet her aunt, she looked at Nona, then to her mother, both had looks of dread on their faces. "What are you talking about?" She looked back to Nona, who had always been straightforward with her. "Nona?"

Heaving out a long sigh, Nona shook her head. "Marilyn is right, it is *one* of the most ludicrous things ever done here." She glanced at Shae's mother then back to her. "Okay, there are worse things, but they're on a whole different level of stupid." Nodding to herself, she continued. "It's been the practice now for close to thirty years, so you weren't even born when it started." She shook her head, "Why it was, I never understood…"

"Because men took over the running of things is why. They don't have a whole brain between the lot of them." Aunt Marilyn snapped.

"Please, Marilyn, lets just get through this." Her mother's soft tone pleaded.

Shae turned so she was facing her mother more. "Mom? Just tell me what is going on." Every muscle in her body was tense. Whatever it was, if it took three of them to tell her, it couldn't be good.

"Think, Shaelan. You *know*. Think of times when things didn't add up right." Marilyn said in a firm tone.

Shae's mother took a deep breath and exhaled slowly, like she was trying to find the words. "What your aunt means, sweetheart, is we, the inhabitants of this village, aren't like other people."

Nodding in slow motion, Shae watched her mother's face. "We live differently, yes…"

"No dear. It's more than that." She paused and looked at Nona, a questioning look on her face, then back to Shae. Reaching out she gently, grasped her hand. "We *are* different, not just in the way we live."

Looking into her mother's eyes for a moment, she still didn't understand. Glancing at Nona, she hoped she'd jump in and rip the bandage off as was her way, because if they continued like this, she was never going to know what they were trying to tell her. "I don't…" she shook her head.

"Oh, bee's ass," her aunt hissed, "baby child, look at your sassy aunt for a second."

Shae turned her head slowly and looked at her aunt's expression. She'd never seen it so serious before.

"You're a woman now. Past twenty-two years, if my math is right, and soon your body's going to…" Her aunt looked to her mother.

Oh god, was this *the* talk? Shae's eyebrows went up. She was long past the sex talk, for crying out loud.

"Your body is going to change." Nona blurted out. "And I don't mean you'll get boobs, although," she smirked and waved a hand at Shae's full bust, "we'd be late on that one if it were." She snorted, then sobered just as fast. "You… we, are not the normal *human* species."

Shae literally jumped where she sat, moving back several inches. "What?"

"Who could have thought this would suck this bad? Now I know why parents avoid this like it's the last thing on their to-do list in life." Marilyn muttered.

Trying to piece together what they could possibly be talking about, Shae shook her head. They had about a minute more before she *demanded* they stop messing around and just get to it.

Aunt Marilyn got up, her shell bracelets clicking together as she moved. Kneeling in front of her, she took a hold of both Shae's hands and leaned forward until she was only six inches from her face.

"Just watch my eyes, baby Shae, and don't go hitting me or squealing like a stuck pig."

Swallowing, Shae did as she was asked, not even wanting to guess what her aunt was up to this time. Her aunt's brown eyes started to change. Which was impossible, yet it was happening right in front of her face. Not the expression in her eyes, but the shape.

Her. Eyes. Changed. Shape.

Shae inhaled sharply when she found herself looking at dark cat eyes.

On. Her. Aunt's. Face.

Blinking, Aunt Marilyn turned to her mother. "Did they go back? Been a long damn time since I did that, was scared I was going to pop an eye out or something."

Shae jerked her hands out of her aunt's and jumped up, practically climbing over the edge of the arm on the chair so she wouldn't knock her aunt over.

"Oh, she's getting it now!"

Her aunt said excitedly from behind her as Shae paced to the window and back in a nervous way. Inhaling through her nose, and huffing it out of her mouth, Shae stopped and stood there looking at the floor. *Inhale… exhale…inhale…logical explanation for what just happened…exhale…* She stood like that for a few more seconds, gathering her thoughts before she spoke out loud. Ignoring the shaking of her arms, she turned around to see her mother and Nona standing, worried expressions on their faces while Aunt Marilyn was grinning like she'd just won first prize. "Okay," she enunciated slowly, "*what* was that?"

Marilyn's shoulders sagged, "Aw, honey, I thought you had it." She sighed dramatically. "I know your smart enough to recognize cat eyes when you see them." She pointed to the window, "don't tell me you've never wondered how come our mountains has a lot of large cats on it." Lowering her arm, she sat down where Shae had been sitting. "You're breaking my heart here."

"Marilyn, shush and eat some cookies," Nona told her as she moved past Marilyn to stand in front of Shaelan. "I'm so sorry for…" she looked over her shoulder at her aunt, "that. We are a shifter clan, child."

Shae knew what all the words meant, it just took a few moments to assemble them inside her head so she completely understood what Nona was saying. "The people in the village can shift into *cats?*" She whispered it more to herself than Nona. It sounded completely insane saying it aloud.

Nona nodded. "Well some don't fully shift," she jerked her head in Marilyn's direction, "like Aunt talks-a-lot over there… and I don't shift no more, I'm old and slow no matter what form I'm in, but yes, the entire village in one way or another are of the shifter species."

Looking from one face to the other of the three women here with her, Shae kept her mouth closed. Lifting her hands slowly, she backed up a few feet. "Just…" she huffed out a breath, "don't speak for a moment," she looked at the floor, "please."

It was completely impossible, what they were saying, and yet she'd seen it. An entire species she had never heard of. Then again where would she hear about it? The local news on the televisions and cable they didn't have? Was that why they secluded themselves up here? From what she'd seen of the world below… this was the only safe way for people that turned into cats to live. It made sense. That part at least.

She turned and went over to the window and looked down at the village. How had she lived here for twenty years and *not* noticed something like this? She'd always had her face in a book or plant… but still this was a pretty substantial thing to miss. Why was it a secret? From the outside world, she got that, but from each other? I mean you would think if your kids were going to turn into cats… Her brain stopped right there. *Turn into cats. I'm going to turn into a cat?* Like the jaguars she'd seen when she was out gathering herbs? *Herbs… oh my god it all made sense!* Why she had to learn medicine for animals and not just the people. The looks on faces at times … the constant hushed tones or stopping sentences midway when she was around. She inhaled sharply.

"*Now* she's got it."

Shae jumped at her aunt's loud statement, she had forgotten about the others behind her. Turning around she looked at the concern on their faces. Her mother had tears in her eyes. "So… I'm going to turn into a jaguar?"

"Just cat, works too," her aunt supplied.

"There's a chance you will, sweetheart. I can't, they're not sure why, as I'm from a true blood line, but yes, you probably will." Her mother offered, her voice shaking. "I'm sorry, I wanted to tell you a long time ago… but the rules…"

"Are a *big* pile of crap," her aunt finished.

Shae shook her head, "I'll get all the details on that later. What I want to know right now is *how?* Is this a mutation, when did it start? How did it start? Is there any documentation, or… or data on this somewhere? If there is, can I see it? I mean, I assume I'm going to be treating injuries or whatever … I need to know the physiology…" She remembered the man she'd stitched up in the jail, *now* she understood how he'd gotten cut. Claws. *Oh my god I'm going to have fur and claws.*

Nona started laughing. "Slow down." She motioned to the chair. "Sit. I know what you're like when you're on a knowledge-seeking quest. We'll answer your questions until one of us fall asleep."

"Don't forget to explain to her about the heat cycle…" Aunt Marilyn mumbled around a mouth full of cookie.

Shae went over and sat down. "You mean like a cat in heat?" She looked at her mother, then to Nona. "That really happens to us?" She held up her hand before Nona could answer. "Wait, am I going to have to go through menstrual cycles and this heat as well?" It was probably not the most important thing she could ask, but *seriously,* females had enough to worry about.

Her mother grinned. "No, you won't. After your first heat or change, you'll only have to worry about that."

Shae sighed, "Oh good." Shaking her head, she took a deep breath. "I don't know where to start…"

"We can answer your questions," her mother smiled at her.

Some of the sadness was gone from her eyes, and even in her present state of shock, that made Shaelan feel better about being lied to her entire life. Well, maybe not lied to, but letting her grow up without knowledge of what she really was, that seemed close enough to lying.

Nona nodded. "I can fill in the medical ones for you. Speed of healing, best herbs…"

"Then we'll tell you the next part of this *crap*," Aunt Marilyn added bluntly.

"The next part?" Shae was afraid she may not cope well with any more information. How much more could there be? It couldn't be worse than finding out you were going to turn into a large cat.

Chapter Four

"I am not marrying… or mating or *anything* with Brock!" Shae stood there with her arms crossed glaring across the room at the three women. "I can't even stand being in the same space he's in." She was shaking as she fought back the tears of rage. They had been trying to console her for an hour now. So, she was some unheard of species and had been living a lie her entire life—whatever. She was going to turn into a cat with furry tail—fine. Be handed off to Brock, absolutely not! *That* was inconceivable.

"Shae…" her mother stood up and came toward her. "This isn't what I want for you. I just… I don't know what to do."

Shae fell into her mother's open arms and hugged her. "Can't you talk to father? There has to be something…"

"He's the alpha of our clan, sweetheart, I can't question his decisions."

Stepping back, shaking, wanting to scream and cry, she looked at her aunt then to Nona. "This is barbaric."

"Mmhm," her aunt nodded, "That Brock, there's something wrong with that one. You can see it when you look in his eyes, if he'll even hold your look long enough to see." She rubbed her hands on her knees, "I'd run away…

fast, to get away from that one." She pointed to her hair. "I got out of mine by being the insane one."

Shae's mouth dropped open.

"Heh, look at her face." She winked. "I didn't just wake up one day and decide to hack off my hair and be the peculiar one."

"No, she was born that way, it just got worse as she aged." Nona quipped.

Shae smiled. "I don't think cutting my hair and dying it is going to work."

Marilyn shook her head, "no that's a one-time showstopper." Her expression was thoughtful for a moment. "He's arrogant, but still one of our species. Something tells me what works on males of our kind might do the trick here."

Frowning, Shae came over and sat on the arm of the chair. "I'm not following. What works?"

"Marilyn…"

"Your turn to *shush*, Nona, you answered the medical things, now let me do what I do." She smiled at Shae, "scheme. Your scent, if he smells another man on you or you're *unpure* in his eyes, he may reject the union."

Her mother gasped. "Are you telling her to sleep around?"

"Huh, no. Just pick one, one time, that's all it takes." She pointed to Shae's mother, "remember a few years back Faye, that big kerfuffle when Ella canceled her mating celebration?" Her mom nodded. "Why do you think that was? Ella had been messing around with… oh, what was his name? Damn aging brain." She waved her hand, "a few nips, not a full mating bite, and some messing around and it takes a month for that scent to wear off completely." She cleared her throat, "or so I've heard."

"That's true." Nona grinned, "the facts, not Ella's ceremony, I don't know nothing about that."

Shaelan sat there as they nattered on about details she cared nothing about. Could this day get any worse? Not only was she going to turn into a cat, but she had to find a man to have sex with or end up married to a man…cat… *whatever*, that made her nauseous.

"So, what are you suggesting she do?"

Her mother's voice had her snapping back to the discussion. "I can't just go sleep with someone. I have to live here for the rest of my life, and the chances of running into them again…" She felt her cheeks heat just thinking of the embarrassment that would follow her forever. Then again, she may end up married, *forever.*

Nona nodded slowly, a smile on her face. "The green-eyed one."

Aunt Marilyn looked around the room then back to Nona. "What are you babbling about?"

"In the yard." Nona said abruptly. "There's a new one. Huge when he shifts according to Earl. Took a long while to knock him out. He's strong. Polite for a… his situation, and he's not from the village."

Shae's mother looked worried, "He has green eyes?"

Who cared about his eyes? Shaelan thought.

"Emerald green, prettiest eyes I've ever seen on a man. They're afraid of him, too, so he's going to be left cooling his heels a long time." Nona said, still nodding her head.

"Emerald green," Marilyn snorted, "Are you sure it's not your eyes seeing things?"

Nona glared at her. "My eyes are fine enough to see the color, it's the rest of me that is failing." She reached over and patted Shae's hand. "Pick him. There's something about him, something noble and trustworthy. He wouldn't even swear in my presence."

Shae's mother sighed loud. "I can't believe I'm going to agree to this. Your father would kill me if he knew."

"He won't know." Marilyn whispered. "We can run interference and Nona can get Shae in there."

Her face was feeling very hot now as they sat here discussing her having sex… with a criminal.

"Pick him, child." Nona said again. "Go to him, ask for his help."

"Well is he attractive even? Do we need to feed her herbs?" Marilyn asked.

"Nothing wrong with Shae's eyes, she'll be attracted, without herbs." Nona stated.

Marilyn rolled her eyes, "How can you be certain…"

Nona turned and glared at her, then waved a hand in front of her face.

"Oh," Marilyn smiled, "Oh my."

Standing up, Shae paced to the other side of the room again. How had her quiet uncomplicated life taken such a complete about-face in such a short time? "Will they know it's him?" She couldn't believe she was considering this. Could she do this? Could she marry Brock? A chill ran over her, that answered both questions. She looked over her shoulder at their puzzled looks. "I don't want him to be hurt because of me."

"Set him free after. Maybe you'll escape with him…"

Nona swatted Marilyn.

"I doubt they'll go sniff the prisoners, sweetheart." Her mother offered up. She turned to Nona. "How are we going to do this?"

We? Shae felt ill and sat down under the window.

"I have to go back down and check on him in the morning, Faye, I'll send Shaelan so she can ask him."

Shae's head popped up. "What if he doesn't find me attractive enough to want to… to…"

Marilyn snorted, "He's a male. Have you looked in a mirror? Those brown bedroom eyes and pouty lips… he'll be drooling, baby child, don't worry about that."

Shae's face heated again. She got up. "I think I need time to process all of this."

Aunt Marilyn looked at the clock. "Oh, look at the time." Her aunt got up. "I didn't realize how late it was getting."

Her mother also got up. "I better get down there before your father comes looking." She came over and hugged Shae. "I'll tell him you're *processing* everything." She shrugged, "I know some that had to be sedated when all of this was told to them." She smiled. "I'm so proud of you."

Not knowing if it was appropriate to thank her mother for a compliment in this situation, she just smiled. For all Shae knew she was going to have a mental breakdown the moment she was alone. She thought back to the girls that had been in some of her classes, discussing their tragic life problems in the library while she was trying to study. They had *no* idea what problems were. Breaking up with your boyfriend because he couldn't remember your anniversary was nothing in comparison to the issue she was about to have.

She lifted her chin and looked around to see that she was alone in the room. She grinned, Nona knew all too well how Shaelan worked her way through a problem. Alone. In quiet and methodically until it was solved. She couldn't do anything about being a shifter, but she sure as hell could chose who she was marrying and control her own destiny.

Chapter Five

Going down the hill the next morning was the hardest walk of Shaelan's life. She was a complete wreck, second guessing this idea with each step. Nona had decided to come with her, to distract the guards so Shae could speak to this green-eyed man. She didn't even know his name. Did she want to know his name? No, she didn't think so. Part of her hoped he turned her down flat. She wouldn't feel slighted if he did. The only problem was, if he did, then she may have to be with Brock for the rest of her life.

"You think any harder on this and *I'm* going to get a headache." Nona said as they neared the bottom of the stairs.

Huffing out groan, Shae looked at her. "I can't help it. This is so bizarre, Nona, I'm still swimming in my own thoughts, trying not to drown."

"I know, child, I didn't sleep a wink last night, turning it over in my mind, but I can't see another way out of this Brock mess."

As they neared the entrance of the prison, Shae turned her head and spotted Brock and her father walking toward her parents' home. A feeling of dread and panic hit her.

"If that's not fate giving you a shove, I don't know what is." Nona said as she nudged her toward the opening gate.

Shae clutched the bag Nona had given her this morning, filled with her own supplies. It should have meant something special to have her own bag, but that had been buried under the weight of what she was about to do.

She didn't hear a thing that Nona and the guard, Morris, said. Her mind was buzzing so loud she wasn't sure if she was going deaf from it. Nona elbowed her in the arm.

"Shae will check the new fella and I'll go see how those stitches of hers are holding out."

Morris stopped and turned around. "Let me see if he's awake, before she goes in. He gave us some trouble this morning."

Nona shook her head, "Tell me you didn't shoot him full of darts again. We can't check the whole body if it's a puddle on the floor."

He laughed, "No, he got a mild sedative in his water earlier, just to make him more amenable."

Shae held her breath, hoping he was awake. She didn't think she had the nerve to come back a second time to ask him.

"You do know he's attached to the wall, Morris, might be a bit unsociable yourself if it were you." Nona said with a flat tone.

Her disapproval made Shae feel better, the shock of seeing the man in here yesterday, the way he was chained up, had bothered her to her core. Criminal or not they were still human… beings, or close enough, she supposed.

They stopped outside a door. She looked at the floor, unable to make eye contact even with Nona. Not waiting for the guard to check on him, she walked in, before she changed her mind. She was almost vibrating as she looked at the man across the small room. His scruffy black hair was hanging in his face as his green eyes were looking over her shoulder, glaring at the guard.

"I don't think…"

Setting down her bag, she opened it and pulled out a small bottle and needle. "I'll just give him a top-up and he'll be easy to manage."

"If you're sure." He stepped in and walked over to him. "I'll hold his arm while you stick him."

Shoot. She hadn't thought of that. "That would be great." She had no idea what she'd even put in the needle, but it didn't matter because she didn't intend to give it to him. Going over, she leaned down, so her long hair hung across his arm. Taking the cap off the needle, she held his bicep and made sure the needle went behind his arm near her fingers. She squirted the contents onto the floor and then straightened and stepped back.

Morris gave her a small grin and stepped back as well.

"Just stand back till he's dopey, child. We're going to go see the other one. I'll see you back at the entrance when you're finished." Nona moved out of the doorway.

"Okay, Nona-Eve." Shae stood there and watched the man as she heard Morris leave. Closing the door, she turned back to him.

He looked at the floor where she'd emptied the syringe and then back to her, confusion on his face. "I won't bite." He said roughly.

Shae was still looking at his eyes, she could see why her mentor thought they were appealing. She had seen green eyes before, but his were a deeper green and very pretty. She didn't imagine he'd appreciate that description. Snapping out of it, she picked up her bag. "Good, I wouldn't want to have to pull your teeth out."

He didn't smile. "I don't suppose I can get any more answers from you than I did that Nona lady?" He gave her a wary look.

Shae knelt beside him to look at his shoulder. "You probably have more answers then I do at this point." His shoulder didn't seem to show any signs of infection. With the low light in the room, she leaned closer to double check. As she did, she inhaled and found his scent oddly appealing, which was strange, considering the amount stink weed they used in this place. That was a small bonus, that his smell didn't nauseate her.

When she had the urge to lick his injury, she jerked her head up and rocked back onto her heels further away from him. She bit her tongue, like it was going to lick him without her permission. *Cat, remember,* she told herself. *Probably a normal animal thing to do. Right?* She exhaled and tried to settle down again. "Has the injury been bothering you?"

"My whole arm, *both* arms, are pretty much f… numb now. I tried to tell that idiot guard this when I couldn't eat… because I can't feel my arms…" He shut his mouth with a click of his teeth.

Standing up, she looked at the chains, they were shortened by hooking the links through some sort of clip in the wall. It was probably against the rules, but rules were the last thing on her mind right now. Stepping behind him, she opened the clip and pulled the link out. His hand dropped to the floor with a clank. "Sorry," she whispered. Moving over she did the same to his other arm.

Squatting down, she looked at the chain attached to the collar. "I don't know how to work this one, I think I need a key." She knelt beside him again, then noticed the scrapes along his jaw. "Yesterday was my first time in here."

"Mine too." He said in a monotone voice, as he rubbed his wrist and flexed his fingers to return the feeling.

Shae cringed at his tone. The chances of him helping her was going to be slim. *If* she ever got up the nerve to ask him. "I'm going to clean up your jaw."

He tilted his head, giving her access.

Pulling her bag over, she got what she needed and gently started to wipe the blood away. He watched her out of the corner of his eye as she did. "I-I, uh…" she exhaled, "I need your help."

He turned his head as far as the collar allowed and looked at her, his brilliant eyes giving her a 'you've got to be joking' glare.

Dropping her hands into her lap she bit her bottom lip. "I know, it's ridiculous." She looked down at her hands, then briefly back into his eyes. "I've only just found out... *what* I am.... My whole life has been a lie..." she felt her eyes well up, embarrassed she almost got up and ran out of the room. She would not break down in front of a stranger chained to a wall. "My father is going to make me m-mate with this man that I don't even know, and honestly can't stand to be near Brock..." She put her hand over her mouth and stared at the floor. "This is insanity. I'm sorry." She capped the bottle and put it back in her bag and started to get up. Pausing, she looked back at his face, to apologize again and then stopped. He was watching her intently, with what looked like compassion in his eyes.

"So, you want me to, what, beat this guy up for you?" He lifted his hands, "Bust me out of here and I'll put the beats on anyone you want."

She snorted. "If you only could."

"What do you mean you just found out what you are?" His green eyes searched hers.

"I'm a... *cat*. Until last night I thought I was just a normal human girl." She held her hand against her forehead, still stupefied. Her eyes started to tear again.

Without warning, he cupped the back of her neck lightly and pulled her closer to him. She forgot how to breathe as his chin touched her shoulder and he inhaled deeply. She thought he mumbled something about stench then he released her. She straightened away, trying to stay calm, and decided that ended her problem of asking him.

"How am I supposed to help?" He lifted his cuffed wrists higher again, to illustrate how impossible it was.

"I thought..." She was shocked he was asking. "I was told." She huffed out a breath and looked at him. "I know nothing about any of this, *nothing*." Her cheeks heated before she could even voice it. "My aunt told me if I smelled of another man..."

"I'm not going to be your sperm donner..."

Her jaw dropped, cheeks flushing. "No. I don't want to get pregnant." She thought she heard voices in the hall. "I need to smell like another man… just… please, help me."

Again, he lifted his hands and jingled the chains and motioned to the door, as if to remind her where they were.

"I'll figure it out… Nona will help… please." She heard Nona laugh outside the door. She leaned close and whispered against his ear. "I'll come back tonight."

"I'll be *here*." He whispered back with a heavy sarcastic tone.

She wasn't sure if that was a yes, but it was all she had time for. Getting up, she clutched her bag against her legs and backed to the door. "Try not to get beat up and drugged again."

He just looked at her, didn't nod or say a word.

Opening the door, she stepped out quickly. She gave Morris a hard look. "I lowered his hands, he was getting pressure wounds on his wrists and the circulation was slowing down. I'm pretty sure you don't want to be dealing with a cripple."

He pulled the door closed and nodded. "As long as he behaves we can give him more room."

Without waiting, Shae started walking back down the hallway. Her heart was in her throat and she was trying not to have a nervous breakdown before she got out. How she was getting back in tonight, she had no idea. She was going to need to be sedated before tonight at this rate.

Calum stared at the closed door for what could have been hours. Lately his life seemed to be taking turns that he never could have predicted. Then again, who in their right mind could possibly imagine *any* of this happening. That was it right there, he was now positive he had some sort of brain damage from hitting his head. Rather than demand some god damned answers, he joked with her.

Heaving out a sigh, he rotated his shoulders to get the blood flowing. At least he could move his arms now, she'd at least given him that. He looked down at his crotch, ok, maybe she gave him a bit more. Because that was *normal,* getting turned on while being held against your will… and what possessed him to smell her, he had no idea. *One of my least brilliant ideas, ever.* Clouding his mind with thoughts like that wasn't what he needed. Whether the drugs they'd hit him with were still in his system, he didn't know, but he was already having a hard time staying alert and focused. Although, right now he was focused on a closed door. He had no idea why checking her scent seemed so important, and he could barely smell over the bloody stench in this place. He thought for a second he smelled cinnamon, but that was impossible, this certainly wasn't a bakery. When she'd looked at him with tears in her eyes, he felt like someone stabbed him in the chest. Calum glanced down at his chest, like he was going to find a knife sticking out of it. He could take on full-grown shifter in animal form, any species going berserk, but a single tear, hell, even the glisten of one and he turned pure coward.

Seriously, *what* was with people not knowing what they were lately? First Rayne… she had a good reason, her parents died before telling her. That *almost* excused the reason Kelsey didn't know, except the fact she lived with other shifters *every* day after that. But this one… whoever she was… as far as he could tell was surrounded by cats, *so* many cats and they even had a fetish for collecting extras and chaining them to walls!

Had he agreed to help her? He went over everything that was said and still wasn't sure. Maybe when… *if* she did come back tonight, he could persuade her to let him go. *Shit.* She said the collar needed a key? Reaching both hands up, he felt his way around the metal collar on his neck. No wonder his collarbone was killing him, damn thing had to be half an inch thick. *Shit!* It did feel like it needed a key at the back. Was that something the guard would carry on him or leave at a desk…

He *really* wanted to pace right now, not to mention he'd lost all feeling in his ass yesterday sometime. Closing his eyes, he concentrated and tried to see if he could hear anything outside the walls of the room. Huffing out a breath, he opened them again. Nothing. This place was solid, unless it was right outside his room, he was hearing nothing.

The door swung open and the guard walked in. "Figured a shower would be good while Shaelan has you doped up."

Calum slumped his head down a bit and tried to look dopey. *This might be my chance to get the fuck out of here.*

The guard stepped closer and held up a rubber covered bar with a clasp at the end. "See this?" He clicked a switch on the handle and sparks arced out of the end. "This is clipped to your collar, so don't try nothing."

Or not. Holy fuck, he'd be a vegetable if he zapped this metal around his throat with that thing, if not completely dead. Well, at least he was going to get to stand up and wash off this stink. Maybe he could figure out more if he got to see outside this room. He relaxed his whole body and fought the urge to beat the guard to a pulp with his own lightening rod, as he moved around to do something with the chains.

"Okay, buddy, it's on your collar so behave like a good kitty." He laughed at his own quip.

He let him lift his arm while he undid the cuff at his wrist. *I'll show you a good kitty just as soon as you take that thing off my neck.*

"Normally there's two of us to take you to the showers, but Shaelan said you'll be docile most of the day." He chuckled, "don't know what she gave you, but it makes my job easier."

He stored that fact for later use. With only one, he may have a shot at this. *Shaelan.* At least he knew her name, that was more than he'd learned the whole time he'd been here.

Calum wasn't faking when he stumbled as he tried to get to his feet. Every muscle was numb or so stiff he could barely move. The guard wasn't overly helpful either, not moving the bar attached to his neck as he stumbled, choking him a few times in the process. *I get out of this and I'm going to beat on every single… male, I come across.*

"Slowly now, you hit the floor and I'll have to call for help to get you back up."

It took a lot of determination to keep his head hung down, so his hair blocked his expression. That guard needed to shut up and not make him do something that was going to get him electrocuted.

Once out into the hall, he walked slowly, staggering a bit here and slight stumble there, so he had more time to look around and see if he could figure out the place.

The walk wasn't as long as he would have liked. All he got to see was a hallway with a door at the end, and four more closed doors before they reached the shower room.

He had him strip and stand facing him with his arms straight out as he clipped his collar to a locked clasp behind the shower. Flipping the water on, the guard went and stood by the door.

Calum looked at the empty soap holders and glanced at the seat at the end of the waist high stall, no soap or shampoo there.

When he finally accepted this wasn't a bathe clean deal, only a warm rinse, he turned to put his face into the spray, which was more of an excited trickle than actual pressure. A movement beside him almost jolted him out of his supposed dopey act. He turned his head to find Dale, one of the men he had been coming to find—chained to the shower wall three feet away.

Dale's eyes widened, so Calum gave a quick shake of his head so he wouldn't say anything to give away the fact they knew each other. He still didn't know what was going on in this place, but giving them information about fellow clan members to use against them, was never a good idea.

"I'm down here." The guard bellowed from the door.

Calum turned to see what was going on… *stitches, shit.* He turned again to get the injured area out of the water. The guard gave them a quick look, then walked out the door and out of sight.

Dale looked over his shoulder at the door, then stepped as close as he could with the length of chain he'd been given. "How the hell did they get you?"

"With two darts."

Dale looked beaten and worn, bags under his eyes. "Oh, damn. Dart barely punctured my coat and I was out."

"What is going on with this place?" He glanced back to the door.

Dale shook his head and wiped the water out of his eyes. "If you don't know yet, I'm sure you'll find out."

"Have you seen Marc or Gene?" Calum stepped back out of the water so he could hear if the guard was returning.

"What? They're here too?"

"I don't know. I tracked you guys here. Now tell me what the fuck is going on." He thought he heard laughing in the hall.

"It's some kind of... breeding farm or... fuck, I don't know what else to call it."

Calum almost gagged from jerking around too fast because collar did not turn with his body. "What?"

Dale nodded. "Swear on my momma's life. They feed you some kind of aphrodisiac herbs and then toss a woman at you while she's in her heat cycle." He frowned. "Both I've been with smelled like my mate. That's not possible, right?"

Calum glared at him. "There's only one. Must be what they've given you." He needed to sit down, or something. *Breeding farm?* They had men, he'd been hit by them, hunted and drugged by them... why the hell would they need to chain up fellow shifters and use them that way? He glanced at the door again. "They're cats? The women?"

Dale nodded again. "Not old, fat or ugly either, from what I can tell in a room that's almost dark."

"Do they ever let us out of the rooms?" He heard voices coming down the hall.

"No. Only here every few days." Dale stepped back under the water.

The guard walked in before Calum could say another word. Turning he leaned a hand on the wall and hung his head under the spray. *Breeding farm.* His brain stuck there. He'd never heard of such a thing. Other than the Tomas family… but they were one-forms and using the shifters as enforcers. What reason could other shifters have to do this? Did that woman, Shaelan, know what went on? Judging by the things she said, he didn't think so. Could he use that to get out of here? She seemed compassionate. Or she just let him believe she was, to get what she wanted out of him…

"You look like your going to slide down to the floor green-eyes, best get you back to your room." He flipped off the water and handed Calum a towel.

Calum didn't even care if he was dry, he just went through the motions. Handing the guard back the towel, he took the clean pants and put them on.

"Be back for you in a minute." He told Dale as he clipped the rod back to Calum's collar.

A fucking breeding farm. Calum walked where he was guided on numb legs. A fight ring he'd heard of. People holding shifters and than putting them in a ring together to tear each other apart for entertainment, but this? This was… he didn't know what, his brain was on pause. This was a lot to digest and later he'd still have to process what he was going to do about it.

Chapter Six

Shae paced to the window. This was insane. She couldn't do this. *Please wake up*. It had to be a dream, this sort of thing didn't really happen. Turning, she looked back to her mother and Nona, they didn't look so sure now either.

"Hope Marilyn gets here soon and enlightens us with her brilliant plan." Nona said with an edge to her voice.

If Nona was having second thoughts, Shae was sure she should put a stop to it.

The door opened and Aunt Marilyn came in looking excited. She held up a bag. "I've got everything we need right here." She went over to the table and set it down, then pulled out some material. She held up a black skirt. "This is for you Shae…"

"Its not a date, Mari." Nona said getting up and going over to look in the bag.

Her aunt frowned. "No. I know that. I just thought…" she waved a hand up and down her body, "you know easy access and all that." She glared at Nona. "Can't be wrestling jeans off then pausing to get dressed after…"

Shae huffed out a breath. "I didn't think of that." Which was true, she hadn't been able to think, period. Going over quickly, she grabbed the skirt and spun on her heel to go to her room. "I'll be right back."

"I've got enough spiked wine in this bag to knock the guard out for a week, baby Shae, so don't you be worrying." She called down the hall.

Shae's hands were shaking so bad as she got changed, she was glad there were no buttons or zips to contend with. "You have to do this," she whispered, "or mate with Brock." She paused. As pep talks went, that did it. "Okay." She went over to the mirror and looked at what she was wearing. Black t-shirt, long black skirt. Well, at least it matched, not that it mattered. Grabbing the brush, she quickly ran it through her long chestnut hair. "Okay," she whispered again, then took a deep breath and went back out.

Clutching the small bag her aunt had given her to her chest, she walked quickly down the hall toward the door the green-eyed prisoner was behind. Her aunt gave her home-distilled whiskey, water, a pouch of stink weed and then snuck her into the building. Shae wasn't sure, but the way she'd done it seemed too practiced, and she had to wonder how often her aunt came here to drink and play cards with the guards.

Her mind froze when she realized she was standing at the door. She stared at the handle. She debated drinking the whiskey. What was she doing? She hadn't really kissed a boy in her life, she'd always been too busy with learning for that. A few pecks when she was thirteen didn't count, and she'd only done that on a dare with Billie.

Her aunt's boisterous laugh echoed down the hall, causing Shae to jump. *Now or never.* Her mind was saying never as her hand opened the door. Once inside she closed it quietly and leaned back against it. Chin still down, she looked at the floor in front of her. It was darker in here than she remembered, must be power down and time to regenerate the storage. Dark was okay, meant she didn't feel so... on display. Exhaling slowly, she moved only her eyes to him. He sat there, his green-eyes locked on her. He could definitely see in this low light and he looked angry.

Forcing her legs to move, she pushed away from the door, trying to remember how to breathe at the same time. "I brought whiskey and water, i-if you want either…" *This is insane.*

"Whiskey."

His voice was low and rasping and she honestly didn't know if his tone was a good or a bad thing. Nodding, she set down the bag and pulled both out then went over to him. His arms were still down as she'd left them, so she realized he hadn't been a problem for the guards. Kneeling a few feet away, she uncapped the whiskey and held it out to him. Her hand was visibly shaking as he looked at it for a few seconds before he took it.

He took a big mouthful of it and then gasped after he swallowed it. "Water," he croaked. She handed it to him. He took a few mouthfuls. "What's that, three hundred proof?"

She had no idea what he was talking about. Never being much of a drinker, she decided now was as good as any time and took a big swallow. It burned a trail all the way to her stomach. She coughed and he held out the water to her. Taking a sip, she lowered it and nodded. "Thanks. That stuff is awful." She set the whiskey aside and stared at the bottle of water in her hands. "I don't…" she glanced at him quickly, then back to the bottle, "know what to do."

The clank of the chains startled her as he moved his arm and placed his hand under her chin, lifting with a gentle pressure so she'd look at him. She swallowed and looked into his eyes. Her whole body was shaking, she didn't know if it was from fear or the way his eyes were searching hers.

"You could start by coming closer."

She nodded nervously.

"I won't hurt you," he whispered.

Setting the water down, she moved over until she was beside him. The hand that had been under her chin now rested against her shoulder, as his fingers played with her hair.

She licked dry lips and watched him. He applied a gentle pressure to the back of her neck with his fingers, so she would lean closer.

"Shaelan?"

Eyes wide that he knew her name, she nodded again. Their faces were close enough, she could feel his breath on her cheek.

"How far do you want to take this, Shaelan?"

His voice was low and sent shivers across her skin. "I don't know how it works." She glanced at his mouth then back to his eyes. "This scent thing." She clarified. His eyes didn't leave hers and that caused her insides to shake.

"Need to get hormones heated for it to be effective." He brushed his mouth over hers, then stopped, their lips barely touching.

"Oh. I don't…" His mouth covered hers this time, kissing her gently.

"Kiss me back," he demanded softly. He grasped the back of her head and waited for her to move.

Bracing a hand on his warm bare shoulder, she leaned closer and moved her mouth over his.

His hand in her hair tightened as he tipped her head to kiss her harder. When his tongue plunged into her mouth and moved against hers, her stomach felt giddy.

Moving closer, Shae ran her hand into his soft, thick hair as she tried to return his kisses. They were dizzying. He groaned in the back of his throat when she nipped his tongue, the sound sent heat through her.

"Straddle me," he growled against her lips.

Raising up onto her knees so she could move over his legs, he grasped her waist and lifted her into his lap. Her insides began to clench when he ran his mouth roughly over her throat. All these new sensations were drowning her. He nipped her neck gently and she moaned and hugged his head to her body.

When he pulled her shirt up, she shivered with excitement from the feel of his palms on her skin. Her bra was undone and his mouth was on her breast before she could think. As he sucked a nipple into his mouth, she hissed out a breath and rocked her hips into him.

He pulled his mouth away and licked across the puckered flesh. "I'll mark you here so no one can see."

She couldn't think to find her voice, so she raised up on her knees to help him reach. As sharp teeth sunk into her breast, she felt a rush of heat between her legs. When he lifted his head away, she grabbed his hair and guided him to the other one.

He teased her nipple and nipped across the sensitive skin, driving her need higher. She felt his hands sliding under her skirt, up her legs, but all she wanted was his teeth in her flesh. He sucked hard on her nipple as his fingers ran along the wetness between her legs. She mewled softly as he stroked her, making her need more.

"Fuck," he panted, "you're killing me."

He nipped her taut bud with his teeth as she felt him moving his pants out of the way. Strong hands gripped her hips as he began guiding her to take him inside her body. He growled against her throat as he controlled her movements.

She didn't know what to do, he stretched her and it should have hurt, but she needed... more.

"Shaelan, look at me," he whispered beside her ear.

She opened her eyes and looked into his lust filled eyes.

"Yes?" He stopped moving completely, forcing her to answer him.

"Please," she hissed, then attacked his mouth with her lips.

Groaning, he gripped her hips with strong fingers and thrust up into her at the same time.

She felt a slight pinch, then was so filled by him she thought she was going to explode. Pulling her mouth away, she leaned down and ran her teeth along the stubbles on his jaw. "Please," she purred.

He lifted her and slammed her onto him. She moaned and threw her head back. He gripped her hair and pulled her face back down to his.

"Ride me," he snarled with clenched teeth.

He guided her for a moment with his hands until she found her rhythm, then he grasped both of her breasts and squeezed. Shae felt like she was going to shatter into a thousand pieces, she just kept climbing higher. He sucked one nipple, then the other, and her legs started to shake.

When he bit into the unmarked breast, she had to clamp her bottom lip between her teeth so she wouldn't scream out in pleasure.

Grasping her hair, he pulled her mouth back down to his so she could moan into it while he took over their movement. She was barely breathing as the orgasm ripped through her, each thrust after that made her moan into his mouth softly. He stiffened and hissed against her lips, as she felt a heat burst into her.

Dropping her head onto his shoulder, she grasped and panted for air to fill her lungs again. Her whole body was pulsing and quivering.

"Water," he gasped.

She grinned in a lazy way and held her hand in that direction, but didn't move to get it.

He leaned, taking her with him and then she heard him swallowing the water. She lifted her head, realizing she needed a drink as well.

After a few sips, she lowered it and looked at him. The silence of nothing but their labored breathing was intense as it dawned on both of them how far they had gone.

"Save some water," he motioned to where they were still joined, "to wash off the blood, so the guards…"

She stiffened and looked down to where they were joined.

Gently, he pulled her bra back into place and reached around to clasp it. His eyes stayed on hers as he pulled her shirt down slowly so she was covered again.

The insides of her thighs were quivering so much, she wasn't sure if she was going to be able to get up.

"Shaelan," he whispered in a barely audible voice.

Her eyes snapped back to his. She bit her bottom lip, not sure what to say or do.

"That wasn't normal. It's not usually so…" he looked at her mouth, "powerful."

She wanted to cry and laugh at the same time. She settled for just nodding briefly. Setting the water down, she grasped his shoulders and started to rise. The feel of him gradually pulling out of her made both of them gasp. She froze, kneeling above him, waiting for the strength in her legs to return.

Reaching up, he cupped her cheek and stretched up to kiss her mouth softly. "Calum," he said quietly, then shrugged, "so you have a name, not a nameless stranger."

She didn't know why he was trying to make her feel better about what she'd just done, but it was endearing.

"You better go." He said abruptly and patted a hand on her hip.

She nodded and slowly got off him, to stand on shaky legs. Picking up the water, she handed it to him as she grabbed the bag and sprinkled some of the herb lightly around the room.

"What is that?"

She stopped and picked up the bag. "Stink weed, covers up scents."

He snorted, "Name's appropriate. It's all I can smell all the time."

She went over and took the water bottle he held out. "I think that's why they use it." Tucking the bottle into the bag, she added the whiskey and then straightened and looked at him.

He shook his head. "Go, before you get caught."

She went to the door and opened it, peeking out into the hall. Glancing over her shoulder at him again, she quickly went out and closed it. Placing a hand on it, she stood there for a second and couldn't understand why she wanted to go right back in.

Her aunt's laugh startled her into action, she ran down the hall with soft steps and ducked past the office they were in. Going out the door, she closed it without a sound and ran for the gate.

She kept running until she was at the top of the hill, looking back down on the yard. *Good night, Calum.*

He sat there in the absolute silence, too stunned to collect his thoughts for several minutes, could have been hours, he had no clue. What had just happened? Calum shook his head, he knew what just happened, what he didn't know was *why.* Hadn't he sat here all day pissed off, deciding he was telling her to get out the moment she stepped in the room?

He rubbed a hand over his face, hearing the chains made him stop and glare at them with abhorrence. Dropping his hand, he glared at the door. Then she stepped into the room, vibrating with fear and anxiety. It had been coming off her in waves so strong it almost choked him. After that, he only planned to mark her just enough to leave his scent on her for a few days. That entire plan went awry when she moved close to him. Then his prison room turned into a bakery. What the hell was with this cinnamon thing? And since when did smelling it turn him on? He'd never felt anything but indifference for it before, sure it tasted okay in pastries or whatever, but... *Seriously, you're thinking about cinnamon?*

Shuffling back against the cold wall, he leaned against it, and pulling his knees up to rest his arms on top. When he kissed her, tasted her, took her scent into his body, he forgot about his plan and decisions. He could still taste her. Banging the back of his head gently against the wall a few times, he blew out a breath. What had just happened?

He'd checked for odd smells in the food they brought him. Had they fed him those herbs Dale mentioned? Now he understood why Dale thought he had two mates. Those were some potent herbs.

It wasn't the herbs that had made him help her though, that had been his own damn soft spot for a female in distress.

He couldn't remember ever seeing a woman look so frightened and yet so lovely. Those soft eyes... when she bit that bottom lip of hers, he may have agreed to do anything.

Damn, what are those herbs?

The marks he'd left on her weren't temporary. He didn't know the finer details about mating, it wasn't largely talked about among males, but he was sure those were permanent mating bites he'd left in her soft womanly flesh. Calum hadn't intended to mark her like that, but he had no control over it. She'd have those long after he was gone.

Shit. He hadn't even asked her about getting him out of here. He tapped his head against the wall a few more times, trying to clear the fog she'd created from his mind. Pausing, he wondered if she'd come back. He opened his eyes and stared at the door, why would she come back? There was no reason to, now.

After she'd looked so stricken by what had happened... ashamed. That hit him harder than all of it. He'd felt so compelled to put her at ease, and he hadn't been lying. Never, in all his experience had it felt like that.

Resting his elbows on his knees, he dropped his chin into his hand and sat. He was in one hell of a mess here, and he wasn't even sure if being chained up was the biggest concern.

Chapter Seven

Shae read the same sentence for the tenth time. She couldn't focus, all she could taste was Calum, even after brushing her teeth. All she could smell was Calum, even after practically sticking her nose in garlic powder to try to stop that. How long would this last? It was very distracting.

Even after washing last night, with soap, Nona had walked by and sniffed the air, then chuckled.

She stood in front of the mirror this morning staring at the bites on her breasts and blushing... her cheeks weren't the only thing that heated when she touched the marks. That was lunacy. They were fresh wounds and should have hurt, not turned her on. She glared at the book and tried to clear her mind.

When her father and Brock stepped into the room behind Nona, the first thought in Shae's mind was *run!* The expression on Nona's face said much the same thing.

Setting the book down, she stood up slowly. "Dad, is everything all right with mom?" He gave her a blank look, almost as if it was weird for her to ask about her own mother.

"Yes. Fine." He motioned to Brock, who stood beside Nona. "We're here to set a date. Need to get this settled before your heat hits. I won't have you whoring yourself."

Opening her mouth, she shut it again quickly before she said the first thing that came to mind. *Bite me*, probably wasn't the best reply. "I've been meaning…"

He walked over until he was right in front of her and lowered his head so they were almost eye to eye. "I won't take any…" he inhaled slowly, his brow furrowed. He repeated the action only this time it was much more obvious that he was smelling her. "What have you done?"

Chalk one up to aunt talks-a-lot, it worked… Her fathers' large hand connected with the side of her face before she could complete the thought. The pain radiated up to her eye. She refused to make a sound.

His eyes were full of hatred as he glared at her, "How dare you do such a thing…"

Nona made a noise of distress causing Shae to glance at her. Brock had a gobsmacked look on his face, not the hard, impartial look he always wore.

"Chief," he barked and walked toward them, "this is for me to deal with."

Her father glanced at him and gave an abrupt nod before giving her another loathsome look. "It will be gone in a few months, son, if there's no *permanent* damage."

Brock nodded, the expression on his face hard again. He stopped in front of her and looked down at her. "Give us a few minutes?"

Her father nodded, as he stepped back.

She looked up at Brock, daring him to just try it when he mouthed the words 'thank you' and his eyes softened into an expression she had never seen on his face before.

Glancing around him, she watched Nona and her father walk out of the house and close the door. When she looked back to Brock, he looked like he was going to cry.

"Are you okay?" His face scrunched up in concern as he tilted her chin up, "what a brutish thing to do."

Shae's face was throbbing and she could taste the blood as her lip swelled, but she just stood there stupefied, listening to him. His voice had gone up several octaves and he looked at her with a completely changed facial expression. Not just his expression, but he was like a whole different person.

"I'm so sorry," he continued, "I've been trying to find a way to talk to you." He wiped a hand across his brow, "*this* is a complete nightmare."

Shae stepped back and held up her hand. "What?" Great rejoinder, but it was the only thing her brain could process to say.

He glanced over his shoulder and then looked bashful. "I like men." He whispered, then practically giggled. "Imagine the horror that is *me*," he motioned the air around himself. "Big scary *he*-cat," his voice was lower again, "is gay!" he squeaked.

Shae covered her face, completely unsure of what to think, or do. Then, she dropped her hands away, mouth wide open. "You mean I didn't have to sleep with…" She blushed.

His mouth made an O, then he covered it with his hand. "Naughty miss. You'll have to tell me who later." He sobered, "seriously, is your face okay?"

The throbbing of her mouth and jaw finally registered and she touched her painful lip. "I'm not sure. How bad does it look?"

"Oh, honey, it's going to be a big puffed-up mess." He came over to her and tilted her chin again. Clearing his throat, he glanced nervously toward the door. "He's going to barge back in here at any second, so here's the deal, I'll buy us some time, you try not to anger him. Okay?"

She nodded. Seriously, what else could she do at this point? She'd had sex with a complete stranger for nothing. Her cheeks heated, okay, not nothing… more like a whole lot of amazing… The sound of the door closing snapped her out of it. She looked up at Brock, who winked at her then his face hardened into the face she was more familiar with.

"I'll see how I feel about this in a few weeks' time." He said in a cold tone, then turned to face her father and Nona.

Shae just stood there, frozen, staring at the floor, not sure what else to do.

"I understand, son. I appreciate you are willing to try. You're a better man then I am."

Shae hiccupped, tying to swallow a giggle at that comment.

"If your done here, Chief, I'd like to look after your daughter's *face*." Nona said in her 'you are excused' tone.

Shae didn't look up until she heard the door closed.

Nona practically ran over to her. "Oh, look what he did to you…" She pulled a cloth out of her pocket and dabbed at the blood Shae assumed must be running down her chin.

"Nona…" Where did she start?

"I know, child, if I'd ever thought he would…"

Shae grasped her hand lightly to stop her. "Brock is not who we thought he was."

"Heh, an asshole?"

Shae shook her head. "No. He's gay."

Nona froze and looked up at her. "He likes… men?"

Shae nodded, and tried to smile, but it hurt.

Nona covered her mouth, her eyes glittering with humor. "Oh, my god, child, that boy needs a medal. The Chief has no idea, does he?"

Grinning, pain or not, Shae nodded. "His voice is… well… it sounds like Aunt Louisa's when he's not pretending."

Nona started laughing so hard, tears started running down her face.

The door flew open and banged against the wall. Aunt Marilyn stood there leaning against the frame, gasping to catch her breath. "Saw them coming down…" she huffed out a breath, "my lungs…" she stepped into the room, "ran my ass off…" she looked from Nona to Shae, her eyes moving over her face. "Oh, my stars, baby Shae, what did he do?" Slamming the door, she hurried into the room. "Nona, go get me the meat fork. I'm stabbing it in that man's heart."

Nona started laughing harder, bending over, and grasping her ribs.

Marilyn stopped and looked at her. "Have you gone mad, woman?"

Nona shook her head and waved a hand at Shae.

She looked back to Shaelan, her eyes wide.

"We just…" she tried hard not to laugh, "Brock is gay," she whispered between giggles.

"He's gay?" Marilyn gave her an odd look, then her mouth dropped. "Oh, you mean he prefers…" she looked at Nona, then to the door. "Your father doesn't know, does he?"

Shae shook her head.

"*Oh*. Oh, now I understand the laughing." She wiped her brow. "Whew! I thought you had finally lost your minds." Panting out a breath, "I'd laugh, but I still can't breathe." She smacked Nona on the arm. "Go get this girl something for her mouth, *be* a healer." She tilted Shae's chin up to look, "and get me a drink. I damn near died running up here." She frowned and then hugged Shae suddenly. "He had no right touching you." She grasped her shoulders and jerked her back so quickly Shae almost tipped over, "Your father hit you, right, not, Brock?"

Shae sighed, "Yes it was, dad. I thought Brock was going to cry."

"I think I need to have Brock come for tea sometime, soon." She chuckled, "He had me fooled." She snorted, "he has everyone fooled." She frowned, "Dammit, I've been outdone."

Nona came back in, "I think you're missing the point, Mari."

Aunt Marilyn dropped her hands away and took the water Nona held out. "The point?" She took a sip, then turned and looked at Shae, then her eyes widened. "Oh. The green-eyed one."

"We sent her down there to sleep with a man and didn't have to." Nona dabbed at Shae's lip with something ointment.

Her aunt went and sat down. "I don't think Shae is complaining it happened…" She inhaled slowly, "and I'd say that potent devil did the job thoroughly."

Shae's face heated.

Marilyn chuckled and waved a hand in a dismissive manner at her, "It's why he's in chains, so he's not complaining, even if he did, no one would listen."

Pausing Nona's hand, she looked at her aunt. "What?" Her first thought was she'd had sex with a man that was imprisoned for a sex crime, then remembered with her aunt, she needed to clarify before she freaked right out because she always started with the punch line first.

Nona's head snapped around and she looked at Marilyn. "You don't think she has enough to cope with the last few days, you had to go and dump that on her? I planned to wait a few days and explain it all to her. In an orderly way."

Shae went over and sat on the edge of the chair beside her aunt. "Explain, please."

The door opened and Shae's mother and Aunt Louisa walked in.

"Leroy came storming in while I was visiting. We figured he knew about Shae…" She shrugged to Shaelan, "Your mom filled me in." Spotting her sister, shook her head. "Sister, I should have known you would be here. Does mayhem follow you everywhere?" She smirked.

Aunt Marilyn smiled, "It's a skill, takes lifelong practice, sister, not just anyone can do it."

Shae's mother gasped, "Shaelan, oh look at your face!" She came running over to her.

Shae really needed to look in the mirror. First, she needed to know what Marilyn was talking about.

"What's going on?" Louisa asked in a soft voice.

Aunt Marilyn laughed, "Brock is gay and I've let the proverbial cat out of the bag."

Stilling her mothers' hand from fussing at her, Shae got up. "Which she was just going to explain." She glanced at the face of the four women present, "and I'm guessing you can all help."

Shae's mother gapped at her. "Brock is gay? Gay, like, he prefers men?"

Nodding, Shae sighed, "I almost stopped breathing when he dropped the act and spoke." She glanced at her Aunt Louisa, "he sounds like you."

"What?" she chuckled, "Oh my goodness."

"Well then." Her mom shook her head. "I guess no marriage?"

Shrugging, she sat back down. "We'll work out a plan later. He bought us some time." Turning she glared at Aunt Marilyn, "You were going to *explain?*"

Several sighs and deep breaths later the other women sat down and Shae waited for one of them to start. Her heart was still beating faster then it ever had before, and if she didn't get answers immediately about why Calum was locked up, she was going to scream.

"We were once part of an alliance … a long time back…" Nona said quietly, a look of deep contemplation on her face, "the alpha didn't like their choices and forbade our clan to leave this territory, until it was sorted out."

"It never got *sorted* out." Her mother added.

"Mmhm," Marilyn bobbed her head, "after the next generation, no one ever found a true mate again…" she looked around at the other women, a sad look in her eyes. "Mates can be anywhere in the world. Condemning us to this territory was handing us all a half life." She shook her head. "You feel incomplete." She motioned to her sister. "You can fall in love and marry, with it not being your true mate…"

"But there's always this small part… wondering." Aunt Louisa said with a sigh.

Nona huffed out a breath. "By the second generation, around your parents' time… maybe earlier … time blurs after a while… the clan was starting to weaken. The fairer ones could no longer shift, fewer of us gave birth to children who could. It was almost as if the life force in our people was dying out." She glanced hesitantly to Shae's mother who nodded, a serious look on her face. "That's when the captive breeding started…"

Shae stiffened. "The what?" She opened her mouth then closed it and got up. "Captive breeding? I thought they were criminals!" She put a hand over her mouth then dropped it. "You mean to tell me we are holding *innocent* men against their will? They've done nothing wrong?" She thought of Calum and pain jolted her heart. No, she couldn't focus on him until she found out what was happening.

Her mother cleared her throat. "They thought that bringing new and stronger blood lines back into the families…"

"So why didn't they marry outside the clan, actually bring new blood lines in?"

Marilyn sighed loudly. "I never thought I'd ever see a man having to be held against his will to mate with a woman." She shook her head. "It didn't work at first, and we sane people thought they'd drop it."

Nona nodded. "They started using the herbs for both parties after a few months… makes both think it's their mate… then successful conception happens…"

Shae tried to process this. Calum had been given herbs to want her the way he did. Her heart thumped louder in her chest. Of course, he had, why else would a man held against his will agree. It was… it was just ludicrous. "What does that mean for the couples? The ones that actually love each other?"

"Those women forced to breed with the *other* blood line… it makes it very hard on their end is what it does." Her mother said with a hard tone in her voice. "It takes several new marks to get the stench of another man off them."

Shae held a hand over her heart. "That's awful." She thought of the marks Calum had put on her, would they be there forever? Had they given him those herbs? She needed to know. Granted there were more important things to wonder about right now, but how would she find out? Shaking her head, she realized that was the least important thing to focus on right now. "Why hasn't anyone done anything about this?"

Marilyn snorted, "Most don't know."

"The elders do, and are too weak to do anything," Nona sighed, "The couples forced into the breeding, are sworn to secrecy or lose their spouse and children. Only the male guards know, and the healer, as well as the alpha and seconds families."

Everyone was silent. The air was heavy like each older woman was mourning what the clan had gone through. Shae tried to grasp what that meant, other than Calum wasn't a criminal yet was a man being held against his will. A man she had asked to help her, and he'd done it so tenderly, with patience… even stopping right before… to ask if she'd changed her mind. "Is every person there innocent?"

Marilyn shook her head slowly. "No, the other side is actually a real jail."

"Oh." She supposed that was good at least, if any of this could be called good. Out of nowhere it hit her. What if they sent other women in with him? What if he did with them what he'd done with her? She jumped up and paced quickly to the window and looked down toward the yard. This horrible feeling hit her in the gut, she felt like she was going to be ill as the thought of him forced to have sex with another woman hit her.

"Nona," she spun around and looked at her, "we have to get to Calum out of there."

Marilyn sat forward like she was going to say something until Nona held her hand up to stop her. "Calum." She said in a soft voice. "That's the fella's name?"

Shae nodded. "It's not right, we have to get him out so he can go home." It bothered her she wouldn't see him again, but she didn't have time to examine why right now.

"How, Shaelan? We can't just walk in and demand he be released." Her mother looked from one woman to the next, "right?"

"No, we can't." Nona said as she got up. Going over to her bag, she picked it up and dug to the bottom of it. Pulling out a small pouch, she set the bag down again. As she walked to Shae, she emptied it into her hand then held up keys. "But we can get him out." She put the keys in Shae's hand and squeezed it shut. Then turned back to the shocked looks on the others faces. "What? I may have set a few loose throughout the years." She nodded to Shae. "Trick is to have them mangle the cuffs so it looks like they broke out."

Nodding, Shae looked down at the keys in her hand. "But how do we get him *out* of the building?"

"That's the rub, isn't it?" Marilyn mused.

A knock on the door had them all freeze and stare, holding their breath. Shae looked at the keys in her hand and quickly tucked them into the pocket of her jeans. Her mom got up and went to the door and opened it. Brock stood there.

He stepped in and nodded to the women, then gave Shae a wide-eyed cold stare.

She glanced at Nona, then back to Brock. "They know." She held her breath waiting for his reaction.

"Oh, thank god," his shoulders sagged, "you have no idea how painful it gets being *that* tense and upright. All. The. Time." He wagged a finger at the women. "I expect you to keep this secret or it's my life, *literally,* that will end." He sighed. "Actually, gives me the fuzzies, that someone else knows…" he waved a hand in the air, "except Garrett, and he's having an identity crisis right now, so boo on him."

Shaking off the shock, her mom jumped up. "Brock, where is Leroy?

"Oh, he went for a run to blow off steam… or whatever." He smiled at Shaelan. "I thought I'd scoot up here and make a plan with the girl while he was gone." He looked at Nona and then Aunt Louisa, his brows drawn together, then pointed a finger at Aunt Marilyn. "What gives? I can smell a scheme in play."

Shaelan brushed her hair back from her face and sighed. "We're trying to figure out how to get Calum out."

His head snapped back to her. "Calum?" He pursed his lips for a second. "We have *a* Calum here?" His jaw dropped, "is that who…"

Blushing, she nodded. "He's one of the captives."

Brock's shoulders slumped down. "Filthy, vile practice *that* is. I want to hurl every time I walk into that place." He straightened, his eyes going wide. "You went to one of them? The captives they force to..." His mouth dropped open, then he snapped it shut and stood there with his hand over his mouth looking at her.

"I didn't know what to do." She grimaced. "I didn't want to mate with you."

"Oh. I'd be offended, but *eww*." He held a hand over his flat stomach. "Thank you. You're forgiven." He huffed out a breath. "I can get you in," he paused, "we'll think of a reason, but…" he shrugged, "I can't break him out of the collar…" He motioned to his body, "Big strong body, but unless I'm in my cat skin, I have all the strength of a worm." He tapped his head, "I think it's all psychological, but what do I know about that? I'm just a big he-cat second in training." He rolled his eyes.

Shae pulled the key out of her pocket and held it up.

"Well then," he grinned at her, "lets go break *a Calum* out." He bowed to the women still looking at him shocked. "Ladies, we will return." Blowing out a breath, he closed his eyes for a moment, then opened them and was the expressionless, cold-eyed Brock again.

Aunt Marilyn started clapping. "Bravo!"

He giggled, then glared at her and cleared his throat. Staring at the ceiling, he exhaled and focused until he was the other man once more.

When Brock had said he could get her in, she hadn't even paused to ask questions. *Now* as they were walking in the door, she had hundreds and no way to ask them.

Earl was the guard that let them in, he nodded to Brock without so much as a question. He gave Shae a curious look.

"We're here to look at options," Brock said, his tone flat and cool.

Shae had to look around as he spoke, so she wouldn't stare at him when his voice was so low and emotionless. She preferred the real Brock.

Earl's eyebrows went up. "Oh. I didn't realize that was a done deal now." He stepped further away from Shae.

When things settled down, *if* things settled down, she needed to find out what the protocol was among shifters—as she was one of them and had no idea. How many people knew she was supposed to be mated to Brock? Probably the entire village knew, it would explain the strange looks she had been getting.

Brock made a small shrug with his shoulder. "Just keeping all options on the table." He looked down the hall for a moment. "If you could keep it to yourself, I'd appreciate it. I don't need flocks of women in my face planning a ceremony and shit."

Earl grinned, "I can do that." He glanced in the office over his shoulder, "Do you need me?"

Brain finally catching up, Shae shook her head. "We'll be fine."

Shrugging, Earl motioned down the hallway. "You know where they are. Give me a shout if you need me."

Brock didn't even acknowledge him as he started walking away. Shae caught up to him after she made sure Earl went back in the office. Brock lifted a finger to his lips, telling her not to speak. She didn't understand why, but did it anyway.

Her stomach was in knots when they stopped at the door where Calum was. Sensing her reluctance, Brock put a hand on her back and gave her a nudge as he opened it.

Standing there, frozen on the spot as he followed her in and closed the door. All she'd wanted to do since she woke up was see Calum, and now she stood here looking at the floor in front of her.

Brock leaned closer and spoke near her ear. "Cat's hearing, he could have heard everything we said in the hall…" he put his hands on her shoulders, and kneaded them, "are you okay?"

A low, lethal growl filled the room.

Shae jerked her head up and looked at Calum, his eyes were on Brock and he wasn't happy. A warm feeling flushed through her as quick at the sharp intake of her breath.

Brock lifted his hands off her. "*Well*, I have a new subject for *my* fantasies for the rest of my life," he sighed softly, "sorry Garrett."

"Calum." She quickly got the key out of her pocket, "he's here to help me get you out of here." His head lifted to look at her, surprise on his face, which turned to furrowed brows quickly.

"What the fuck happened to your mouth?" He demanded.

His voice was low, and until that moment she had no idea that dangerous and menacing appealed to her so much.

"It wasn't like that last night." His eyes were focused solely on her face now.

Shae fumbled with the keys in her hands as she went over to him, trying to figure out which one was for the collar. "It was pretty dark in here…" She knelt close to him.

He stopped her movement by cupping her chin gently and turning her face so he could look at it. "My mouth was all over yours, I would have felt *this* and tasted your blood." He hissed. "Who did this to you?"

Pulling from his grasp, she jingled the keys, "let me get the collar off." He turned as much as he could so she could try the first key. It worked. Opening it, she eased it off his neck, her heart pounding when she saw the red marks on his skin.

Calum was on his feet, pulling her to him before she could think. She sucked in a breath when she realized how big he was standing up. He had to be close to six foot five, at least. Grasping her chin lightly, he tipped her face up so she had to look at him.

His green eyes were hard. "Who the *fuck* hit you?" He lowered his face closer to hers, "they're dead."

"Be still my heart," Brock squeaked, "no, seriously it's skipping all around inside me…"

"Brock, not now." Shae hissed.

Calum's head snapped around to look at him. *"This* is *the* Brock?"

Huffing out a breath, she lifted one of his hands to look at the cuffs, "Apparently, Brock is very good with secrets."

"Heh," Brock chuckled, "don't mind me being here, continue with the he-man thing. It's very stirring…"

She paused to watch Calum look him up and down for a moment before he turned and looked back down at her. With a touch, softer than a feather, he cupped the side of her face and lowered his head to lick over her swollen lip. Never could she have imagined a fat lip could feel so sexy. Lifting his head, he looked at her, his eyes searching her face.

"We're going to continue this conversation about who…"

It dawned on Shae where they were and why they were here. "Let's get you out of here first." She held up his arm, "do you think you can break these? Or mangle them a bit?" She looked nervously over to Brock, then back to him, "so it looks like you broke out?"

He grunted and pulled his arm free from her. Looking down at the collar, he growled quietly. Bending down, he picked up the offensive piece of metal and grasped it in both hands.

Shae stood there, her jaw slack as she watched him twist the collar like it was made out of rubber, not steel. He dropped it with a clank and then held out his arms and clenched his fists. With a low rumble coming from his chest, she saw the muscles in his arms moving, growing. The metal around his wrists protested the pressure, emitting a soft squealing sound, then the one popped open and clattered to the floor, followed by the second one a mere breath later.

"Oh my…" Brock sighed.

Rolling his shoulders, Calum gave him a quick glance then was right in front of Shae again. "What about my clansman?"

She couldn't think as she looked up into his eyes that were a brighter green now, more cat than man. She cringed when she realized he was waiting for an answer. "One of your clansman are here?"

He nodded, as he gently brushed her hair over her shoulder. "There might be more, I tracked three this way, I saw Dale in the shower."

"They let you shower together in here?" Brock asked. "I should have faked being a guard and not a second." he mused.

Shae turned to look at him briefly, he shrugged. "We can't just run down the hall calling out names and freeing everyone."

Calum clenched his jaw, then spun to look at Brock. "Why doesn't someone challenge the alpha and put a stop to this?" he snarled.

Brock's eyebrows shot up. "Yes, right" he rolled his eyes dramatically, "everyone will follow a gay alpha." He snorted. "There's so much male pheromones around here, most days I walk around stoned from it."

Shae's nerves were vibrating. "We'll look for them, but first we need to get you out of here." She turned to Brock, "how are we getting him *out* of here?

Brock huffed out a breath, "we'll get him to the back door, it's not far. Let him out into the forbidden area…"

"Will anyone be there?" She'd always been warned about going there, the whole village had been, but she never understood why. One more thing to add to the list of things she needed to find out.

He shook his head. "Only one that goes there is Jerome and he's on a supply run."

She nodded. "Okay." Her stomach was bubbling with the idea of getting Calum out, she felt ill thinking she would never see him again, but there was no other option. Turning, she was surprised how close he stood to her, his green eyes moving down over her. She thought she'd seen him inhale subtly a few times. "Let's go." She whispered, trying to keep the emotion out of her voice and failing.

He grasped her hand and nodded, then looked at Brock. "Lead the way."

Brock glanced at their hands and sighed. "Let me check." He turned and opened the door then stepped out. With a stiff posture, he glanced in both directions, then motioned for them to follow.

It was the longest, tensest, thirty feet in her life as they moved to the door that Brock stood holding open. She was shocked when they stepped through and were outside.

Brock kept half his body in the building and motioned to the right. "Do *not* go that way. I don't know how you got up here, but avoid *that* way."

Calum nodded, then looked down at Shae. His hand tightened on hers as he pulled her closer. "Come with me."

Shae shook her head, "I-I can't…"

His eyes search hers for a moment, "I'll be back, *with* help." He whispered.

She stood there motionless as he gently kissed her cheek and released her hand.

They both stood there in silence and watched as he ran, fast, into the tall overgrown weeds.

Tugging on her arm, Brock pulled her back into the building. He grimaced at her. "We're going to look for his clansmen?"

She nodded. They hadn't asked names, but she had said she would. So, they were.

An hour later she sat at Nona's trying to stomach a cup of tea. Her whole body was shaking, thinking of what they'd done. They did find one more of the captives that knew Calum, his name was Marc and he had been the man she'd stitched up on her first visit inside.

He was gone. Calum was gone. She sat there taking deep breaths and trying not to cry. She didn't know why she wanted to cry. They'd done a good thing, now Calum could go home. He said he'd come back, but why would he ever risk that?

"Shae, child?"

Nona's voice brought her back to reality. She looked at her.

Patting her hand, she offered a soft smile. "It will all work out, child."

Marilyn nodded from where she sat across the table. "I had a vision once," she said, in a soft hushed voice she rarely used, "in it was Shae, leading our people to freedom and ending the tyranny and cultism our proud clan has been forced to live with." She didn't say any more than that.

Brock moved from where he'd been leaning against the wall and bent down to hug Shae tightly into his chest. "It wouldn't surprise me." He straightened and started for the door, "I have to get back before the chest-beating-chief returns. Prepare my story in case Earl yaps and says we were there." He stopped and gave Shae a smile, "He said he'll be back… and I believe he will be." He winked, "a big rawr for that one." With that he left.

"Who will be back?" her mother asked?

Shae stared into the cup she held in between her palms. "Calum. He said he'd be back with help." She looked up at the women around the table, both hope and fear were in their eyes.

Chapter Eight

Calum pulled the bag with his phone out of his pack, then tossed the pack into the car. His hands were shaking, and he was exhausted, having never run that fast and far in animal or human form. It had taken him a lot longer than he would have liked to find the direction his car was in. Popping the trunk, he went to get something to eat and some water. *Then what?* He had no idea.

He chewed the dry protein bar without tasting it as he looked back up the mountain. He couldn't just drive away and leave Dale up there, or the other two if they were also chained to a wall. Shaelan, he couldn't leave her either. He shook his head and tossed the rest of the bar into his trunk as he opened the bottle of water. Why hadn't he made her come with him? What was going to happen to her when they discovered he was missing? He growled as he pictured her swollen mouth and bruised jaw. If someone had done that to her for having his scent, then what the hell would they do to her if they found out she'd helped him escape?

Drinking the entire bottle, he crunched it up in his hand and then pitched it in the trunk as well. "Fuck," he rubbed his hands over his face and heaved out a breath. Dropping his hands onto his hips with a smack, he looked around him. He couldn't go back up alone, he'd already proven how useless that was.

What if… she'd gotten Dale out? Would he even be strong enough to shift and hightail it out of there? He'd looked pretty run down. "Shit," he hissed out a breath between his teeth, "could this get any more fucked up?" Sighing loudly again, he slammed the trunk and went and climbed in the driver's seat. He had to get help. Closing the door, he started the car, then grasped the steering wheel and glared at it.

Looking out the window of the car, he tried to think this through. This was what he did, he was the enforcer of the group he'd grown up with. When there was a situation, he came up with the plan. This was *the* situation of all screwed up situations. As it stood right now, he had no plan and no idea what to do.

"Fuck!" He smacked his palm against the wheel and turned the car off. How long were these damn herbs going to be in his system messing him up? He wasn't at all comfortable with the possessive feelings he had toward Shaelan. He would protect any female, been raised to do nothing less than that… but this… this was on a whole new level. He'd tried to ignore it as he booked it down the mountain, but even on four legs it nagged at him to the point he'd stopped a few times, debated about running back. Which was the stupidest thought he'd ever had… in his life.

He grunted, "If it's so stupid, why the hell are you going back up there?"

Shaking his head, he got out of the car and went to go get some protein bars and water to put in his pack. He'd be calling in the cavalry before he moved from this spot, *this* time. Have some back up en route in case he didn't make it back. Again. Where could he send them though? He jammed the bars and water into his pack as his eyes surveyed the various outcroppings and plateaus he'd just come down. Had to be somewhere he could watch for them, and others. He was not getting shot again. The thought of being chained up… he'd go out fighting this time. To the death, if need be.

Staring at the phone, he waited until there were bars and sent his location. He typed quickly, trying to fit it all into a short message that he hoped they'd figure out. Only he could end up on a mountain where the signal seems to come and go with the breeze. Hitting send the second time, he prayed it got to them and wasn't lost floating around on a signal in the clouds for the next thirty years.

Sealing the phone in the bag, he put it back into the pack and zipped it up. He had to stay on two legs for most of the foreseeable future. He didn't know what area they stalked to shoot animals full of darts, but surely, they wouldn't shoot a man. Would they? Grabbing his sunglasses, he shoved them on his face and hoped he didn't look anything like that green-eyed, naked man they'd chained up.

He had to check that Shae was okay and then get back to the lookout location, where he hoped they would join him after he'd left the directions in his car. Even if Devin used his jet to get here, it would still take them a day, at least, maybe more, depending on what was going on back home.

If they had managed to get Dale out, Calum figured he'd drag him back down the mountain, even it meant he was away from Shae, to get his clansman to safety. As much as he didn't want to leave her—*why* the hell that was he'd figure out later—he felt the obligation to look out for one of his own men, first.

Shae paced past Nona again.

Nona sighed, "You have me almost praying someone gets sick, so we have an excuse to get outside of these walls."

Stopping, she clutched her head between her palms. "I know. I'm sorry. I just…" She went back to the window and looked out it. "What's going to happen when they discover him missing?"

Nona shrugged, "They probably already have by now." She motioned to the window. "What do you see going on down there?"

Checking again for anything that seemed out of the ordinary, she crossed her arms to hug herself. "Nothing unusual."

Nona chuckled, "That's what you want to see. Now if you see them hiking up that hill in this direction, then we have something to worry about."

"Do you think he made it?"

Nona made a thoughtful noise, "size and shape that one was in, he'd probably run all the way home by the time they found his empty cell."

Shae nodded and hoped so, but didn't at the same time. She'd felt ill and jittery since she had watched him disappear into the weeds.

"Are you okay, child?" She heard the chair scrape back on the floor, then Nona was beside her pressing a hand against her forehead. "You're quite warm." She turned Shae's chin and looked into her eyes, then poked her in the arm. "Mmm."

Shae grimaced, "What is it?"

Nona gave her an odd look. One Shae couldn't identify. "How are you feeling? Aside from worrying they're going to find out you let their green-eyed man go?"

Shrugging, she huffed out a breath. "I'm just anxious and have the jitters." She scowled, "hasn't exactly been a normal last few days."

"Was quite the homecoming." Nona continued to stand there and look at her. "I'm afraid we may have stirred the pot too soon."

"I have no idea what that means." Which, she decided was normal, half the time she really didn't understand what Nona was saying when she used her little sayings.

"It means I think you're coming into the change." She blew out a breath, "we may have caused it by sending you to…" She clasped her hands together, "the time you spent with your Calum."

My Calum? She'd ponder that later. "You mean my," she lifted a hand, not knowing how to say it without turning three shades of red. "I'm starting to change into a cat because of being near another cat?"

"Mmm," Nona nodded slowly, "something like that." She, too, turned to look out the window. "Your mate can bring that on faster." She gave a small shrug. "Or could just be your age and it's your time."

"I doubt he's my mate," although the thought pleased her immensely, "you guys said that was almost unheard of now."

"In the clan, yes, but he's not from here, is he?" She turned and went into the kitchen.

Shae watched her then turned back to the window. She couldn't just stand here and keep turning this over an over in her head, she'd have a breakdown. "I'm going to go for a walk, Nona."

"Seems a good idea, child, I'll get dinner started." She called from the kitchen.

Standing at the back of the room, Gage looked around at all the leaders and members of other clans that were present. Things were finally coming together to shut Tomas down, and he couldn't wait for the day it all came apart for the crime family that had wreaked havoc among the clans for close to four decades, maybe longer. They didn't have the exact date it started or anything, just an idea when shifters started disappearing.

Turning, he smiled to see Kelsey and Rayne standing back observing all the alphas in the room. Honestly, if any of them knew those two women like he did, they'd be afraid. His phone vibrating in his pocket had him pausing to pull it out. He opened and read the text, then read it again. Glancing over at Devin, he saw he was frowning at his phone too. Waiting for him to look up, he motioned to the exit with his head. Devin nodded and started walking in that direction.

Stepping out into the hall, Devin turned and looked at him. "Did you…"

Gage nodded and looked at his phone again. "Yeah…" he scowled at the message again.

"What does it mean?"

"What's wrong?" He looked up to see Kelsey and Rayne coming out the door.

"Message from Calum."

Rayne looked relieved; Kelsey smiled. "So, he's okay?"

Gage looked at Devin, then back to his lovely mate. "Uh… we don't know…"

She frowned, "What does the message say?"

He glanced at his phone and read the message one more time. *Pinging location. Directions in my car. Send females and backup! DON'T SHIFT!* "He's either in deep shit or…"

"…having a bachelor party." Devin finished for him.

"What?" Rayne and Kelsey exchanged a look, then Rayne went over and pulled the phone out of her mate's hand to look at it.

Gage stood there, his arms crossed and watched them both study the message. They didn't understand…

"Calum doesn't ask for backup… ever…" Devin said in a quiet tone.

Gage nodded. "He *is* the backup…"

"…the quarterback, wide receiver and fullback…" Devin stated in a matter of fact tone.

Rayne gave him a blank look. "In non-sports lingo, please."

"Did you get the ping… or whatever?" Kelsey asked glancing at the phone over Rayne's shoulder.

Devin sighed, "Yeah, at the same time as the text."

She looked at the phone once more, "So… he's sent you the location of his car and from there further directions to where he is."

Nodding, Rayne continued, "He needs backup, but shifters are in danger of being discovered there so stay in two-leg form…"

"…and women are needed to either look less suspicious…" she glanced at Rayne.

Rayne grimaced, "or there are other women involved and a feminine presence is required…"

Devin gave Gage a wide-eyed look then threw up his hands. "How… the *hell*… did you get all that from his cryptic message?"

Rayne shrugged, a slight smile on her face.

Going over, Kelsey wrapped her arms around Gage's waist and leaned against his chest. "So, when do we leave?"

Gage looked down at her. "Oh, no. You're not going anywhere…"

She bit her bottom lip and looked up at him for a moment. "Are you going?"

He looked at her mouth then back to her eyes. "Yes." He knew there was a trick in here somewhere, just by the expression on her face.

"Then I'm going." She stated as she stepped back from him.

He shook his head. "No. Absolutely…"

"What if my cycle returns and you're off on some mountain?" She raised both eyebrows at him and dared him to answer. "We don't know how often it will for me, yet."

Gage looked to Devin, who shook his head, he was on his own with this one.

"Should you be going into some unknown situation… with your social standing?" Rayne asked her mate.

Devin frowned at her. "It's Calum. Period. End of discussion."

She huffed out a breath. "Fine then. When do we leave, and who else are you bringing?"

"We?" He glowered.

Rayne went over and leaned into him, her voice soft. "Yes, Kelsey has a very valid point. I've never yet come into …

whatever it is you call it with a wolf. What if that happens and I don't know what to do or…"

He raised a hand to stop her from saying the next part. "Fine. But if one hair on your head so much as gets a split end, I'm taking it out on Calum's… hide, once we find out what the hell is going on."

Rayne turned to look at Kelsey. "We need good shoes this time."

Kelsey nodded. "Yes. And food! No wildlife snacks."

Devin looks at Gage, then snarled. "I'll go fill Dad in and you," he pointed to Gage, "find two more males to take with us."

Gage nodded his head once. "Scary or stealthy?"

"Both." Devin barked as he went back into the gathering.

Chapter Nine

Backtracking for the third time, Calum stopped and looked around. He hadn't run over any waterbeds or stone, so he hadn't come in this direction. Normally, picking up trails was his thing, just not today it seemed. If he hadn't been running to escape, he may have stopped and looked around. The only reason he knew he hadn't been here was he'd run over everything in his bare, human feet and would have remembered this.

Closing his eyes, he tried to recall what he'd heard. That, he had been paying attention to, listening for someone following him, sounds of nature around him—like echoes, so he didn't run off a cliff—he exhaled slowly and tried to remember. That didn't work, he had nothing.

Opening his eyes, he looked around again, he thought maybe he'd been running East, because he'd had to turn when the sunlight in his eyes obscured his sight, so he could make sure he had a clear path in front of him. Turning again, he found his bearings and started in a new direction.

A little while later, he spotted a ridge that seemed familiar, but he'd thought that about a dozen things so far, so he may be wrong about this one too. Huffing out a breath, he pulled off his pack and got out some water. Once he was through this ordeal, he may actually be tired of hiking. He doubted it, but a break may be in order.

Taking a quick drink, he put the water back, swung the pack back on and inhaled to start out again. A smell hit him, causing his insides to churn. It was the smell of death and rotting flesh. Not the same as an animal carcass rotting. Moving cautiously, he followed the scent. Instinct was telling him to go the other way, but this was something he had to check out, for his own peace of mind, if nothing else. The odor was stronger, and became more rancid as he approached a small knoll. Crouching down, with the silence he had honed for years, he went up.

He reached the top, and quickly looked over it to see if anyone was there. Bile rose in his throat as he looked down the other side. It was a ditch, not a knoll, and there was a mass grave at the bottom. Holding his hand over his sensitive nose and mouth, so he wouldn't taste it for days, he carefully navigated his way to the bottom. Once he reached the grave, he squatted down on unsteady legs and looked at the pile of bones laying there. Human remains, years worth, if the quantity and wear was any sign, lay in a heap.

As his eyes skimmed over the mound, he froze and stared at a decaying body. It was on the top, it had recently been tossed here. Rags covered the lower half, in a material he recognized as the same he had been wearing earlier that day. He stood slowly to see better, without disturbing the resting place of the others, then lowered his hand from his face as his heart mourned what he saw. There was a metal collar around the decomposing body, and a tattoo on the arm that he knew all too well. He knew it because he had harassed Gene for a week when he couldn't shift after getting it, so it wouldn't heal and vanish.

His chest ached for his friend and clansman. He couldn't afford to pause and bury him right now. Not today, when they could be out looking for him, but he would be back. Pulling off his pack, he reached inside to grab his phone so he could take pictures of everything around this location, ensuring he would be able to find his way back. As he moved around to get different angles, he looked back at his friend and almost dropped his phone when he saw a wound on his forehead. A bullet hole. He'd been shot. Calum snapped a few pictures of the bones, careful not to take any of Gene, no one wanted to remember him that way, and put the phone back in his pack.

He climbed back up the ditch and looked once more, before jogging in the direction he'd originally been heading. Devin and Gage had better come here prepared to fight, he thought as he increased speed, because someone was going to pay for his friend's wasted life.

He slowed down and inhaled deeply, trying to rid his system of the stench and replace it with the fragrant scents of nature. The thought made him think of Shaelan and cinnamon… he needed to get her out of this place, for her own good, until he found out what the hell was going on. Using captives for breeding was one thing—a ten on a warped scale of bad, but shooting them in the head after meant her life could be in danger, and she didn't even know it.

He'd completely lost his mind, Calum decided as he watched her walk toward a long wooden staircase leading up a steep incline. He was in a tree—a *tree*, the tallest he could manage to get in as a man. Deciding it was better to stay in that form, he'd gone back across the forbidden area, after he located it, and then climbed a damn tree when the village was in sight. He had a good idea now why it was called the forbidden area. Whoever was responsible for the bones out there, didn't want anyone to know what they were doing with the captives.

His ego was getting a little more than bruised these past few days, he'd never encountered so many doubts and issues in his life, not to mention losing his way in the wild. That hadn't happened since he was a young boy.

When he'd finally gotten up in the tree, scratches and all, he'd been shocked to see the place he'd been held was so built up. How was a village this size up here, full of shifters and no one knew? He knew all the clans, and not once had he ever heard of one in this area. Especially the feline shifters, he knew of every family spread out all over the map.

Calum made sure he stayed tuned into the elements, staying downwind of the settlement. It would crush what was left of his pride, if he was caught *and* treed.

He'd been watching Shaelan for quite a while now, it appeared she was just wandering around with no purpose, stopping from time to time to talk to people. The lady with the neon pink hair had been a surprise, but then again *surprise* seemed to be this week's theme.

He studied the stairs she was climbing and wondered if she lived in that house at the top. It was starting to get dark, surely, she wouldn't just wander up there without a purpose. Glancing around, he checked out the terrain and looked for a way to get up there without walking through the middle of the village.

It was the first time in Calum's life he'd used his skills to stay off other shifter's radar, in a serious manner. Devin and Gage used to think he'd lost his mind when he'd practiced for hours. He stiffened and ran that through his mind again… He may have just lost his mind this last twenty-four hours.

To recap, I am up a tree, spying on the people that held me prisoner to have sex with their women in heat, and after getting out I come back on my own accord.

Yeah, he'd lost it alright.

Looking down, he wondered how many more scratches he was going to get while climbing down from the tree. Sighing, he moved his pack around to his back and started the slow careful descent. Getting out of a tree without a sound wasn't as easy as most would think. Someone his size getting out of a tree silently was going to be a miracle.

Nona paused, the spoon halfway to her mouth and looked into the hall, then shook her head and continued to eat.

"I didn't see Dad or Brock, do you think they're out tracking him?" Shae pushed the food around in the dish, not tasting anything.

"I doubt they'd still be out. Logic predicts, even to your father, he's long gone by now." She rolled her eyes, "If there's news your aunt will sniff it out and come tell us." Nona added then looked down the hall again.

"I hope so." She whispered, but didn't really. Since this afternoon, she'd had a heavy feeling inside her and she couldn't really shake it. Watching Nona look down the hall again, she set her spoon down. "What is it?"

Shaking her head, Nona looked at her. "I keep hearing a clinking noise." She set her spoon down and stood up, "we don't have anything that would *clink* in the hall."

Shae followed her. "Something rattling outside maybe?"

"I don't know what. There's not a strong wind tonight." She stopped. "Do you hear it?"

Holding her breath, she cocked her head to the side. "Maybe." This better hearing thing she was supposed to get, hadn't arrived yet, it seemed. She opened Nona's door and looked around, listening. "It's not in here."

Nona checked Shae's room then closed the door.

They walked to the only room left, the supply room where all the herbs and medicines were kept.

Both walked in and stood there listening. There it was again, Shae heard it this time. Nona pointed to the window and then looked around and picked up a broom and nodded for Shae to go check.

Not sure what good a broom was going to do if the sound was outside the window, Shae went over to the window, almost wishing she held something too. When she peeked out it, she paused and looked back at Nona, then back out the glass. Calum was standing there looking at her. Hurrying, she opened the window. "Are you insane? What are you doing here? You're supposed to be at the bottom of the mountain far, *far* away by now."

"I did get back to my car…"

Nona leaned out the window beside Shae, "Maybe having this discussion while hanging out the window is a bad idea."

Shae jolted, forgetting that having an argument outside a village of people that had sensitive hearing could be easily overheard.

Nona pointed to the back of the house. "Go around to the deck back there."

Calum nodded and ducked back down behind the shrub, heading in to the back of the house.

Closing the window, Shae opened her mouth and looked at Nona, then closed it and held her hand over it.

"Not too bright, your Calum." She chuckled.

Shae ran to get to the back door, she opened it as he stepped up onto the deck. "Get in here," she hissed. He walked by her, she closed the door and spun around. "What are you doing here?" She paused to notice he wore boots, jeans and a black t-shirt. "Why did you come back?" The panic in her voice was clear.

Calum gave her a lopsided grin. "No one saw me."

Forcing herself to relax, she rested her hand on her stomach to settle the butterflies that had taken flight when she'd seen him. "I'm more worried about them smelling an outsider hanging around."

"I stayed downwind…" He stopped when Nona walked in.

"Would you like something to eat?" She asked politely.

Shae's mouth dropped open, had she lost her mind too?

Nona grinned, "Relax, child, no one comes here for social calls but your aunts or mother, it's fine. He probably hasn't eaten today." She walked out again.

Shae closed her eyes trying to settle her nerves, but when she opened them, he was standing right in front of her. She looked up at him, and for some reason, having him close made some part inside her feel calmer and in other areas of her body, so not tranquil.

"How are you?" he asked hesitantly, "I didn't hurt you last night, did I?"

Lost in his eyes, she felt her cheeks heat and shook her head. "You came back to ask me that?" She let out a shaky breath. "No. You didn't."

He reached and touched the side of her face with gentle fingers. "Good." Leaning down he kissed her swollen mouth lightly. "We still need to talk about who hit you."

Shae sucked in a breath, when she realized she wasn't breathing in just air, and with it, his scent. Leaning closer, she inhaled again. His smelled... she didn't know what, safe but dangerous...

Nona cleared her throat.

They jumped apart from each other. Calum turned and motioned for Shaelan to go first.

She stood by the table and watched as he took off his pack and set it on the floor, then eased his large body into one of the chairs. With his size, he made the chair look like it was a miniature, a problem she was sure he was more than used to. She'd been surrounded by large men her entire life, but for some reason Calum seemed... bigger. Frowning at her own stupid thoughts, she quickly sat on the other side of the table, afraid to be too close to him.

He nodded politely when Nona set a bowl of her stew in front of him. "Thank you." His eyes flicked to the dish in front of her.

She hadn't even remembered she was eating before seeing him out the window, then realized he wasn't going to eat until she did. Nona came back in and set a drink in front of him, then sat down and started eating like this was a normal thing. Shae picked up her spoon, only to put it down again and lean over the table. "*Why* are you back here?"

He took a bite and nodded to Nona. After he chewed and swallowed, he looked at her for a moment. "Answers." He shrugged, "mostly." Grinning, he searched her eyes, "I would have called, but you didn't give me your number."

Nona snorted and then stopped when Shae gave her a blank stare.

"We don't have phones here." She told him in a quiet voice, trying not to smirk at his sense of humor. *This is so not the time for joking.*

"Good thing I came back then." He took another bite, his eyes only leaving hers for a second.

"I can still smell the stink weed on you," Nona said, breaking the staring match they were having.

He huffed out a breath, "*that* is the worst plant I have ever smelled."

"There are worse, but they make a body ill after too long." Nona set her spoon down and pushed the dish away. "They tried a few before they found one that didn't make everyone ill or break out in a rash." She shook her head slowly.

"You give them the plants?" His tone was serious now.

She shook her head, "No. I wouldn't have nothing to do with that part of it. I look after the health of the fellas. That's my part." Nona played with the grain pattern of the wooden table, not making eye contact. "Might have keys too… accidentally set the odd one lose, from time to time."

His eyebrows went up. "Thank you for that." He took another bite and then glanced at Shae, his eyes moving over her face. "So, do you know how long these herbs will take to wear off." He slowly turned back to Nona to wait for an answer.

Shae's brows drew together, she glanced to Nona. He'd known he was drugged when he was with her? She couldn't look back at him now.

Nona's looked at him with surprise. "The breeding herb?"
He nodded.

"Heh," Nona grinned, "you weren't given any of that. They had no idea what they were doing with you. Herbs only work for short time, least we'd have howling men chained up all the day long. Only give them to the fellas right before, they wear off fast."

The silence was long as he sat there looking at Nona. When he turned to look at Shae, his eyes were softer than they had been. "Interesting." He mused quietly.

Shaelan could feel her cheeks getting hotter. *No herbs? So, all of last night was… real.* She was almost squirming the way he was looking at her now. He was sitting perfectly still, watching her, she wasn't even sure if he was breathing. She needed to change the subject, or at least start an audible one. "I found two of your men. Marc and Dale." She shook her head trying to clear the other thoughts out. "I'm sorry, but there's no Gene here."

Calum set his spoon down and reached to pick up his pack. He pulled out a cell phone and tapped the screen a few times, then dropped it on the table in front of her. "I found Gene."

Shae picked up the phone, then gasped. "Where is this?" Her breath caught in her chest, "Who are all these people?" She looked back to him.

He shook his head. "There's a few collars there... Gene's was still clasped around his *neck.*"

With shaking hands, Shae handed the phone to Nona.

"He was shot in the head," Calum added quietly.

Nona dropped the phone on the table like it had burned her hands. She covered her face with shaking hands. Dropping them, she looked at him. "I asked…years ago… they told me they let them lose after serving their purpose." Exhaling a shaky breath, she pushed the chair back and got up. "My god. What have they done?" Picking up her dish, she walked into the kitchen.

Shae watched her walk out, then looked back to Calum.

"I'm sorry," he said, the pain clear on his face, "I didn't know if she knew."

Shaking, she exhaled, trying to ease the pressure on her chest. "I don't think anyone does." Taking another ragged breath, she tried not to cry in front of him. "I'm sorry about your friend." She clasped her hands in her lap, tying to steady them. "I just got home from school, two weeks ago… I-I didn't know… anything," she whispered as a tear roll down her cheek. "Excuse me, I n-need a moment." Pushing back from the table, she quickly headed toward her room.

Her chest felt like it was being crushed, she couldn't catch her breath. Before she could reach the privacy of her room, Calum was behind her, stopping her. The tears were rolling down her face as his strong arms wrapped around her and pulled her gently against chest. "We didn't know…" she whispered, leaning into him.

He didn't speak, just ran a hand down her spine in a soothing gesture as she sobbed quietly. Shae couldn't believe she was falling apart in a stranger's arms, because he was, despite what had happened between them. Taking a deep breath, she exhaled slowly and tried to calm down.

"Just breath with me, listen to my heartbeat." He whispered, his breath against the side of her head.

She could feel each breath he took, hear the pulse of his heart as it beat. Never before had she felt such peace, which was completely absurd, but she'd take it over the overwhelming sorrow that had been choking her a few moments ago.

"That's it." His warm hand ran over the back of her head.

When she realized her arms were wrapped around his waist, squeezing him, she stiffened. She hadn't even known she'd done that. With his other hand, he coaxed her to look up at him. Hesitantly, her eyes connected with his. She didn't understand the look he was giving her. Her heart stuttered when he gently wiped the tears on her cheek away with his thumb.

He lowered his face to hers, "there's things we need to discuss…" his lips brushed over hers lightly, "but the sight of you distracts me…"

His tongue brushed over the swelling in her lip. "Discuss?" Was the only word she could vocalize with him being this close.

He smirked, "Yes." Leaning down, he pushed his face into her hair and inhaled slowly.

It was the most erotic feeling, which, she thought only confirmed she was indeed a shifter. *Shifter ... my father.* "You need to get out of here before they find out you're here."

Straightening, he frowned at her. "You keep trying to get rid of me and its going to give me a complex."

She blinked, and stared up at him. "I just want you safe."

Kissing the top of her head, he turned with his arm around her and started guiding her back to the table. "We want the same thing."

Nona stood there, staring out the window when they walked back in. "We can't let this continue." She said, so quietly Shae barely heard her.

"Then we're on the same page." Calum said firmly. He sat down at the table again, still holding Shae's hand.

Turning, Nona looked at their joined hands then sighed loud. "We have a few other concerns as well."

Dragging her eyes from him, Shae looked to Nona, "Oh?"

Nona made one of those noises she made, letting Shae know it was a deep thought moment. "You're starting your change…"

"We don't…"

Calum nodded, "She's close."

Frowning, she looked down at him. "How do you know?" Everyone knew more about what was going on with her body than she did lately.

"My cat can sense it." He said in a hushed tone, a contemplative look in his eyes.

Glancing from him to Nona, then back to him, Shae lifted a brow, "that's a thing?"

He chuckled, "It's a thing."

His eyes moved over her face almost in a caress, Shae had to curb the urge to sigh out loud.

"I think there's a bit more…"

The door opened and Aunt Marilyn breezed in, as was her way.

Calum was on his feet so fast the chair banged to the floor in a clatter, pushing Shae behind his large frame at the same time, before she could react.

"Woah, big fella," Marilyn raised her hands up, "I'm the harmless aunt."

Shaelan peeked around Calum and gave her aunt an annoyed look. "I almost had a heart attack."

"You?" She closed the door, then stood there with her hands on her hips, looking Calum up and down. Then she pointed a finger at Shae. "*You* are brilliant! Hiding him up here while their best trackers chase their tails. Ha!" Then she slumped her shoulders. "Dammit, I've been out done again. I must be getting old."

"He did leave," Nona said with a smirk, "then he came back."

Aunt Marilyn's jaw dropped, "well, aren't you the ballsy one?"

"I suppose." He said in a low voice.

He was still half in front of Shae, she realized. Placing a hand on his arm, she looked at him. "It's okay, Aunt Marilyn won't tell anyone you're here." His eyes searched her face for a moment, then he relaxed, becoming slightly less rigid.

"Heh, I could stand up here waving a bright flag and they still wouldn't see it." She mumbled and moved toward the table, her eyes moving up and down, then stopped on his eyes. "Damn, do you have any… older brothers with those eyes? Not too old, mind you." She extended her hand, "Marilyn." She laughed, "or crazy Mari, as they call me around here."

Calum looked at her hand, then slowly extended his and shook hers. "Calum, and I don't see why they would, your color choices are perfectly sensible."

"Ha!" She turned to Nona, a big grin on her face, "I vote he stays and we send Leroy away…" glancing at Shae, she scowled, "any father that does that to his daughter's face needs to…"

A low, feral growl came from Calum. He turned to Shae and cupped the back of her neck and head with his big hand. He pulled her toward him, lowering his face to be level with hers, green eyes burning. "Your father *hit* you?"

His voice was so low it sent shivers all through her body. "He was angry…"

"We do *not* harm our women. For. Any. Reason." He whispered in a venomous tone, while he looked at her swollen mouth. Calum straightened, without releasing Shae and looked at Nona. "Who is this Leroy, and why hasn't he been banished for harming a female clan member?"

The surprise was clear on her face, "he is the alpha." She said slowly.

A long, drawn-out growl of frustration came from Calum's throat and Shae felt her knees go weak. Leaning against him, she ran a hand lightly over his chest, trying to soothe him, even while she was wondering why she felt compelled to do so.

"My word," Aunt Marilyn said breathlessly.

"I think we need to talk." He said firmly to Nona.

Aunt Marilyn dropped into the nearest chair, nodding with a dumbfounded look on her face, one that Shae had never seen before—ever.

"We do for sure." Nona agreed as she moved over to her chair.

Calum didn't release his hold on Shae, guiding her to sit in a chair, then pulled another close to her and sat down. He blew out a breath and rolled his muscled shoulders a few times, then leaned on the table and to look at Nona.

"I am not leaving until some things here are settled." He glanced to Shae briefly before continuing. "And I should tell you, I've called for help, they'll be on their way."

"Help?" Marilyn sat forward. "Who?"

Nona raised a hand to stop all talking. "Show her the pictures before we climb too deep into this."

"Pictures?" Marilyn's voice was still quiet for her.

Her aunt sat perfectly still and waited while Calum picked up his phone and brought up the horrible pictures of the grave he'd found. Shae watched as sadness wiped her aunt's usual carefree expression away, as she stared at the screen.

"They never let any of them go home." She set the phone down and looked to Nona. "Did they?"

Nona shook her head. "I don't think so."

She watched her aunt close her eyes and rock back and forth in her chair for a few seconds, processing the information. When she opened them again, Shae was taken back by the disgusted expression in them.

Then her head snapped to Nona-Eve. "Are any of the women caught, that they've been sending into the yard?"

Nona gave Shae a quick look, then shook her head. "Not yet, that I know of."

Shae frowned but kept quiet, until she knew what was going on.

"Good." Aunt Marilyn nodded, "good. Even if they are pregnant already, hide it. Don't tell anyone." She pointed a finger at Nona. "Get them to agree not to tell anyone… buy us some time."

Unable to stay quiet any longer, Shae glanced from one to the other. "Time for what?"

Nona tapped the phone on the table. "To stop them from being there."

"Oh." Shae shifted to the edge of her seat and leaned on the edge of the table. "Brock and I can go…"

"No." Calum said abruptly.

Eyebrows raised, she turned to look at him.

His expression softened. "You are not putting yourself at risk again."

She opened her mouth to answer, but her aunt interrupted before she could.

"That's not a permanent solution, baby Shae. We need to stop this, not stall so they can bring in more people." She clicked a fingernail on the blacked-out phone screen. "No more will be added to *that*." She flicked the phone down the table. Then turned to Calum. "Who is on the way to help?"

Calum leaned back in his chair and crossed his arms over his chest. "A few of my friends." He gave Shae an odd look, but continued, "The next in line for King of the Alliance, one of his seconds and a few more."

"The alliance?" Nona asked, a tone of excitement. "It still exists?"

He frowned, "yes."

"Are these friends large shifters like you?" Marilyn asked.

Calum nodded. "The *prince*," he smirked, "is a wolf, but no one will mess with him."

"He's that mean?" Marilyn inquired, looking a little too excited.

Grinning he shrugged, "yes and no." His expression sobered, "I'm one of his seconds and my friend, who is a large tiger, close to twelve feet in length, is his other." He shrugged, "You mess with him, you mess with us. Not to mention the entire alliance of clans."

She made a big 'O' with her lips and nodded abruptly. Shaking her head, she turned to look at Nona. "The alliance still stands, and from the sounds of it, stronger than ever."

Nona sighed. "I caught that." She looked briefly at Calum and Shae then clasped her hands on the table. "We were part of the alliance, back when it was formed. The alpha, at the time, wasn't happy a wolf was in charge and refused to be part of it."

"Mmhm," Marilyn flung both arms out, "we've been forbidden to leave the mountain territory since then."

Calum sat there, stunned by the information dumped on him in the last hour. Never in his life could he imagine some of the things they told him. Then again, he *had* been chained to a wall, so he supposed the rest wasn't so far from unbelievable. The alpha of this clan, from his grandfathers' time, had quite clearly been insane, and since then the depravity had spread through the generations like cancer.

If Calum had been anyone else, they would have broken his friends out of their chains and got out of here fast, leaving the alliance to come in and clean up this atrocity. There were complications to doing just that. Firstly, he wasn't ever able to walk away when others needed his help, even if they didn't know they did, and this clan clearly needed help. Secondly, Shaelan was his mate, he knew that for sure now, and he'd marked her as such.

There was no other explanation for the range of emotions he went through being near her. The lecture he gave Devin not too long-ago kept flashing through his mind. He'd ridden him hard for marking Rayne when she was unaware, and now he'd done the same damn thing. Yes, she had asked him to mark her so she carried his scent for a few days, but what he'd done, that was never leaving. In fact, if he had his way, he'd be renewing his scent on her frequently. Which brought him to another snag, she had just found out about her own heritage… adding a lifelong mate to that may not go over well right now. How did he find out where she stood with that?

"Calum?"

He blinked and turned to look at Marilyn. "Yes?"

She smirked, "You've been sitting there staring at Shae for so long we thought you'd fallen asleep with your eyes open."

He cleared his throat, "No ma'am, *wide* awake."

"I was saying, we need to get you somewhere safe for a day or so…"

That made his mind focus again, "Come again?"

"You can't stay here." Shae whispered, "or you're going to end up back in chains."

He snarled, "They can try."

Nona got up, picking up the cups on the table. "She's right. You can't stay here… until we get more involved in this, get the ducks in a row…"

"There's something else…" Turning he looked at Shaelan, his eyes wandered over her. His cat rubbed gently across his skin, almost purring, which he didn't know he was capable of.

"Heh," Nona gave her head a shake, "I'm well aware."

Shae got up to help her. "Aware of what?" She took the cups from Nona's hand. "That my change is coming… or however you say it?"

"That too." Nona nodded, "but I don't believe that's what he's referring to."

"It's plain as day." Marilyn added looking entirely too happy.

"What?" Shaelan looked from one woman to the other. "What is?"

He stood up slowly to move in her direction, she was giving off that aura again, the one of pure anxiety. His cat demanded he comfort her. Calum was in synch with that, but he hadn't planned on broaching the subject in front of the others. Hell, until a he found out he hadn't been given the breeding herb, *he* hadn't even known what was going on. The guys would never let him live *that* down. Taking the cups from her hands, he set them on the table and gave her a hesitant look. "You're my mate and you bear my mark," he smirked, "*two* of them." He loved how she blushed as he reminded her.

She looked down at the floor, then back to him. "Is that why I feel so…" she lifted a hand, like she didn't know how to say it.

"Yes." He wanted to pull her against his body and remind her of it, but they weren't alone, and he had already proved he had issues controlling himself where she was concerned. The fact that he stood here with her in the village was testament enough. As her dark eyes caressed his face, it was all he could do to keep his hands off her.

"Did the temperature in here just go up?" Marilyn said loudly.

Nona huffed out a breath. "I think it did, Mari."

Calum cleared his throat and jammed his hands in his pockets like a bashful teenager. He tilted his head and watched Shaelan. "I know all of this is a lot to swallow in such a short time, but I can't change that." He paused, trying to figure out if that look on her face was a good or a bad one, for him. "I can give you time to digest all of it." He sighed, "or try to."

She was wringing her hands together in front of her. "Okay."

Her voice was barely audible, even with his acute hearing. He realized the only way he could give her time, would be for him to leave again. If he stayed near her, he would not be able to keep his hands, mouth, or teeth, off her. Turning his head away from her, he looked at Marilyn. "Where were you thinking I could go?"

She looked a Nona, then smirked. "The caves."

Nona nodded, "No man will go near them, so that's the perfect spot."

"Caves?" Shae looked at her aunt, "we have caves?"

Marilyn threw her head back and laughed, "Yes we do. It's a cave the women—that don't want to breed—go when their heat hits." She shrugged, "how do you think us older ones got out of being tossed in a room with the men in the yard?"

Shaelan's brow furrowed. "Are there women there *now*?"

Laughing harder, Marilyn shook her head. "definitely mated to him if your looking at me like you want to scratch my eyes out." She sobered when Shae's expression didn't change. "No, baby Shae, there are no women there right now."

Shaelan was blushing again and biting her bottom lip, Calum wanted to lick it. She had to stop doing that or… yeah, he needed to get out of here and give her time to work through all this.

"Okay," she finally answered, avoiding Calum's eyes.

Leaning closer, despite just deciding he wouldn't go near her, he lifted her chin so she would have to look at him. "No male near you but Brock… and even he's questionable right now." He waited until she gave a little nod. "I'll try to give you time, but if I smell another man's scent on you… I can't promise they'll survive." Her eyes went wide. "*And* if anyone lays an unkind hand on you again, I *will* kill them." Waves of anxiety hit him again. "I know that sounds uncivilized, and it may be, but clan have their own laws and the two most important are you never mess with someone's mate and women are to be cherished, nothing else." She nodded again, her eyes locked on his and biting her lip again. He bent his head and inhaled her scent, that cinnamon fragrance that was her, and an aphrodisiac to him. "I better go," he whispered against her ear, "or I won't be." Straightening up, he meant to step away, he really did, but his legs weren't doing as ordered. He looked at her swollen lip and decided it was the only thing stopping him from taking her mouth the way he wanted. Grasping her chin, he tilted her head up and kissed the side of her mouth, then the other side before licking across her lips so he wouldn't hurt her. "I'll see you when my friends get here." *Devin and Gage, you better be hauling ass.*

"We'll keep her safe, Calum." Nona assured him.

He released her and stepped back before he could change his mind. Turning, he grabbed his phone off the table and his pack off the floor.

"I'll take you to the caves," Marilyn said, "none of the patrols so much as look at me." She snorted, "in fact, any man sees me and runs the other way."

"That's their loss." He told her, and he meant it.

"Damn. I can't wait to meet your clan." She said as she moved to the back door.

He gave Nona an abrupt nod. "Thank you for the food, and everything." That was one strong lady, she'd been going against the alpha all along, and the man didn't even know it.

"Calum."

Just hearing Shaelan say his name, had him stop and turn to her.

"Be careful, please."

The worry on her face made his cat rub against him. He winked at her, "they no longer have the element of surprise."

Backing toward the door, so he would leave, he held her look until Marilyn closed the door after him.

Turning, he inhaled slowly, checking around them. He could smell the whiskey Shaelan had given him on her. "You have some of that whiskey I can bring with me? It's going to take something to keep me calm while I'm away from her."

She laughed and patted him on the back. "Honey, where do you think I make it? You'll have a whole distillery of it, if needed."

Chapter Ten

Calum left the cave before dawn to get to the ridge where he sent Gage and Devin. The 'cave' as it turned out, was an actual cave, with several extras added, Furniture, cabinets and in one corner, a distillery, that he had no idea how Marilyn got to run without power. It felt like a cabin that was made out of stone. Part of him didn't want to know how she did it, she was… he couldn't think of a word to adequately describe her.

He hadn't slept more than a few minutes. Instead he paced or stood in the entrance of the cave fighting his own instincts to go back to Shaelan. His cat was as conflicted as he was, understanding why he couldn't, but not being at peace with the facts. He wasn't used to not being in synch with his cat, since his very first shift both halves had always been connected with the same destination in mind. He was battling with himself in the last day, while keeping his cat contained so he didn't go back. If he'd been able to shift and burn off the emotions riding him, that would have made his life less tense as he waited for backup.

Traveling was a little easier, now that he knew what to look for. Marilyn explained how they got the drop on shifters they tranq'd had made his ego feel less damaged. Now that he knew to check up in the trees and not down, he was able to move with more confidence and speed.

He paused and looked down the ledge he'd just climbed. Needing the physical exertion to burn off his impatience, he'd taken a short cut and gone up instead of around. During the climb his mind bounced all over the place, but always ended up back on Shaelan. One of the many things that had him swearing in frustration. How the hell Gage had lived with this torment about Kelsey for so many years, he had no idea. Then again, maybe he did, he'd left his mate more for her safety than his. The main problem in this entire situation was her father... he'd had to leave so he wouldn't do anything epically stupid that would put her in harm's way. Not that what he'd just done was smart either, climb a shelf on a mountain covered in burrs... his clothes did not deflect them like his fur, he'd discovered. At least he'd have something to do while he waited for the guys to get here, pick burrs out of his hair, clothes and boots.

Double checking his location, he nodded and got back to getting to that ridge. Devin and Gage had until dark to get their asses on this mountain, then he was going back to the village—with or without them.

Shaelan set the book aside and got up to pace around the room, again. She'd done that at least ten times now, trying to work off the uneasy feeling that was plaguing her. Before that, she'd stood out on the small deck behind the house and stared off into the trees. Had she hoped to see Calum? Yes, then again, she would have had a fit if she did. He needed to stay away. He *had* to stay away.

Rubbing her hands up and down her arms, she looked from one to the other. Every few minutes her skin felt like it was crawling with something. If it were just her arms, she'd say she was anxious, but the feeling was on most of her body as well.

"You are wearing me out, just watching you today."

Nona's voice made her jump. She blew out a breath. "I'm sorry. I can't sit still."

"I caught that." Setting the knife down, she pushed the tray of herbs away and grabbed the edge of the table to assist her in standing up. "Your cat is riding just under your skin…" she came over to her and rested a cool palm on Shae's arm, "you're away from your mate." She gave her a soft smile. "You have every right to be uneasy." Patting her arm, she chuckled. "Some day, when all this settles down I'll tell you about my first change." She winked at her. "I damn near ripped Mari to shreds." Shaking her head, she went over to the window. "It's a small blessing she can't shift…" glancing at her over her shoulder she raised her brows, "we can't control the woman, imagine the cat." Jerking her head toward the glass she grinned again, "speaking of… here she comes, half the length of the stairs ahead of your mother, Aunt Louisa and…."

When she stopped speaking, Shae went over to look for herself. Her mother had her arm wrapped around someone. It was Billie. Shae turned and ran for the door, leaving it wide open in her wake. She ran down the stairs as fast as she could manage.

Her mother stopped walking and Billie looked up to see her. She started running up the stairs, two at a time, her long black hair flying out around her like a cape.

Shae stumbled down the last few steps to get to her, landing in her arms when she stopped. They squeezed each other tight, both panting and shaking from the exhilaration.

"I wanted to see you…" Billie gasped, "I had my first heat… and…" She buried her face in Shae's neck and squeezed again.

"…I didn't know yet, so you couldn't." Shae finished for her, just as breathless.

Billie nodded, then paused and inhaled in an obvious manner. She leaned back and covered her mouth, a tear rolling down her eye. "Oh Shae, they sent you in there too?"

It took less than a heartbeat for Shaelan to understand what her friend meant. "Oh… no." She hugged her to her again. "Come on. We have to talk." Billie just nodded.

Aunt Louisa and her mother ushered them up the steps as they clung to each other, awkwardly tripping every few feet.

Shae glanced at the other faces in the room, all were tear-stained.

"Bastards," Aunt Marilyn hissed. "No one has ever been brave enough to explain to me…" she glanced at Billie, "in detail, what it's like."

Billie sniffled and shook her head. "I don't blame…" tears started flowing again, "I don't even know his name."

"We'll find out." She couldn't believe what Billie had gone through. It wasn't at all like it had been for Calum and her. These herbs they used on people made them frantic, almost mad with need… it was vile. A shiver ran down her spine. They had to stop this before more women were hurt. Looking from Billie to her mentor, she waited until Nona looked up. "We have to tell them the rest."

Marilyn moaned, pained, "everyone has a right to know what's been happening under our very noses for so long." She shook her head. "Barbarism is what it is."

Her mother set her cup down on the table and looked at Marilyn. "What are you talking about?" She dabbed a hand on her cheek, wiping the dampness away.

Shae inhaled slowly and blew out a long breath, gathering her words. "Calum found a mass grave of remains, of bones…"

"Bones?" Her mother frowned, "what kind of bones?"

"Our kind, Faye, the remains of shifters." Nona supplied in a quiet voice.

"What do you mean?" Billie asked, her voice shaking.

Shae wrung her hands together, trying to keep it together enough to explain. "One of Calum's missing clansman was there, still wearing his collar…" she swallowed the lump in her throat, "he'd been shot in the head."

Her mother jumped up so fast she jarred the table, causing the cups to rattle. "What are you saying? The cap... men released are killed?" Her voice was high pitched. "That's … that's impossible. They go home." She said quietly, confusion in her tone.

Getting up, Shae went to her mother. She hadn't expected a reaction like this from her.

"Oh no." Billie gasped.

With a hand over her mouth, terror in her eyes, her mother stood there shaking her head back and forth. "No…" she inhaled a ragged breath, "no, I can't accept that."

"Mom?" Shae put a hand on her arm to steady her. "It's okay, we're going to put a stop to it…"

Her mother looked at her, but wasn't really seeing. "I always thought he went home. I was at peace with it that way." She shook her head. "How could I be so stupid?"

Pulling her hand back like it had been bitten, Shae looked over at Nona, who was looking at the floor, then to her aunts, no one would make eye contact with her. Something broke inside her in that moment and Shae slapped her hand on the table, sending cups clattering. "What aren't you telling me *now*?" She knew she was yelling, but after the last few days, she really didn't care. Chancing a glance to Billie, she saw confusion on her face, and felt just a tiny bit better that she wasn't the only clueless person in the room, for a change.

Standing there with her hands on her hips she watched the older women in the room glance to each other, they kept looking to her mother, so clearly this was for her mom to tell. Taking a deep breath, she tried to be calm enough to ask, even though she wanted to demand. "Mom?" Her mother didn't look at her. Shae studied the emotions on her face, they went from shame to anger, to mourning. It could only mean one thing. "Mom, is he my father? Leroy, is *he* my father?"

Her mothers teared eyes jumped to connect with hers. She shook her head. "No."

Shae put a hand on the table to steady herself. "*Who* is?"

A hollow expression replaced the sadness in her mother's eyes. "I don't know his name… they… they were numbered and the names in the book are," she exhaled a ragged breath, "*was* his assigned name." Her mother sat quickly, as if her legs had given out. She stared past Shae's shoulder, her eyes glazed, not seeing anything. "It's your middle name. Kel, only we add more to them, depending on the sex of the baby…" she gave her a guilty look, "Kelani. It's how they keep track, so half-siblings don't mate."

Shae's legs gave out, she dropped down to the floor and lowered her head onto her knees, hugging them. "*Finish.*" She growled, unable to feel anything but rage.

"Shae…" Nona said softly.

Lifting her head, Shaelan glared. "I want her to finish explaining *why* a man that has hated my very existence for my *entire* life has been masquerading as *my* father." Nona sat back in her chair again. Turning slowly, Shae looked at her mother, the woman that had, up to this point, been the only pure and unmarred thing in her world. "Finish," she whispered hoarsely.

"I had a mate, not a true one, but we loved each other." She nodded, looking down at her own hands. "He had been injured, in a fight…" she glanced fleetingly at Nona, "He was the true alpha of the clan and…" she exhaled a slow breath, "and we were discussing putting an end to the captive breeding…he didn't agree with it." She finally looked at Shaelan, tears filling her eyes. "But…we couldn't conceive, so I consented to participate in the breeding program." She offered a shaky smile. "We just wanted a child to love." The words garbled as she continued, "Your fa-Leroy killed my mate in a challenge to become alpha…" she swallowed a sob, "my family had always led…" She held a shaking hand over her mouth, "he didn't know I was carrying you when he took over…" she shook her head several times, "he let me keep you when he found out." Her whole body stared shaking, "He thought he would be seen as strong and virile when it was revealed that I was pregnant so soon after…" She shook her head several times, "but he never truly accepted that you weren't his." Her eyes pleaded with Shae, "I would have died before I gave you up."

Shae didn't know how long she stared at her mother. She rocked her whole body gently as she hugged her knees tightly. "Where's this book?" Her voice sounded hollow, even to her own ears.

"I can get it," Nona said softly.

She didn't turn to look at her, "I want to see, with my own eyes, if I have siblings I didn't know about."

"You do." Her mother said in a sad tone. "That boy you liked we forbad you to hang out with. Kellan is his middle name."

She had a brother. No father. Her entire life was one lie after the other. "Does he know?"

Her mother shook her head. "Only the elders know, outside of the alpha and maybe the second family."

Shae nodded her head in time to the rocking motion of her body. Stopping herself, she pushed to her feet and stood there for a moment. Forcing her numb legs to move, she walked to her room and closed the door. Locked it, then she slid to the floor and leaned against it. Outside it she heard someone else do the same thing, and knew that Billie was there. She didn't think she could face even her right now.

She stared at the bookshelf, not really seeing it. Her heart physically hurt, but she couldn't form a tear. *So many lies.* Her entire world was one lie after another. Shae felt rage move through her, and she jumped up, screaming as she swatted at the books on the shelf. They flew in the air, clunking into whatever they hit. Picking up the shelf, she heaved it at the wall and then spun around and flipped her mattress off the bed. Her dresser was next, the drawers were pulled out and flung across the room. She stopped and stood panting, and shaking. *Calum*, she wanted to see him. Not even he could fix this ness. She screamed again, making a noise she had never before heard in her life. The sound of a lonely, wild animal.

"Shae," Billie's voice came through the door. "Shae, please let me in." She pleaded.

The tears fell so fast now, she blindly stumbled to the door and placed her cheek against it as she reached to unlock it.

Chapter Eleven

Kelsey stopped and turned in a circle, taking in the vastness of the mountain. "I can't believe the guide only brought us this far."

Rayne adjusted the strap on her backpack. "I'm surprised he came this far."

Jake went past, giving Kelsey a wink, "I'm just enjoying the holiday from the shop."

She couldn't blame him for that, in all the years she'd known him, he rarely left the clan's area. Catching up to Rayne, she glanced back at her mate, Gage, "He said ten minutes and we should be at Calum's car." Jesse walked by her, she didn't know him very well, but the others trusted him, so she would until he gave her a reason not to. She'd asked Gage, quietly, what clan Jesse was from and since then had wanted to ask him to shift. Just so she could see a leopard up close. Of course, she didn't because this wasn't a casual vacation they were on.

"I'm more concerned with the *way* he said 'this is as far as I dare go. Good luck to you.' He looked scared." Jesse said, pausing to adjust the laces on his boots.

Gage and Devin exchanged a look that had Kelsey and Rayne stopping to stare at them.

"What *aren't* you telling us?" Rayne demanded of Devin.

Devin exhaled and stopped walking, just looked up the mountain. "There used to be a clan in this area," he started walking again. "When the alliance was still in it's infancy."

"Did they move?" Jake asked.

"No, they just vanished. None of those sent to check on them ever came back." He looked around again. "Anyone sent up to investigate never came back either. So, they stopped sending people."

Kelsey stopped and looked at Rayne.

Gage looked around then back to her, "What is it?"

She waved a hand toward the bottom of the mountain. "That village we were in…" she looked at Rayne, "it had voodoo vibes."

Rayne nodded.

Gage rubbed the back of his neck. "What are *voodoo vibes* exactly, Kels?"

She rolled her eyes at him for not getting it.

"I think she means creepy as shit." Jesse offered.

Jake laughed, "Voodoo vibes, creepy as shit… this is *so much* better than the shop."

Shaking his head, Gage caught up to Kelsey and looked over her head at Devin. "Was it a big clan?"

Devin shrugged, "Large enough," he pointed in the direction they were walking, "this mountain was their territory, according to alliance archives."

"Clan of what variety?" Rayne asked as she stepped around some long grass like something was going to jump out of it, while trying to tame her long blonde hair enough to pulled back from her face.

Devin moved over to walk beside her. "The cat variety."

Jake stopped so fast Kelsey almost walked into his back. He turned, a serious look replacing his usual easy-going one. "Okay, I'm with the ladies on this one. We're going to find Calum, who has tracked disappearing members, of the cat variety… to an area where an entire clan vanished…"

Kelsey glanced at Gage who was glaring at Jake, probably because he was agreeing with her and Rayne.

"There's his car," Jesse said, relief clear in his voice.

Gage walked quickly to the car, checking the area around it as he went. Then he went to the front tire and reached behind it to pull out the keys.

Kelsey raised her eyebrows and looked at Rayne, who had much the same expression.

Opening the door, he leaned in and lifted the floormat, and pulled out a piece of paper.

"Why do I feel like this is some system you guys developed early in life?" Kelsey asked.

Rayne laughed, "I'm sure it's nothing we want to know about."

Devin and Gage exchanged another of their looks, confirming what Rayne had said.

"Fine." Kelsey tucked her hands in her pockets, feeling anxious standing still. "Does it say why he's there?"

Rayne nodded to her question. "Why we shouldn't shift, or why we women were required to come?"

Devin looked up from the note, "It's one piece of paper, hun, not a journal."

Jesse looked over his shoulder at the note then glanced around them. "We need to get going and see how far we can get before dark."

They walked for an hour more, as the sun started to set. Rayne and Kelsey walked close together feeling like this was a repeat of their ordeal a few weeks earlier.

"I have noticed one thing since being able to shift." Kelsey said out of the blue, "the mosquitos don't bother me."

"That is a plus." Rayne agreed. "The insects in Devin's forest are the size of birds."

Devin chuckled from behind them.

Rayne glanced over her shoulder at him. "The local creatures don't seem to know who you are, Devin."

Kelsey glanced into the growth of weeds beside them to see small eyes watching them.

"I'm nothing to them, hun. They're the real deal, not shifters."

Rayne sighed, "if that was supposed to make me feel better, you failed." She stumbled over a branch and grabbed Kelsey's arm to stop from falling. "They could still stop stalking us and respect our personal space." She let go of Kelsey's arm and reached down to adjust her boot. "Next time, we need to break in our boots *first*."

"This is the *last* time." Devin mumbled quietly. "We *are* in their territory… and Cal said no shifting." He reminded her.

Kelsey stopped. "They're creeping me out and getting on my nerves." Putting her chin down she focused and growled deep in the back of her throat. She heard scurrying in the grass and nodded. "Much better."

Gage walked over and put his arm around her. "Growling like a tiger in the middle of the bush would be announcing our presence and almost the same as shifting."

She sighed, "Sorry, not knowing what's going on has me on edge." Leaning down, he kissed the top of her head. "I wished we knew more."

Jake stopped and looked around them. "We have to be getting close…" he held up his hand and the other three males immediately surrounded Kelsey and Rayne. Jake shook his head, "there's someone moving around out there, but it's not steady movement."

Jesse nodded, "no shifting what-so-ever?" He whispered.

"Not until we know why." Devin answered.

"I hate being in such unfamiliar territory, Dev." Gage pulled Kelsey back into his side.

"So do I." Devin agreed, then motioned for them to walk again. "We're almost to the ridge he mentioned in the note."

Kelsey tried to use her new hearing and ability to scent around her, but her nerves were so jumbled and her heart was pounding so fast she couldn't focus. "If anything happens, we could go up in the…"

"*No* trees." Gage squeezed her into his side.

Jake, who was in the lead, suddenly crouched close to the ground. The other five immediately did the same.

"I hate this *shit*." Devin hissed.

"Agreed." Gage whispered, then nudged Kelsey. "You girls get in that tree over there."

Kelsey hissed, "but you just said…"

"Go." He nudged her again.

"Come on Rayne." Kelsey grabbed her arm on the way by.

"But I don't…" A branch snapped from behind them. "climb." She moved past Kelsey. "If I rip my pants I'm going to be pissed." She hissed quietly.

Calum leaned against the tree and shook his head as he watched the women climb. He could have called out for them to stop, but didn't. He'd stepped on the branch, just to see what Gage and Devin would do. Now that he had them on edge, maybe they'd stop making more noise than a marching band.

Gage suddenly stood up, hands on his hips. "Calum, you bastard, I can smell you."

Calum grinned and started walking again. "Could you guys make any *more* noise?" He kept his voice low, knowing the shifters would hear him. Marilyn had said this area was clear of village patrols, but he wasn't taking anything for granted while on this large hunk of dirt. Stepping out of the taller plants, he nodded to Jesse and Jake. As backup went, they were two he trusted.

Stopping in front of Gage, he cleared his throat. "You may want to get your women out of the tree now, we have to get to the cave."

"We're going to a cave?" Jake asked.

Calum nodded, not feeling like explaining just yet.

"Cool." Jake looked excited by the idea.

He waited for Rayne and Kelsey to have both feet on the ground, then turned. "Let's go, I don't like being out in the open in the dark."

Gage put a hand on his shoulder to stop him from walking. "If your anxious, then I'm feeling all nervy too. What the hell is going on?"

Devin cocked his head and studied him. "Did you find your men?"

He had no idea where to start to explain any of this, and he definitely wasn't going to stand here and chat. They needed to get back to the cave. He nodded. "Yeah. I'll try to explain, but we have to get moving. Now."

Rayne came over, pulling at leaves tangled in her hair. "We can't shift to speed it up?"

Running a hand through his hair, he debated on it for a second. "Better not. I don't think they'd be interested in the rest of you, but as I've already escaped once, I don't want to do it again." He growled softly, "I'm not fond of chains."

"*Chains?*" Gage immediately pulled Kelsey closer.

Devin nodded as he grabbed Rayne's hand. "Lead the way, and we'll talk when we get where we're going." He nodded to Jesse, "You and Jake take the rear and watch our backs."

Calum started walking back the way he'd come. He felt better knowing he wasn't alone. It didn't feel better with Shaelan still in the village with her insane father though, but this was a start.

"Are you okay?" Rayne asked him, keeping her voice down.

He snorted, "I'm in one piece if that's what you mean. I had stiches in one shoulder, but it healed when I shifted yesterday." Looking over his shoulder, he caught the look between the men. "Let's pick up the pace, if you think you can jog for a bit?"

Kelsey caught up to him. "You have my adrenalin pumping like crazy, so I'm up for that." She brushed past him and started running without having any clue where she was going.

"Me too." Rayne answered, following Kelsey.

Nodding, he swung his pack around to his back and started jogging after them so he could take the lead.

They were only about thirty feet from the entrance when he heard a low yowl, from a jaguar announcing its presence. He stopped and crouched down, looking in every direction he could. Without turning to look, he knew the others would be low to the ground now as well. Calum inhaled, trying to find the direction of the cat. Turning slowly, he waited. He saw the eyes coming toward them in the dark, shrugging out of his pack, he braced himself for a fight.

He heard a warning growl from behind him and recognized it as Gage's voice. Out of the trees, a large male, with a coat almost as dark as his own started walking toward them. Hadn't Nona said no males come near here… Huffing out a breath, he stood up slowly, not wanting to make any fast moves. "Brock?" he asked quietly. The cat turned in a slow circle as if to say, 'look at me'. Sighing, he looked behind him to the others. "It's okay."

Brock came bounding over in long strides and rubbed against his leg. He refused to pet a male cat. "Are you patrolling?" Brock chuffed in response. He started walking toward the cave entrance. "We're almost there, guys."

He turned to see Brock walking in a circle around Jake. "He likes women." Calum said and then almost laughed at the wide-eyed look Jake gave the cat as he stepped away from him.

"He's beautiful," Rayne said going over and stroking a hand over his coat. Devin growled. Lifting her hand away, she rolled her eyes at him. "Not the same species, don't get your tail in a knot."

Kelsey chuckled and caught up to Calum. "You have a lot of explaining to do."

Nodding, he motioned for her to go into the cave. "Yeah, I do. And it's going to get messy."

She stopped and looked at him. "Messy like tears or like tie-Gage-up-so-he-doesn't-do-something-stupid, messy?"

"Hey, *Gage* can hear you." Gage said as he stopped beside her.

"Both," Calum answered and motioned again to the cave.

Jake came over and walked beside them. "Missing clans, a dark mysterious cave, voodoo vibes and creepy as hell, how bad can it be?" He snorted and walked in.

When they'd all gone in, Brock bounded over. "Thanks for keeping lookout. Please go watch out for Shaelan."

Brock looked at him for a second, then took off into the dark.

Calum heaved out a deep breath, wishing he could shift and go run off some of the frustration that weighed on his shoulders, as heavy as the ground he stood on. Running his hand through his hair, he looked at the entrance and knew he had to keep it together to fill the others in on the last few days of his life, and prepare them for the hell that was going to be the next several.

He watched Gage pace by again, and figured he'd give him a few more minutes. Turning, he looked to Devin, who hadn't moved a muscle since he went and stood in the entrance. He hadn't seen Jake or Jesse, both had gone outside and not yet returned. It was hard, the unspoken commonality among all male shifters was when they had a problem to work through, or an emotional upset, they shifted and ran it off. Being here, shifting was too dangerous, so that left them trying to sort it through the hard way. A way, he'd recently learned, that was not easy at all.

The biggest problem he was having right now, he hadn't yet told them everything. They didn't know about what happened to the captives once 'released', and he hadn't found a way to explain to them about Shaelan's existence, or the fact that the alpha was her father.

Pushing away from the wall, he went over and looked at the water and the bottles of whiskey beside it. Having tasted the potent brew, he opted for water. Getting a cup full, he turned back and saw Kelsey coming toward him. She stopped a few feet away, and it was then he realized she completely understood the way it was in the life of a shifter now. Mated females didn't get too close to males, aside from their mates.

Hopefully Kelsey and Rayne would help fill in some blanks for Shaelan. Her village had taken the shifter norm and misconstrued it, or created some bastardized version, and he wasn't sure what rules or protocol they followed, if any at all. That's why he wanted the girls to come, his patience only went so far when it came to explanations.

Somewhere in the back of his mind, he knew Devin would come personally, not just send others, and he knew Gage would arrive as well. He didn't know Kelsey and Rayne as well as the men, but he knew enough to understand that there was no way their mates would be coming without them.

He blinked, realizing that Kelsey had spoke to him. "Sorry?"

She gave him a sweet smile. "I asked if you were okay?"

"Yeah." He motioned to Gage still pacing around. "I'm giving them time to absorb what I told them before I pile on more."

Brows furrowed, she glanced at her mate. "There's more?"

Nodding, Calum finished what was in his cup. "Unfortunately, but the waves of anger coming off them was getting a little intense, so I thought I'd wait before continuing."

"A bad kind of more?" Rayne asked as she got up.

Taking a deep breath, he debated on lying to them, but decided it wasn't worth it. "It's not good."

"Let's get on with it then." Devin said from entranceway. "Jake and Jesse are standing watch, so if we can move close to the door, they'll be able to listen."

Calum moved without comment to his pack and pulled out his phone, then went and sat by the doorway. If he stayed on his feet any longer, he was going to drop. Sitting on the ridge all day watching for them, and wondering about Shaelan had exhausted him, both emotionally and physically. More than once he wanted to go to the village, but didn't want to take a chance on anything happening to his friends that were here because he'd called.

When he realized Gage and Devin were looking down at him, he sighed, this wandering mind thing was getting to be a bit much. Both of them looked like they were barely holding it together, he could see the rage brewing. Unlocking his phone, he brought up the pictures, and without a word of warning he handed the phone to Devin.

"Am I looking at what I think I am?" Devin asked, his voice shaking with emotion barely held in check.

"Its where they take the captives after they're done with them." He couldn't look at the women to see their faces, or he might lose it. "Gene was on the top, collar still on..." He glanced quickly to Gage as he studied the pictures. "With a bullet hole in his head."

Kelsey and Rayne both gasped. He closed his eyes unable to watch another female hurting over this. "I still have to go and bury him." Opening them, he watched Gage hand Jake the phone where he now stood in the entrance.

"We'll do it together after this is resolved." Devin said icily. He stood with his hands on his hips staring at the dirt under his boots. "Those bones could be any number of clan members reported missing over the years. The alliance will have records of any jags missing." He shook his head. "I don't know if they can ever be confirmed though."

Calum shook his head. "I don't know if they have records of any kind, they don't exactly ask your name and address when you regain consciousness and are chained to a wall."

Gage squatted down and looked at him. "They have to have some kind of help, or warning system or... something." He looked up to Devin who agreed with him. "If they got you, they *had* to have help. You're a ghost on four legs when in the bush."

"They're in the trees, that's how they get the drop on you." He shook his head, "but, yeah they have to have someone warning them, I doubt they sit in trees all day waiting for a chance that a shifter wanders by."

"What about that voodoo vibe in the village?" Kelsey asked quietly.

Nodding, Calum still avoided looking at either woman. "I thought about that village too, while I cooled my heels today watching for you to get here."

"The Alliance will dig into it." Devin heaved a loud sigh. "So, what are we going to do?"

"Can you go in as a representative of the Alliance and hold them accountable?" Rayne asked Devin.

He shook his head. "Even if I'm holding a copy of the blood oath in my hand, I doubt that would get us far. The elders that made the pact, won't still be living." He rubbed his forehead. "This mess is the alliance's fault, they just gave up and it got out of hand…" his voice trailed off, no one needed to be reminded how out of hand it now was.

"How many people are there?" Gage shrugged, "can we get in without being seen?"

Calum took his phone when a somber-faced Jesse stepped inside with it. "It's a big village, too many for us to handle alone, from what I saw."

"Do we call for more backup?" Devin wondered.

"I don't know." Calum rubbed a hand over his face. "I'm exhausted and can't think straight. Marilyn and the medicine woman said to give them a few days to get their ducks lined up…" he shook his head at Gage when he raised an eyebrow to him using that phrase, "so I'm guessing they'll start from the inside and we'll have to see how far they get." He thought of Shaelan, all he wanted to do was see her to make sure she was safe.

"What else?" Gage asked with a hard edge to his voice. "What else haven't you told us?"

Taking a deep breath, he exhaled and dropped his head down. "My mate is in that village."

Gage stood up, "and you left her there?", he was close to roaring.

Opening his hands, he gave him a blank look. "I couldn't stay and end up back in chains. What the fu…"

Jake stuck his head in the entranceway. "A woman is coming this way."

Calum got up quickly. He wanted it to be Shaelan, but hoped it wasn't at the same time, not her out wandering around in the dark.

"With a pink hat on..." Jesse's low voice said from somewhere outside the door.

Calum snorted. "Marilyn, and that's her *hair*, not a hat." He shook his head when Jesse's head appeared in the entrance and looked at him, his eyebrows almost to his hairline. "You'll see." He smirked.

Marilyn didn't disappoint when she came in. "Whew! I need to get me a horse or some damn thing..." She lifted a foot from the floor and bent her knee a few times, swinging it back and forth. "Almost broke this off in a damn hole I didn't see soon enough..." She stopped and looked around at everyone, then smiled as if she was the hostess at a party. "Oh, good you made it. Brock told me company had arrived, so I brought food." She held up a worn, honest-to-goodness picnic basket.

No one moved or said a word, just looked at her. Calum stepped over and took the basket. "Thanks, Marilyn." She grabbed a hold of his chin when he would have stepped away and pulled his head down close to hers.

"You look like something the cat dragged in." She laughed, "Ha, maybe not cat..."

He straightened up slowly, "It's was a long day."

"I don't doubt it. Mine has been damn gruelling. I'm all tuckered out. I've talked to almost every female old enough to have boobs about what's been going on." She was looking everyone over from head to toe as she spoke. "Another day and we'll have a full uprising in the works. Doesn't matter the nature of a body, none likes choking down lies and deceit." She smiled at Kelsey, then Rayne. "My *word*, your women are absolutely lovely. I mean, just gorgeous." She glanced from one male to the next. "Who's the royal one? Do I kneel or curtsy or something?"

Calum smiled at the horrified expression on Devin's face. "I don't think that's necessary, this time."

Marilyn's pink head bobbed a few times. "Okay, then. Let me sit this aged ass down and I'll fill in some details." She walked by them and headed into the cave. "A sip of whiskey might be needed too, I'm thinking." She waved a hand over her shoulder without looking at them. "Tell those two statues outside to come in. No male comes near to this part of the mountain, they're all petrified the cats in heat will drag him into the depths of this cave of *spirits*." She sat down and winked at anyone looking at her, which was everyone. "A little story we concocted to make sure this space was only for us women." Her loud laugh rang out, echoing off the stone walls surrounding them.

Shaking his head, Calum held the basket out to the stunned looking Kelsey, and motioned for everyone to go in. "What did you mean another day and you'll have a full uprising?" He walked in to sit down, and try to relax his tense muscles.

She waved a hand in the air, "Several of the women will be coming here in the morning so we can talk it out." She shrugged, "we don't know a damn thing about bucking the system, never mind overthrowing it." Ruffling her bright hair with one hand she grinned, "this is the only bucking I've ever done." Frowning, she looked at the floor, "Okay, I'm lying… I have Ronald smuggle magazines and stuff in with the supplies. Then pass them around the village to keep us up-to-date on world events." Waving that off, she looked up suddenly, then bobbed her head a few times.

In the back of his mind he had to wonder if the magazines she referred to were tabloid rags… but didn't have energy to explain to her that the news in those was less than accurate. The woman plain exhausted him, just listening to her. He started to lower his tired as hell body into one of the chairs. "How's Shaelan?" His heart thudded in his chest when he said her name.

She glanced at every person there, but didn't once make eye contact with him. Then began picking imaginary link off her skirt.

He froze. "What's wrong?"

Clasping her hands in her lap, she cleared her throat. "She had a rough time today…"

"The change? Is she okay?" He stood up, "Fuck! I shouldn't have left her there…"

"No, no. Wasn't her change coming, well it could be in the background but…" She took a shaky breath.

When he saw her eyes tear up, he turned to run for the entrance. Before he could reach it, Jake and Jesse grabbed him. "Let me go," he growled. He was dragging them, their boots sliding across the stone as he continued toward the entrance. Devin appeared in front of him, pushing back on his shoulders. He growled a low warning. Prince or not, that was his mate and something was wrong. "Dev, move…"

Laughter like he'd never heard filled the cave. He saw the confusion on Devin's face as he glanced over his shoulder. It was a male's laughter. Huffing out a breath, he shook off the men trying to hold him and turned around to see Gage almost doubled over laughing and pointing at him.

"About. Fucking. Time." Gage gasped between bursts, "You asshole!" He straightened and tried to sober up. "How many years have you rode my ass about this mating *stuff*?" He chuckled, "and now it's your turn." He looked to the roof of the cave, "thank you," he whispered.

Growling low and pacing away, Calum rolled his shoulders and tried to walk it off, so he wouldn't go running back into the chains waiting for him at the village. "Bastard," he hissed, only to hear Devin chuckle quietly.

"Whew! That was exciting!" Marilyn said loudly. "Damn, I love you guys." He heard her sniffle and turned to see her facial expression go from smiling to distraught. She looked right at him. "Please don't leave us here to live like this anymore." Rayne and Kelsey were in front of her comforting her before he could reply.

He looked at Gage, then to Devin, both men's expressions reflected what he was feeling. No way in hell they were leaving this clan to live like this.

Jake stomped over and sat down. "I'm never leaving the shop again." He wiped a hand across his brow and scowled at the floor by his feet.

"You said something about whiskey?" Jesse said suddenly, looking to Marilyn. He pointed to the bottles, "Is that it?"

She nodded to the women to let them know she was okay, "You need to bring me a bottle there handsome. I have to get through explaining to the large, angry, green-eyed one what transpired today to upset everyone, and most especially his mate."

Calum slid down the wall, and exhaled, trying to bring his cat under control. His whole life he'd kept to himself. Stayed out of trouble, never stirred any up. In the last few days his entire world was a mess, not just a simple one, but a fucking mess, one he couldn't even see clear enough to fix. Not feeling any more settled, he looked at Marilyn. "Tell me."

Chapter Twelve

"Calum, please, for the sake of my sanity, sit down." Jake growled.

Turning, he looked at Jake, then realized everyone was staring at him. "Sorry." He glanced to the entrance again. "Walls are closing in on me." Rubbing the back of his neck he went to start pacing again and stopped himself. "She said morning…"

Gage heaved a loud sigh, "It's been dawn for about ten seconds. Sit the fuck down and let me pretend I'm still sleeping."

"Won't someone wonder if a bunch of women leave?" Kelsey asked in a sleepy voice. "I mean how bad is it there, are people free to come and go, do they monitor everyone?"

Calum had been wondering the same thing for the last hour, and was still kicking himself in the ass for knowing before he left his mate there.

"Someone better bring coffee, or I'll go end this tyranny once and for all, single-handed." Rayne moaned.

Devin chuckled the nodded. "And she would too. Vicious she-wolf without her caffeine." Rayne smacked him.

Jesse came wandering in. "There's a group coming. Will take them a bit to get here though, they are only halfway down the hill on the other side of the ravine."

Calum frowned at him, he'd just checked a few minutes ago and could see no one from this location.

Smirking, Jesse pointed to Kelsey, "used her tree-view trick."

"Later on," Calum said as he turned toward the entrance, "I want more details on *that* adventure."

Devin stood up and stretched. "Figured you had enough going on right now, you don't need to go even the score on that front too."

Calum paused and looked at him. "They abducted your mates, that is *my* business and someone will pay for it…" He backed up a step closer to the entrance. "I just have to clear up a few other things first."

"Yeah, like deal with his *mate!*" Gage chuckled.

Snarling at him, Calum turned back to watch for the women. If Shaelan wasn't with them, he was sending someone back to get her. It had almost killed him being away from her this last day.

It felt like hours, as he stood there watching in the direction of the village. He knew it was quite the treacherous path to navigate, having done it in the dark, and if they had Nona or other elders with them it could take a while. He exhaled loudly, again, and jammed his hands into his pockets as he stepped few more feet away from the cave to see if he could spot them.

He heard the others come up behind him, but didn't turn to look.

"Not a word," Rayne said in warning, most likely to Devin.

Calum had at least been right about something in all of this. Gage and Devin were never going to let him forget how he'd harassed, lectured, or ribbed them about mates. Ever. He still hadn't told them how he met his mate, or that he'd marked her. There just weren't the right words without it sounding bad, especially in front of the women. Mostly, he was going on instinct with all of this. His knowledge of true mates was limited, so he relied on his gut. Which right now was tied in knots.

When he caught a brief glimpse of pink, he started moving in that direction. There was only one thing *that* color on this entire mountain.

As they got closer, he counted a dozen heads moving through the gulley that lead up to the cave. There was only one he was interested in seeing at this point, and when he spotted her it was like the light from the sun was only shining on her.

He glanced behind him to see everyone had followed. Jake and Jesse were looking all around them, keeping watch for anyone coming from another direction.

Unable to look away any longer, he turned back to see Shaelan had stopped walking and was looking up to where he stood. His cat rubbed over his skin, his heart jumped up into his throat. *Fuck staying out of sight.* He moved out of the shelter of the trees and started in her direction while at the same moment, she dropped what she'd been carrying and started running up the hill.

His feet slipped a few times on the steep incline, and he slid a few feet, but he kept going and didn't slow down until she was almost in front of him. She threw herself into him with such a force he landed on his butt on the hill, still holding her, he sat up and buried his face in her hair. *Cinnamon.* Cat and man were back in synch, and a feeling of contentment came over him.

Leaning back, he grasped her head to see her face. Her jaw was slightly bruised and her lip was still healing, but the swelling was gone. Her eyes moved over his face in the same way. "Are you okay?" He searched her eyes, trying to see for himself. She shook head, then dropped her head to hug him tightly again. She snuggled her face into his throat and his cat started prancing inside him, excited by having her this close.

"So many lies," she whispered.

He ran a hand over the hair hanging down her back. "I know. Your aunt filled me in." He smirked, "then the guys held me back from coming to you."

She leaned back. "I wanted to see you too, after I found out." She bit her lip for a second, "I don't understand any of this, Calum."

When she said his name, he dragged his eyes from her mouth. "I know." He sighed, "this is not how it's supposed to be."

"I don't want to be away from you again. That's the only thing I know for sure, even if I don't understand why."

She closed her eyes briefly and his heart jerked in his chest when she opened them and he saw they were filled with sorrow.

"It's horrible, what the women go through... and probably the men." She took a shaky breath. "My friend Billie was with one of your clansmen. Dale. Another woman was with Marc..." She looked behind her. "Shoot, my bag." She turned back to him, looking panicked. "I have the book of all the men, women and babies since it started."

"We'll get it and we'll deal with all of it..." He looked at her mouth again and lightly grasped her chin. As he lowered his face to kiss her, a shadow moved over them. Pulling her closer to him to shelter her, he looked up to see a woman with black hair grinning down at him.

"Hi. I'm Billie."

Shaelan sighed and turned while still sitting on him to look at her. "My bag..." Billie held up a cloth bag. "Thanks."

She moved to get off him, and whether he agreed with it or not, he realized they weren't going to get any more alone time right now. Standing, he set her on her feet and grasped her hand. Leaning down, he whispered, "tell me someone brought coffee."

She grinned. "We're not *that* uncivilized up here."

He hugged her against his side, tucking her under his arm. "Then your clansmen are safe from *the* Rayne."

Billie looked up at the sky. "Not a cloud in the sky."

Calum chuckled. "This is going to be a long meeting."

As they reached the cave, he was relieved to see everyone settling down outside. The thought of so many being in there together in such a small space would have had his cat on edge. There was a reason he spent so much time alone, he wasn't big on crowds. He noticed Shaelan wasn't rushing over to be in the middle of them either, she seemed content to stand aside and holding his hand. Which was good, as he didn't plan on letting go, not just yet.

She exhaled. "I suppose you should meet my mother." Her voice was filled with tension. "I know it's not her fault, she just tried to keep me safe," she looked up at him, "but it's hard right now."

He felt like he was falling into her eyes, and actually had to blink to kick his brain back in gear. "I think she had to go through a lot and do what she needed to, so you both survived."

Shaelan continued to look at him for what felt like an eternity, he didn't know her well enough to understand what the changes of expression on her face meant. He stood there, not breathing while he waited for her to speak.

"I suppose she did," she said quietly.

Dragging his eyes away from her, he surveyed the women present. When he reached one with high cheekbones and a refined aura, he studied her for a moment. She kept looking over at Shaelan, every few seconds. He leaned down, "is that woman in the blue sweater your mom?"

She gave him a shocked look. "How did you know?"

Calum smirked, "Same beautiful face as yours." He shrugged, "and she keeps looking at you with that motherly look they get when they're checking if you're okay."

She laughed quietly.

When she suddenly stepped in front of him, he jerked his head up to see why. Rayne and Kelsey were heading their way. He knew he was standing there grinning, simply because she'd moved to block him from other females, but he didn't care. Squeezing her hand that was still in his behind her back, he leaned down. "They're coming to see you, not me."

"Me? Why?"

"They're my two best friend's mates." He was trying not to push his face into her hair, now close to his face. "Both had similar situations as you... in not knowing they were shifters." He clarified.

She turned, "Really?" Heaving out a breath she leaned closer to rest her head on his chest. "You don't know how much better that makes me feel. I thought I must be the stupidest person *ever* for not noticing."

He rested his chin on the top of her head, as he cradled her into his chest. "I think your situation and clan took things to the extreme, but no, you're not stupid."

"Calum, can we borrow your mate for a few moments?" Rayne asked sweetly.

He hadn't realized they were going to take her. He frowned.

Kelsey grinned at him. "We're just going to go get you some coffee and introduce ourselves."

"Promise we'll bring her right back." Rayne added.

Gage and Devin started walking in their direction, he gave Shaelan's hand a quick squeeze and released it. She took Rayne's outstretched one and went with them, after a quick look over her shoulder at him. Giving himself a mental shake, he looked back to find serious expressions on the men's faces. "What?" he asked when they were close enough he could say it quietly.

Devin waved his phone around. "Pulled this out to check for a signal and see if I can reach dad and one of the women said she's seen Jerome with a phone before, but had no idea what it was until now."

"A cell phone? But they don't..." he scowled. "Son of a bitch. They do have people feeding them info about shifters coming up the mountain."

Gage nodded. "Meaning they probably know we're here. We had one of the villagers bring us up."

"Fuck." Calum turned around so his back was to the women and stood with his hands on his hips. "and they know my car, that you went to."

"Yeah, so they're going to know we were coming for you." Gage said quietly.

Calum glanced at the phone still in Devin's hand. "Is there signal?"

He shrugged, "Not the best, but I could get through to Dad if you think we need to go that route."

He nodded, "I think that the more outside of here that know, the better." Looking over his shoulder, he found Shaelan. "There's a book with a list of women, captives and babies born. Make sure someone takes pictures in case it gets lost..." Shaelan was smiling at something Kelsey said. "This is going to get very messy." He turned back and motioned with his head. "Lady in the blue sweater is Shaelan's mother and the alpha's... wife." The word mate meant too much to his culture, he didn't feel the man had earned the title.

Gage blew out a breath, "from what Marilyn told us last night, she's with us."

Devin nodded, "but she'll be the most vulnerable, aside from Shaelan that is."

"I want my men out of chains, we can't do anything until we know they're clear." Calum looked again to check on Shaelan. "And we need to know numbers, weapons, and just what we're up against down there."

"Agreed." Gage said in a hushed tone.

"Let me go wander around to grab a better signal and call dad. I don't even know where to start to explain all of this to him." He mumbled.

Calum nodded, as he watched Nona coming toward them. "Take Jesse with you. None of us go anywhere alone."

Gage nodded and motioned to get Jesse's attention. "I'm going to go chat with Marilyn, she may think she's unequipped to help here, but she's mistaken. The things that woman knows and does..."

Chuckling, Calum glanced over to where she was chatting with some of the other women. "I would have been scared to death to deal with her in her youth."

"Same." Gage said with a grin as he moved over to talk to her.

He checked on Shaelan once more before he found Nona standing in front of him.

"You two need to resolve *that*, soon." She said with a knowing expression on her face.

He rubbed a hand over the back of his neck. "Which part is *that*? Me losing my sanity, or are you talking about some other part?"

"Heh," she nodded, "no that's the part I meant."

Jamming his hands in his pockets, he looked down as her eyes moved over his face, appraising him. From the look, it wasn't good and he wasn't fooling anyone but himself, pretending otherwise. "I'm trying to give her time."

Nona folded her hands in front of her and glanced at Shaelan for a second, then looked back to him. "You think time is going to clarify and settle the emotions ripping through the two of you?"

He glanced over at Shaelan and let out a quiet breath. "No ma'am."

"She's the strongest person I've ever known." She smiled, "Marched up my hill when she was just a child, against her fathers' orders, then asked that I train her to be the clan's next Nona," she winked at him, "it's a title, not a name. She's fought against that man every day since. I think when she struggled for the right to go get a more advanced education, it was the start of her preparing, without even knowing it, that she'd need the strength to change her life. All of our lives."

"I didn't know…"

She gave him an annoyed look, "You think she ran up that hill when she saw you because she felt like going for a jog?"

Calum tried to think of something intelligent to say, but couldn't, so he shook his head 'no'.

Nona nodded abruptly. "She had her revelation yesterday, tore her room apart and screamed like a vengeful creature…she sat on the deck staring into the night for hours after that, even fell asleep there. Her animal took her out there to watch for yours, I believe." She looked him up and down. "She doesn't need time, she needs a man strong enough to let her be who she has to be." Sighing, she searched his eyes, the expression in hers softening. "Only one thing will clarify it, make all the pieces fit together." She pulled the collar of her jacket down to expose an aged bite mark next to her collarbone. "And after that, you'll both be stronger and ready to face this head on."

He looked at her neck again, even though she'd already covered it back up.

"He died a long time ago, before we grew a single wrinkle together." She said quietly.

"I'm sorry." He couldn't imagine finding Shaelan then losing her. He couldn't even stay strong for a day without her right now.

"So am I, every damn day still, *but* having had him in my life, even for that short a time, has given me the strength every day since."

He stood there, still trying to process it, then looked around at everyone. "We can't…"

She nodded, like he'd already finished speaking. "Talk to Mari, she'll have a place you can have some quiet time together. Take the night, while we get a plan in place and get you and her settled so you can help finish this then free her people."

Calum looked down at her, then nodded briefly. "I think the strongest person I've ever known is standing right in front of me." He meant it too.

"Heh," she grinned, "sweet talker." She waved a hand in Mari's direction. "Go talk to the crazy one and go to your girl before you distract everyone from the task at hand, stalking her with your eyes every two seconds." She walked away chuckling.

Shae watched him as he stood there talking to Nona, she couldn't help that her eyes kept going back to him.

"I'm afraid you're getting the biggest brooder of all of them," Kelsey said with a grin.

"Oh?" She glanced back at him. "Did he…" She clutched the thermos against her chest and tried not to blush. "Did he tell you how we met?"

Rayne shook her head. "No, I think he started to, but Marilyn came storming in."

Shae grinned, "Yes, she does that well. It's a skill, according to her."

"It is something." Kelsey said quietly. "So, how did you meet?"

She had no idea why she had brought it up, but now that she had there was no way out. She huffed out a breath, "I may die of embarrassment explaining, but…" She looked back to him for a second. "I'm training to be the next medicine woman for the clan, and I went in to check his shoulder." She pursed her lips, "actually there's more before that. I was being married off to a guy I didn't know…"

"Oh my god, does Calum know? Is the guy dead?" Kelsey asked leaning closer.

Shae shook her head, "No, he's not. That's a story for another time." She grinned. "A strange one, then again, I guess to you two, my whole world is."

Kelsey snorted, "Oh we may be tied with that one."

Rayne nodded enthusiastically. "Nothing in our lives could be close to normal before we found out we were animals."

They both looked back to her. She felt a kinship with these women and it made her feel weepy inside. Exhaling, before she changed her mind, "So, I asked Calum—and just so you know, this was Aunt Marilyn's idea—to mark me," she blushed, *shoot*, "so I had another male's scent on me…"

Kelsey held up her hand, "Wait, you did this while he was chained up?"

Shaelan nodded and was sure her cheeks were flame red now.

Rayne covered her mouth, then dropped her hand away. "And he did."

She noticed it wasn't a question, but Shae nodded anyways. "Both of us thought he had been given the breeding herbs at the time." She blew out a long breath. "I was just…" she looked over at him. "I don't know if it was him, or what, but I just wanted to climb right inside him."

Rayne placed her hand on her arm. "We both know what you mean, trust us, we've been lost in that mating animal magnetism ourselves without understanding it."

Shae fanned her face. "What is *that* all about, right?"

Kelsey looked at her for a long moment. "So… his mark is on you, but you didn't mark him?"

Her eyes tracked to him again. "No." She looked back to her. "I don't even understand it all. I mean is there a process or something?" She blushed. "Besides *that* part?" Shae still didn't know why she was telling two strangers. Then again, who else could she talk to? Her mother? Absolutely not. Her aunts, no and Billie had just gone through a horrible ordeal, so she was out too.

"It makes so much sense now." Rayne said softly.

"Yeah." Kelsey agreed

Shae looked from one to the other. "What does?"

Kelsey shrugged, "The way he's losing his mind right now because you're twenty feet away from him. This morning I thought he was going to wear a path in the rock with all the pacing."

Shae interrupted her, "I don't understand."

Blowing out a breath, Kelsey gave her a soft look. "Until you accept and mark him, his cat is going to be riding him hard and clawing at him from the inside…"

"That's a thing?" Shaelan glanced back to Calum, again.

Rayne nodded. "that's most definitely a *thing*." She reached out and rested a hand on her arm. "After you've shifted the first time, you will understand all the animal parts to this bizarre and wonderful world."

"I feel like this is a major exam and I didn't even read any of the material on the subject." Shae hugged the thermos again. "I just, I don't like being away from him, but I don't understand any of this." Kelsey and Rayne both nodded at the same time.

"The way it was explained to me is this," Rayne said quietly. "Fate doesn't pair two mates that don't belong together. None of the elders know of even one time a mismatch was made. It will all fall into place when you're both truly mated."

Shaelan nodded, and then turned to see Calum walking toward them. Butterflies took flight inside her stomach, like they did each time he looked at her. She blew out a breath. "I swear his eyes are the prettiest thing I've ever seen."

Kelsey giggled, "oh, tell him that."

"I'm going to see what Devin has found out from his father." Rayne said. "We'll talk to you later about the marking *process.*"

"Oh, mmm, yes." Kelsey offered quickly. "I need to go talk to Gage about getting some chains..." She giggled.

Shae knew they were just leaving to give her a few moments alone with Calum, and she was glad they understood. Now if she could just figure out how to talk to him about this without blushing to the color of a bright red apple, she'd feel better.

Calum stopped in front of her and looked at the thermos she was clutched to her chest. "Keeping it warm for me?"

She laughed, "Sorry, I got caught up talking to Kelsey and Rayne. They're very nice."

He nodded slowly. "They kind of scare me." He smirked, "but they aren't mine to deal with."

"I am?" She wanted to wrap her arms around him, so she continued to hug the thermos so she wouldn't

"You are." He agreed. Motioning to the cave, he held out his hand. "I'd like a few minutes to talk to you, without so many eyes staring at us."

She took his hand and followed him inside. Her eyebrows shot up when they walked in. "The *cave* has furniture?"

He nodded and kept walking to the back of it. "and a distillery."

"Aunt Marilyn strikes again, I'm sure." She commented. He stopped when they were well away from the entrance and turned while still holding her hand.

"I know a lot has happened in the last few days…" he shook his head, "to both of us…"

She watched his mouth as he spoke, remembering what it had been like when he kissed her and then felt her whole-body flush, just thinking about it.

"Shaelan, if you want me to get through this, stop looking at my mouth that way." He whispered.

Her eyes flew to his, "sorry." She shrugged, "I can't help it." Biting her bottom lip, she continued to look at him, waiting for him to continue. He pulled the thermos from her hands and then grasped the back of her head and leaned down. When he brushed his mouth over hers, she was afraid that he was going to stop there, so she wrapped her arms around his neck and kissed him so he didn't.

With a growl, he wrapped his arms around her and lifted her up to his height. His mouth was hard and demanding as he took over the kiss.

Needing to be closer, she wrapped her legs around his waist and grasped his hair so he couldn't stop kissing her. Her insides heated when his tongue stroked hers.

Breaking the kiss, his mouth traveled down her throat. "If I can find a safe, private location…" he ran his teeth along her jaw, "will you spend the night with me?" He ran his tongue over her flesh, "get to know each other…"

Shaelan moaned as his mouth moved to nip her ear softly. "Yes." He turned and leaned her against the wall, rocking his hips into her. She gasped as sensations moved through her.

He gripped the back of her head and titled her face up to his. "You'll be coming back with my mark—where everyone can see it." His breath brushed over her lips as he watched her. "So be sure."

She could see the vulnerability in his eyes as he waited. "I am." Never had she felt more certain than about being with him.

He growled low in his throat and took her mouth in a rough, scorching kiss.

"Knock knock…" Someone called into the cave. "Sorry, Cal, I drew the short straw… Dev's back from talking to his dad, and requires your presence."

Calum pressed his face into her throat, his breath as out of control as hers.

"Give us a minute and we'll be out, Jake." He lifted he head and grinned at her. "I honestly only intended to talk to you." He gently lowered her until her feet were on the ground.

"I'm glad you didn't just talk to me." She felt her cheeks heat up and bit her bottom lip.

He groaned, "It's going to be a long day."

Chapter Thirteen

Calum looked over his shoulder for the hundredth time, making sure no one was following them. He knew Jake had said he'd keep an eye out, without invading their privacy, but he trusted nothing on this mountain until the sick bastard running the village was taken down.

"No one will follow us," Shaelan whispered, her arm brushing against his as they walked. "Aunt Marilyn gave her word and I believe her."

He grinned, "Yeah, I don't think I'd want to be on her bad side." He wanted to hug her against his side, but knew if he touched her right now he'd be laying her down in the long grass... Shaking his head, he focused on calming his cat down. If he pranced around any more inside him, Calum's ass was going to be wiggling as he walked. Like he was sure Brock's did when no one was looking. *Hello?! Get your head together!* Glaring at the ground, he sighed. He was a mess. Going to be with his mate and thinking about a gay jaguar... He was going to be with his mate for the first time, he didn't count being chained to the wall, neither of them knew then. He was nervous, which was honestly the first time in his life he'd had this feeling.

Shaelan stopped walking and stood still. Calum was immediately turning to see if she sensed something he didn't.

"Sorry," she whispered. "I'm just…" She gave a loud sigh. "So much to process today." Her cheeks turned pink, "and I'm a little nervous too."

Heaving out a heavy sigh, he offered her a smile. "To be honest, I'm a mess too, if that makes you feel any better."

She looked him up and down. "You don't show it."

He snorted, "Good to know." Reaching over, he pulled the blanket she'd been hugging out of her arms and tucked it under his arm. "How much further is this 'retreat' of your aunt's?" He wasn't sure what to expect, knowing what he did about the woman. An hour 'that way' hadn't been the detailed directions he would have preferred either.

Shaelan turned and looked around. "Shouldn't be much further. It's right at the edge of our territory's boundary in this direction, she said we couldn't miss seeing it."

"I'm almost afraid to find out."

Shae laughed, "me too. She keeps things interesting though."

"That she does." He agreed and walked as close as he dared to get without touching her.

"I can't believe everything that's going to happen in the next day or so. I hope it all goes the way we've planned." She blew out a loud breath. "Do you think Aunt Marilyn and Brock will be able to do it? I always thought the darts were for injured wildlife… like, *real* wild animals."

Calum ran a hand through his hair. "If they can replace the ammo with blanks and empty darts, we'll stand a better chance." If they managed to do that inside the village, the only unknown factor would be the ammo that was carried on the supply run. This Jerome that ran the escort—was the same Jerome that was the only clan member that went into the forbidden area. Calum and he were going to be having a serious discussion about Gene's death. The chances of Jerome being alive at the end of it were slim.

"I don't know what you're thinking, but my insides are rolling around from the vibes coming off you." She said quietly.

Snapping out of it he glanced down at her. "Sorry. That would be your cat feeling the anger I do." He realized again that the things he took for granted, she wasn't aware of. "That night you came to me, your fear and anxiety almost smothered me."

Her eyes went wide, "is that what it is? It's so weird, these feelings I keep getting, that I've never felt in my life. At times, it feels like my skin is crawling, but nothing is there."

Careful to keep his distance, he reached out and ran his hand lightly down her back. "Your change isn't far off if your getting *that* feeling. Get used to it, your cat will do it often. Especially when they want your attention. After a while it will feel strange if you can't feel their presence inside you."

She huffed out a breath, "I'm scared, but excited at the same time. I don't even have a clue what to expect. There's been no time for questions or answers since all of this started."

Stopping, he swore under his breath. He should have left her with Rayne and Kelsey tonight, so they could help her understand more. It angered him that his mate was being pelted with so many things she couldn't grasp. "We can go back and you can talk to the girls…"

She grabbed his arm. "No. I didn't mean that. I want to be here. I just have a lot of questions."

Searching her face, he saw she meant it. She did want to be here, but he could also see the under- lying confusion in her sexy eyes. "I can try to answer them… as long as they're not female questions, we're good." She smiled up and him and he his heart stutter.

"Thank you." Pursing her lips together her eyes moved down over him for a moment then stopped at his neck, her brows furrowed.

"What?"

"I just realized…" her eyes flew back to his, "Rayne and Kelsey…"

Her hand moved to cover her one breast, he tried not to let his eyes follow the movement, but failed.

"They were explaining the mating bites?" She asked.

That got his attention back on her face. "Marks. What about it?"

She gave a slight nod. "Mating marks. I can't mark you."

His heart, he was sure, stopped beating all together. Swallowing, he found his voice. "You can't?"

She shook her head, looking puzzled, then opened her mouth baring her teeth at him. "I don't have fangs… sharp cat's teeth, like you."

He heaved out a breath so loud, he felt his shoulders drop a few inches in relief. "You will soon enough, your change isn't far off." *False alarm.* His cat settled back down inside him.

Stepping closer, she looked up into his eyes and he felt his whole world still. "You don't understand." She whispered, causing his eyes to flick to her lips then back to her eyes. "You said I would be bearing your mark in a visible location…"

He nodded, completely distracted by her scent, her eyes softly holding his, her lips moving…

"I want you to bear *my* mark when we go back." Those plump lips pouted, "but I don't have the sharp teeth to do it."

His whole body shuddered at the image that gave him. Her marking him. Him carrying her scent permanently. Swallowing, his mouth suddenly dry, he ran his finger lightly over her bottom lip. "We'll figure out a way." He'd never meant something as much as he did then. If he had to claw up his own neck so she could lick it and fill his system with her scent, he would do it.

She blushed again and smiled up at him. "Okay." Fanning her face, she blew out a breath. "I get so hot when I…"

Moving fast, he placed a finger over her lips. "Please…" The lust in her eyes was killing him. "Don't say or do things like that until we're there." He titled his head and looked her up and down, "I'm already having a hard time keeping my hands to myself."

She nodded, her cheeks flaming.

He straightened up and stepped back, motioning for her to walk. "More questions?"

"Only about a thousand." She answered quickly.

Chuckling, he nodded. "Ask away."

"I think I should maybe avoid some that might be related to…" she fanned her face, "some things. Let me change subjects here." She stopped briefly to look around, and check their direction.

He loved that she knew direction in the middle of nowhere, oddly, he found that a turn on. *Wrong topic. Focus.*

When she started moving again, she gave him an apprehensive glance. "Are you planning on being back in the morning when they get your men out of there?"

He nodded, not voicing how much vengeance he had inside him. When Devin had told Calum that his father had ordered that they were to hold *until* the alliance got there, he was not happy. It was agreed they could try to get their men out, not having them on the inside would give Leroy no hostages to use against them.

"I can't believe Earl and Morris have done the job for this long and don't agree with any of it." She shook her head, "I mean, it's good they don't agree, and if anyone can talk them into helping the men escape it will be my aunt, but, how could they *do it* for so long?"

Taking a moment to contain the emotions he was feeling, he spoke quietly. "Like your mother, they only did what they had to do to survive." He reached for as much as he could remember, with all the tranquilizer in his system. "They only struck out at me, when I went for them first… from what I can remember."

"I suppose, they were only doing their job," she looked him up and down, "and defending themselves, but still…"

she lifted her hands then dropped them again. "I couldn't do it. I didn't make it two days before I broke all their rules."

He laughed, "If it helps, I agree with all the rules you broke."

She chuckled, "of course *you* do. You *are* the rules I broke." Sobering, she sighed, "As terrifying as all this is, I'm glad it's going to be ending. I could not have done my job and treated innocent men that were being held against their will."

"Speaking of that, Nona told me you will be the next *Nona* when she retires."

"Hmm," she exhaled a sharp breath, "Nona-Shae. It still sounds so wrong to me. There will only be one Nona to me, and that's Nona-Eve."

It had been plaguing him since Nona had told him, his mind struggling to process the details, with everything else going on. Stopping, he looked down at her, then dropped the blanket on the ground. "We need to stop here, while we're out in the open, and talk about some things." He winked at her, "Once we reach the *retreat*, I won't be talking."

"Oh." She nodded and sat down.

He could see the second he said it, she had closed herself off inside. "It's not bad. There's just some logistics we need to discuss." His cat wasn't at all happy with this pause in motion. Calum had seen what had happened between Devin and Rayne when he wasn't upfront, and he was *not* going to go through that. He studied her face, that beautiful face. Sitting down, far enough away, so he couldn't grab her, he looked at her again. "Sometime I'll explain the alliance and how it works, and everything else you don't know, but what you need to be aware of right now is…" He loved how she watched him, so focused on what he had to say… Shaking his head, he smirked. "I'm really struggling to keep my hands off you."

"Talk faster," she whispered, as her eyes flicked to his mouth for a moment.

Closing his eyes, he reined in his thoughts, then opened them to continue. "Devin will be the next alpha of his clan, but also the leader, or king, of the entire alliance of clans."

She nodded. "You briefly told my aunt that, I believe."

"Gage and I are his seconds..." he paused to see she grasped the concept of the word. "Not all the time, but there will be times I will have to be with Devin, for his protection, or in an official capacity." He had spent his whole life supporting this notion and now, for the first time ever, he was feeling doubt.

"I understand that." She huffed out a breath. "A king, it's a whole world I don't understand, but I'm looking forward to learning more about it."

She actually looked excited about learning. He found that endearing as well.

She inhaled sharply. "Oh. I get where you're going with this. I'm going to be my clans' Nona and you're the King's second..." She rubbed her forehead with two fingers. "I guess long distance relationships don't work in the shifter world."

Running his hand down the length of his jaw, he gave his head a quick shake. "I can honestly say I've never seen a mated pair apart for longer then a day. Except in extreme circumstances, when it couldn't be avoided."

"Oh."

He watched her face and could actually see how fast she was processing thoughts. She was something to watch, his mate, smart and beautiful... Cursing silently, he fought to focus again. "Once the alliance is involved in your village, and they *will* come in and help in any way needed, you'll have more freedom but..."

She nodded, then stopped and looked at him. "I don't know." She shrugged, "this is so far from my experience, the alliance and how things should be, I don't know where that will leave me when it all settles."

Calum, didn't like to see the uncertainty in her eyes, he slid closer and drew her into his arms. "We don't have to decide anything right now. I just wanted to be open with you about my position and responsibilities."

She hugged him tight. "You have no idea how much your honesty means to me." She tilted her head up and look at him. "There hasn't been a lot of that in my world." She stopped and pushed her nose into his throat and inhaled slowly. "I love the way you..."

Growling, Calum dropped his arms away and leaned back from her. "We have to go."

Frowning, she sat there looking at him. Then she smiled a slow smile, her eyes sparkling, cheeks flushing. Without another word, she stood up and shook out the blanket.

They both stood and stared at the small wooden shack. It was lopsided, with rough boards, not finished or altered to even fit properly. It looked like a small hunting hut, about ten-foot square. Calum had both hands resting on top of his head as he looked at it. "She painted the door pink."

Shaelan giggled, "Guess that's her way of marking her territory."

He laughed. "Do we dare look inside?"

Nodding, she started walking. "With Aunt Marilyn, it wouldn't surprise me if we opened the door to a solarium and swimming pool."

Pulling the key out of his pocket, he unlocked the lock and flipped it open. Opening the door slowly, they both leaned in to look and then sighed at the same time to see a sparsely decorated room. There was no furniture to speak of, only a blanket, few pillows and small wood stove.

"Well, that was anticlimactic, wasn't it?" She asked stepping in.

Swinging his pack off his back, he opened it to get some candles he'd taken from the cave. "I'm actually relieved."

She nodded. "Yes, I think we've both had enough surprises in our lives lately."

Calum snorted, "agreed." He lit a few of them and placed them on the small stove. Setting his pack by the door, he took the blanket from her hands and spread it out on the floor. Kicking his boots off, he shoved them out of the way.

She closed the door and leaned back against it, looking at him. He could sense the anxiety coming off her. "Don't worry about the details right now." His eyes moved slowly over her, "Don't worry about mating protocol, or what happens later on." He tapped a hand on his chest. "Follow your heart, the rest will work itself out." He held out his hand to her, "Let me show you how it's supposed to be—now that I'm not in chains and you don't think I'm some sort of monster."

She looked at his hand for a second, then shrugged out of her jacket, dropping it where she stood. Her shoes went next before she finally reached out, placing her hand in his. "I never thought that."

He wanted her to come to him on her own accord, *needed* her to, so he didn't pull her toward him. Even his cat had stopped and was waiting. "You did when you came in to treat me. I could smell your fear, even over the stench of the stink weed."

She stepped closer and nodded, "I'll admit I was scared, but I had been led to believe you were some sort of dangerous criminal." She inhaled subtly, "but it wasn't all fear, it was…"

"My scent turned you on." He squeezed her hand lightly, encouraging her to take those last few steps.

"Yes," she gave him a heated look, "and that scared me more than thinking you were some horrible person." She confessed.

"Let me show you, love." He whispered.

The way she was looking at him, caressing him with her eyes had every muscle in his body tense. She bit her bottom lip and his hand started shaking, as he fought to not drag her against him. When she took her other hand and ran it over the side of her breast, rubbing where he knew his mark lay, he'd never gotten so hard that fast in his life.

"Will there be biting?" she whispered breathlessly.

Dragging, his attention away from her heaving breasts, he looked at her with lust riding him hard. "There will be biting." He said with a hoarse tone.

"Good," she dropped her hand from his and, in one motion, pulled her shirt over her head and dropped it to the floor.

He was sure the zipper on his jeans was going to pop as he stood there, with his hand still held out to her, watching. He could see his bites through the pale material cupping her breasts, her darkened nipples, hard and wanting. Ripping his shirt over his head, he tossed it to the floor, and closed the distance between them. Grasping her by the waist, he lifted her up to his height. "I wanted slow…"

She licked his throat, making his knees almost buckle. "I don't think we can." She nipped at the sensitive skin of his neck and he felt his cat go completely still, waiting. "Show me slow in twenty years." When her tongue stroked over is neck again, he growled deep in his throat. "When you growl…" she moaned softly as he shifted her up higher. Wrapping her legs around his waist, she leaned back and looked at him. "I want to claim you. I want to be yours."

He'd planned on it, later, first he'd intended to drown in her for a while until the need wasn't weighing on him to the point he couldn't think. He tried to remember if there was anything other than he had to let her, of her own free will, mark him first. Her hot tongue licked over his jaw.

Dropping to his knees before they gave out, he buried his face in her throat. "Clothes off before you do, or we're going back in rags in the morning…" His restraint was already stretched to it's limit. Calum's cat was quiet, knowing she had to make the first move in mating, but as soon as her mouth marked him after saying she accepted him… he knew his cat would take over.

He watched her stand and shimmy out of her jeans. If his control snapped… he didn't want to hurt her. Moving toward her on his knees, he held her hand as she kicked off the pants. She stood before him in nothing but a pale see-through bra and pantie. His senses were spinning out of control from the scent of her. "You have to be ready so I don't hurt you…" He could barely form words.

"I am," she panted, then reached around and unclasped her bra. Sliding it free of her arms she dropped it.

Crawling closer to her, he ran his tongue up her leg. With shaking hands, he slid the skimpy cloth down her legs so she could step out of them.

He could barely breathe. He raised up and nipped her hip softly. She grasped his hair with both hands and hissed out a breath. If she didn't mark him soon, he wasn't going to make it. Inhaling, he growled softly in his throat and then stood up so he wouldn't screw this up and bite her thigh. She *had* to make the first move, he reminded himself.

Shoving his pants down his legs, he got out of them fast, then looked to see her drop to her knees in front of him. With a hesitant, shy look in her eyes, she bit her lip and ran her hands down his waist and over his hips while looking up at him. It was the most erotic thing he'd ever seen. *Holy hell.* Grabbing her hands, he pulled them away before he lost it.

Dropping to his knees, he lay on the blanket, pulling her with him. Keeping her close, he kept his arm loose around her waist, even though he wanted to pull her tight against him. He watched her lick her lips nervously. Was kissing her breaking the rules? He couldn't remember. She nibbled his bottom lip and he growled again.

"I was told you're not allowed to touch me." She whispered against his mouth, "until after I mark you. I didn't believe it was true until now."

He could taste her scent on his tongue, "It's true." She pushed on his shoulder so he'd roll onto his back. She shifted until she was on her hands and knees over him. He didn't dare look anywhere but her eyes. Clenching his hands into fists, he kept them on the blanket.

"But," she licked her lips, leaning down close to his face, "I can kiss you, right?"

"Yes." He looked at her lips, then back to her eyes when he started to lift his head.

With the tip of her tongue she ran it over his lower lip. "You can kiss me back?"

He nodded, unable to form any words as the heat from her breath brushed over his mouth. It felt like an hour as she stayed right there not moving. He growled, "Shaelan."

"I love when you growl," she whispered against his lips.

He was jut about the break the rule and grab her, when her mouth touched his. Lifting his head, he turned it and took over the kiss, plunging his tongue into her mouth and filling his senses with her taste.

She nipped his tongue and trapped it briefly as she lowered her body onto his and rubbed over him. He could feel how wet she was as she slid over him, and had to squeeze his hands until they hurt to prevent grabbing her.

When she pulled her mouth from his, he tried to catch his breath. She pushed her breasts into his chest as she reached down between them, and grasped his engorged shaft. He stopped breathing completely and continued to hold his breath until she slid him inside her.

The air left his lungs all at once. *So tight. So wet. Fuck-ing torture.* His growl was closer to a roar as he turned his head to bare his throat to her. She moved up and down slowly and he saw stars behind his eyelids. "Accept me." He hissed out. *Fuck.* "Claim me." His growl sounded more like a whine, "on my jugular, it will mark."

He was a heartbeat away from grabbing her head, when she lowered her mouth to his neck and licked over the skin. She moaned against his ear as she slid him deeper into her body.

"You're mine," she whispered against his throat.

When her teeth clamped down on his skin, he growled, it should have hurt with the amount of pressure she was using, but it only made him and his cat reach a frenzied state of arousal. He didn't wait until she let go of the flesh between her teeth before he grabbed her hips and thrust up into her.

He rolled her onto her back, her mouth still attached to him and slammed into her again. She moaned and let go, then licked his wound several times before grabbing a handful of hair and dragging his mouth to hers. He tasted blood and his cat screamed in victory. He wanted her on her knees, but Calum wanted her to moan for him first.

Thrusting faster, he leaned down and grasped her breast, running his fingers over the mark as she whimpered with need.

Shifting to his knees, he pulled her hips up with him and continued to pound into her. When she reached her hands up to touch her breasts, his rhythm faltered. She thrashed her head back and forth and moaned as her body started to convulse tightly around him. Slowing, he let her ride it out for a few moments. Imprinted in his brain forever would be the image of her orgasm, she was so sexy and erotic.

When she was panting to catch her breath, he pulled out and flipped her onto her stomach. Lifting her hips, he drove into her and she rewarded him with a deep moan. Leaning over her, he pushed her hair out of the way and nipped the side of her neck.

She was pushing back into him almost as hard as he was thrusting, reaching around her, he grasped her breast and kneaded it.

"Mine," he growled against her skin.

He bit into her neck, right above her collarbone, so everyone would know she was forever his.

She squealed in pleasure, then her body clamped down on his and his name was growled out in the most sensual way he could imagine.

His whole body was rigid as he exploded inside her, the intense heat washing over him. He released her neck and tried to bring oxygen into his lungs, and gasping each time her tight inner muscles convulsed around him.

They were mated forever and he honestly didn't know a time in his life he'd ever felt this serene inside.

Chapter Fourteen

If she knew how to purr, she would have. Shaelan lay there with her head on his chest, listening to his heartbeat under her ear. "Calum?"

"Hmm?" He ran his hand gently up and down her back.

"Will you shift for me?" She leaned up on her elbow and looked up at him. "I've seen cats around here all my life, but didn't know they weren't wild animals." She smiled at him. "I'd like to see it happen."

Rolling onto his side, he pulled her up against him and looked at her. She loved the way his eyes connected with hers so much, so she could see he was paying attention to her. "I just want to know."

He smiled. "I get that." Kissing her mouth softly, he sighed. "Give me a few minutes more to just hold you."

Leaning closer, he licked over the mark on her neck, bursts of heat went through her whole body, making her hiss out a sigh of contentment.

"Let me replenish my oxygen deprivation first," he said with a lazy smile. "Whoever came up with that no touching thing, never had to go through it personally."

"Poor man." She teased.

He chuckled, then sobered, and played with her hair between his fingers. "Actually, it was so women have the control. It ended the practice of forced mating."

"Forced mating is how I ended up coming to you." She said softly. His eyes caressed her face and she honestly could say she felt loved, just from that look.

"That's very true. Let's hope yours is the last everywhere then." His eyes hardened briefly.

Leaning closer, she inhaled deeply, then smiled. "You do smell different now."

"As soon as you go through your first change, I think we should renew it," he said with a soft laugh.

"Yeah? Just once?" If he felt like she did when he bit her, the two of them were going to be walking around with bites all over their bodies.

"Often." He gave her a lazy grin.

She went to snuggle into him and he tensed and pulled her closer into the shelter of his arms, then froze. Moving slowly, he sat up and held a finger over his lips so she wouldn't speak. Shae tried to focus to see if she could hear anything, but her heart was beating too loud to hear anything outside.

"Hellooo." Someone called out.

"Brock?" She looked at the door.

Calum's face expression turned serious in an instant. "Something must be wrong."

She nodded and got up, looking around for her clothes. Giving up, she grabbed the blanket and wrapped it around her, as Calum pulled his jeans on. Picking it up so she wouldn't trip, she went to the door.

Putting his hand against the door, he gave her an odd look. "He would have shifted to run here, so he's going to be naked."

"Oh." She jerked her hand back and held it against her chest. Pulling the blanket off, she held it out to him "I'll be out in a second."

Stepping outside, she saw them talking quietly. "What's wrong?"

Brock turned and huffed out a breath. "I am *so* sorry to disturb you. Like, *really* sorry." He pouted. "But we need your brain and Calum's tracking skills."

"What happened?"

Calum came over and put his arm around her.

"Billie, ran off into the night. We've looked everywhere we could without raising alarms." He waved the arm not trapped under the blanket around. "She was afraid they were going to find out and kill…" he glanced to Calum.

"Dale." Calum supplied for him.

"Find out what?" She gasped, "she's pregnant?"

Brock nodded vigorously. "Yes. Nona said no one would notice in the next days, but Billie panicked." He held his hand to his forehead for a second. "We think she was trying to get to the cave, but got lost and just kept going. You and she used to be attached to each other, is there another place she would go?"

"Let me get our stuff." Turning she went back inside and looked around for her shoes. Calum came in and hugged her from behind.

"We'll find her. Devin is already out looking, as a wolf he can scent just about anyone." He released her and picked up her jacket and handed it to her.

She stuffed her bra into his pack and looked around for her other shoe. Calum took the bag and tied his boots to it. "What are you doing?"

He smirked at her, "looks like you get to see me shift. I'll feel better escorting you back on four feet rather than two." He tapped a finger to the side of his nose, "And, I can pick up scents better."

She nodded, "Oh, okay."

He pulled his phone out of his pack and did something with a button, then held it out to her. "Do you know how to use it? In case we need backup," he assured her.

She took it and look at it. "Slide my hand across the screen to unlock it?"

He nodded. "Then just hit that red button on the bottom of the screen and a list of names will come up. Hit Gage or Devin, it will call them."

"Okay." She tucked it into the back pocket of her jeans. She scowled and pointed a finger at him. "We better not need backup."

Sighing, he came over and grabbed her chin and kissed her hard on the mouth. "You look so sexy right now, my fierce kitty."

Smacking him on the arm, she grinned. "Get the key for the lock and put the candles out."

"Yes, love." He pulled the key out of his pocket and handed it to her, then took off his jeans. "There's a flashlight on the phone too, slide the top of the screen down."

Shae hadn't seen a lot of naked men in her life, but if she were to guess, she'd say she'd gotten really lucky in that area with him.

"Stop looking at me like that." He growled.

Blushing, she shrugged and took the jeans he handed her. "I can't help it, you look *really* good naked."

"Can I look?" Brock called from outside.

"No." Shae answered, shaking her head.

"Sucks to be the gay one." Brock grumbled.

Shaking his head, Calum winked at her. "Don't forget to put the candles out."

Before she could answer, the sexy naked man turned into a very large, black jaguar. The snapping sounds his bones made seemed painful, but if it were he wouldn't have done it so quickly, she figured. She stood there with her mouth open as the last of the fur appeared on his body. He stretched and then nudged her with his nose. She ran her hand down across his face. He was so soft. "Oh, Calum..."

Brock leaned in the door. "You're just a sexy beast in every form, aren't you?" He tossed the blanket in the door, "my turn."

Shae grinned and picked up the blanket. "I can't wait to do that too." She looked at her feet. "It's going to be a long run back." Calum nudged her hip with his shoulder and went out the door.

She was exhausted, but refused to slow down or complain. Brock was ten feet in front of her and Calum ran alongside her, briefly moving out, around, or weaving behind her to the other side.

He made a soft noise and Brock answered in kind, then both stopped. Huffing out a breath, she stopped and stood there panting. He rubbed his shoulder against her leg, almost pushing her over in the process. When he did it again she realized, he wanted her to sit down. "I'm fine," she gasped.

He made a low yowl and bumped her again.

"Fine. For a few minutes, only." She leaned her head against his side as he stood beside her. "We have to find Billie."

Brock turned and lay down, his sides heaving as he looked out into the night.

"There's a river," she blew out a breath, "we used to hide under a ledge and talk for hours..." she shook her head, "I don't know the direction from here though." Looking around, it dawned on her how dark it really was, and wondered how she hadn't been falling over her own feet this whole time.

Brock sprung to his feet and made a soft noise in his throat.

"You know where I'm talking about." He made another noise and pranced on the spot. She nodded and used the body of her mate to pull herself to her feet. "Let's go." Calum looked up at her. "Please," she whispered. He shook his large head, but moved out of the way. She ran her hand down over his coat and started after Brock again.

By the time they reached the river, she was falling over her feet more than she was walking. She'd had to stop running a few minutes before, her entire body was numb. Brock stopped suddenly and sat down, facing the other side of the river. Turning, Shae looked around, he was pointing out the ledge. "That's it." She looked from one large body to the other. "Let me go, seeing you guys might spook her."

Calum rubbed against her, but moved so she could pass. Finding the best place to cross, she used rocks that weren't completely immersed in water and was honestly surprised Calum hadn't splashed in after her when her footing slipped a few times.

Getting both feet on the dry bank, she looked at the area under the overhanging rock. "Billie?" She called out quietly. "It's Shae."

"Shae?" Billie stumbled out of the darkness and toward her. She almost knocked Shae into the river as she landed into her arms and sobbed against her shoulder. "I don't want him to die because of me."

Shae squeezed her. "He's not going to die." She ran her hands up and down her back, she was cold. "Come on, Calum and Brock are on the other side. We'll go to the cave."

Billie nodded, her teeth chattering together.

It was a long slow walk back to the caves. Calum knew Shaelan was exhausted, but she refused to stop and rest until her friend was returned to the cave and warm. As they neared the entrance, Nona and Marilyn came charging out of it. He stopped and looked at them, he had to wonder for a moment how intimidating that duo must have been in their youth. They put the fear into him more than once since he'd met them, and that made him pause and think of what Shaelan was going to be like by their age. He was going to have his hands full, something told him.

Devin came out of the trees in his jeans and bare feet, and gave him a relieved look as both girls went by him.

He realized Shaelan was standing at the entrance looking back at him and holding up his jeans. What he wanted to do was go hunting and find someone to kill, he had several options in that department, but the look on her face had his paws slapping the earth in her direction instead.

Nona handed him a hot cup of tea as she looked at his neck to the mark his mate had left. "You want some salve for that wound?" Her lips twitched as she tried not to grin.

It had been the first thing he'd done when he'd shifted back. Checked to see that it hadn't healed over and disappeared. Seems that fate knew it wasn't an injury, and left is as raw as it had been before he'd changed. "No ma'am."

"Heh," she chortled, "smart man after all."

He motioned to Billie. "She going to be okay?"

Nona nodded, "Her health is fine. The mental stuff, is not too steady."

He blew on the hot liquid. "My clanmate will look after her, if she'll let him." He knew Dale would, knew that any one of his clansman would step up. If not the women in their clan would beat them ten different ways from Tuesday.

She looked at him for a long moment. "It almost brings me to tears how noble your men are." She shook her head sadly. "Been a long damn time since we've had any of the likes of that around here."

Pausing, he looked over to Shaelan to see her talking a mile a minute to Billie and Rayne. Glancing back to Nona, he shrugged, "I think your men will step up once the noose isn't around their necks." He couldn't imagine what the males had gone through in all of this. Yes, the women withstood the worst of the treatment, but to stand back and tolerate it to survive, and then look after them through it, he doubted he would be that strong.

She tapped him on the arm lightly, "I do hope your right." With that she went toward the entrance.

Before he could go to Shaelan, Marilyn appeared in his face, blocking his way.

"I brought some clothes and shoes for your men tomorrow."

Dressing them hadn't even occurred to him. "Appreciate that." He'd wondered more than once where their cars and other belongings had gone. He was going to make a point of being present when they caught up to those helping Leroy and Jerome.

She rubbed her hands together in an anxious way. "All hells going to break loose when they find them gone."

He nodded. "I know."

"Earl and Morris won't be safe. I'm going to hide them once they get your men out the back." She looked over to where Billie and Shae were sitting. "I'll find somewhere in the village or near enough to, leave Billie in some peace staying here."

He hadn't thought what it must be like for Billie and other women to see the guards after what happened, he suspected that the shame and fury would follow them for years. "We'll do what we can for the guards when this is over." He took a quick sip. "It's good they're helping." He left unspoken what would happen to those that didn't.

She laughed, "Earl has a thing for pink." She winked at him. "And Morris, he would have left the village years ago, if there had been a way." She wrung her hands together. "After his folks vanished." Clapping her hands together, she gave him an excited look. "I won't see you tomorrow during all the action, *I'm* the distraction inside the village that will give them time to get gone."

Sucking in a breath, he debated on asking for details, then decided it might be better for his sanity if he didn't. "I wish you luck."

"Ha, they're gonna need it, not me." Turning, she went to where Nona waited for her by the entrance.

Blowing out a long breath, he watched them leave.

"That woman scares the hell out of me." Jesse said, as he stood up beside him.

"Agreed." Calum gave him a nod. "You heading out at first light to meet up with the alliance?"

"Yeah. Can't tell you how happy I was to find out there's a road on the other side of the mountain. Dev sent his father the details." He ran a hand through his curly hair. "That walk in the other way gave me the creeps, felt like insects crawling all over me the whole time."

Nodding, Calum wondered if Devin's father would be able to get to the truth of who was helping Leroy for all these years. If they disappeared, they'd always be wondering if it was happening somewhere else. "Just get there safe and back again."

"Count on it." He looked around. "I'm going to try and find a quiet spot to grab a quick nap. Never been in so much commotion for so long in my life."

"I'll see you in the morning." For the fourth time, he turned to Shaelan but found her walking toward him.

"Billie's going to go try to rest." Her eyes moved from his neck to his eyes a few times. "I'm exhausted."

He studied her eyes as they stroked over his neck again, he felt his body stir. "Most of me is as well."

She blushed, "Well with this many people in here, *most* of you is going to have to behave."

Nodding slowly, he winked. "Most of."

He looked back at his sleeping mate one more time, then gave Gage a shove to get moving.

Once out in the opening and far enough away to not be heard, he looked back again. Shaelan wasn't going to be happy they had left this early without waking her. He didn't know how he knew that, he just did.

"I'll be lucky if Kelsey doesn't stab me later." Gage murmured.

Devin nodded, "I'll be doing penance for this too, now."

Running his hands through his hair, Calum huffed out a breath. "We have no idea if this is going to go smoothly. We may have to think fast and adjust..." he looked from one to the other, "we can't be blamed for trying to keep our mates safe."

Devin and Gage exchanged a knowing look.

"Keep telling yourself that," Gage told him as he started walking.

Devin shrugged, then turned to follow. "This mating *stuff* is complicated."

Calum caught up to them, checking over his shoulder ever few feet, "I barely survived the mating part, so I'll take your word for it."

Gage made a point of looking at his neck in an obvious manner, "I think your throat took the brunt." He whistled, "so glad Kelsey bit me after her first change."

Calum ran his hand over the tender area of his neck. "I'm not talking about this." He grinned briefly remembering how he felt when she did it. "I meant that bullshit of no touching… what the hell is that about?"

Both men nodded.

"Right there with you. I'm just glad we only have to go through it once." Devin said quietly.

"Longest wait in my life." Gage mumbled.

Shaking it off, Calum pointed to their right. "We have to go in that way to be in the forbidden area."

"Where the grave is?" Devin asked, his tone serious again.

"Yeah." Calum clenched his jaw, thinking of Gene.

"They'll pay for it." Gage said, his tone lethal.

Calum flexed his hands a few times, feeling his fingers vibrate with claws that wanted to emerge. "Nothing done to them could ever make up for the years of despotic treatment they've put their own people through."

Devin clasped his shoulder lightly. "The alliance… we'll heal what we can."

Nodding, Calum exhaled the flash of emotion riding him. "Let's just get those men out. Then I'm free to kill the bastards who are responsible."

Chapter Fifteen

Shaelan paced toward the back of the cave and looked at Rayne and Kelsey, looking as annoyed as she felt. "I can't believe they left without a word."

"I can," Rayne said softly.

Kelsey nodded, "It's pretty much their M.O., but that doesn't mean we have to like it."

Billie adjusted the laces in her shoes as she hugged her knees into her chest. "I just hope they get out safely." She glanced to the entrance. "Why didn't... Jake?" Kelsey nodded, "go with them."

Pulling her hair back into a ponytail, Kelsey dropped her hands and then rolled her eyes. "Gotta leave someone here to keep us under house-cave arrest."

Rayne groaned. "Look how well *that* turned out last time."

"Right." Kelsey mused quietly.

Shaelan decided if she had to wait she may as well be distracted. "What happened?"

Kelsey sighed and sat down. "Your life isn't the only messed up one." She glanced to Rayne who nodded. "Aside from the secret of what we are..."

Shae slid down the wall and looked from one to the other. She could see the emotions changing in their eyes as they thought about it.

Rayne grimaced, "It's a very tangled web to explain it *all* from the start, so we'll just say there is an organization of criminals…" she tipped her head and looked at Shaelan, "a mob-like family. Really bad."

Shae nodded, "I just spent two years off the mountain for school, so I understand. A crime family."

Kelsey's head bobbed a few times. "Okay, so this supreme family of *asshats* abduct shifters and enslaves them. As their goons, muscle… whatever…" She pointed to Rayne, "*she* was engaged to the head of the family before she escaped."

Eyes wide, Shae glanced at Rayne, only to see her nod.

Rayne waved it off, "I could write an entire book about my ordeal. We're getting off topic here. Gage and Devin left us under house arrest at Kelsey's while they ran off to save the day." She rolled her eyes in a dramatic way. "These guys show up asking for directions," she grinned, "your mountain is easier to navigate then the roads at Gage and Kelsey's place."

"True," Kelsey laughed. "So, we end up abducted by these two guys."

Shae and Billie both gasped.

"Until…" Kelsey points to Rayne, "she shifts and threatens to bite this guys'…" she cleared her throat, "bits, off." She starts giggling.

"Long story short," Rayne continued, "leaving us under guard didn't work out that well for them last time."

Jake appeared in the entrance, his arms crossed over his chest. "Which is why no one is going to go in or out of this cave until they…"

Brock came barreling into the cave, knocking Jake out of the way. He tossed Nona's medical bag toward Shaelan. "Your going to need this." He leaned on his knees for a second and huffed a few times trying to breath.

Shaelan grabbed the bag and got up. "What's wrong."

He waved his hands and swallowed, still trying to breath. "Nona is on her way… but she says they'll get here before she can." He straightened and looked around. "I need blankets," he squeaked, "and some shoes."

Rayne scrambled up and held out the blanket she'd been sitting on. "What happened?"

Clutching the blanket to his chest, he blew out a breath. "Jerome beat the bejesus out of one man…" he tapped his chest a few times, "I threw up in my mouth when I walked in on it." He gave Shae a distraught look, "I couldn't blow my cover… so I just distracted him enough to leave." He took the shoes Kelsey held out. "They're carrying him here." His eyes grew large. "I have to get this to them." He waved Jake out of the way, "Faye and Marilyn have the whole village in motion to keep them occupied, so they can get here." He called out over his shoulder then was gone.

Shaelan's heart was beating so loud in her chest, she couldn't catch her breath. "We should…"

"No." Jake hissed. "If you girls go running to them, it's going to distract them." He rubbed a hand over his face. "They'll be focused on every sound, scent and breeze around them right now in order to get them back here as fast as possible."

"You should go help them, Jake." Kelsey rushed over to him. "We won't move from this cave."

Rayne nodded, "At least go watch their backs until they can get here."

He rubbed both hands over his face. "I don't even know…"

Shaelan snapped out of it, "I can point you in the right direction." She clutched the bag to her chest. "Please, just go watch and make sure Jerome doesn't come after them."

Billie was on her feet. "You *have* to go help."

Jake looked from one to the other, indecision plain on his face. "If I leave you and…" he looked from one to the other again, "*Shit.*" He pointed a finger at Kelsey. "No one leaves this cave."

She nodded. "Go."

Shae ran to the entrance and pointed, "head that way, there's a ridge you can watch from. They'll be coming from the East."

He went by her. "Stay in the cave, I won't survive an angry Cal."

Shae watched him running until the long grass swallowed him up. She turned and looked at Kelsey who was pulling her shoes off. "What are you doing?"

Kelsey paused and looked at her. "Going to climb a tree to keep watch." She shrugged, "I do that better as a cat."

Billie shook her head before Shae could reply. "A tiger?"

Kelsey nodded.

Shaelan went over and stood there shaking her head. "A tiger would stand out here like a flashing sign." She looked from Rayne to Kelsey. "So would both of your hair color, without shifting."

Billie nodded, then took a deep breath. "I'll go. I can shimmy up that tree outside." She looked to Shae, "I live here, No one is looking for me, so I'm invisible."

Kelsey huffed out a defeated breath. "You're right. We'll stand in the entrance and you can call down to us."

Rayne went toward the entrance. "Hurry. My heart isn't going to beat properly until I can see those men are safe. *All* of them, including my own."

Calum stood and traced the landscape with his eyes, watching for any sign of movement. He couldn't scent anything, but that wasn't surprising with his nostrils filled with the scent of stink weed and blood.

He glanced to see Brock helping Marc get some shoes on. That was a smart call, grabbing something for their feet. When he'd run over this rough ground, he'd only been inside for a few days and filled with too much rage to feel anything. These three men had been in a hell of a lot longer. They'd been drugged, underfed and their muscles were so sore from sitting, they were barely able to navigate. He didn't know how long Chad had been missing, but he knew his two clansmen had been gone close to a month now. Gene had vanished first and that was about six weeks ago…

Chad's moaning had Calum looking over at him. He didn't know the man, but he knew his clan leaders. Hopefully Chad was the only missing from that family, because there were no more captives inside.

When Brock and the guard had flung the door open, dragging Chad between them, Calum had to hold Gage back from attacking the guard. Brock quickly explained that Jerome was on some sort of rampage and took it out on him. He didn't need to wonder what the rampage was about. Chances were Jerome knew all about the people that had come up the mountain to get him, and hadn't been able to find hide nor hair of them since. Calum had this nagging thought that kept about how long would that last? They couldn't stay in the cave much longer.

Gage and Devin moved Chad to get the blanket under him, another good idea on Brock's part. With almost every part of him swollen or bleeding, they'd had to stop constantly, because they were causing him more pain trying to get him to safety. With the blanket, they could use it like a stretcher and carry him. It was still going to hurt, but would minimize any further damage.

Gage nodded to Devin, and they lifted it together. Chad moaned, but quieted once they had him off the ground. Marc and Dale got up on unsteady legs and started walking slowly beside them. He turned to look at Brock, who was sweating and covered in blood, as he stood watching them leave. "You need to get back. Grab a shower, fast."

Brock nodded, then turned eyes full of misery and guilt toward him. "I feel like a coward for just letting Jerome leave."

"His day will come." He motioned in the direction of the village. "Get back and make sure Marilyn doesn't do something stupid."

He clasped his face between his palms, his eyes huge. "Oh my god, I have to get back." He waved a hand at the men walking away. "I'll come to the cave later." With that he took off running.

Checking as far as he could see, Calum assured himself no one was looking for them, yet, then turned to head back to the cave. He caught up to them quickly.

"How much further?" Mark asked, sounding winded already.

Calum didn't like how the gash on his ribs looked. It had been stitched up and had healed over, but the fact that it *was* there, reminded him they'd been in chains and unable to shift. "At this pace, half hour or so." He checked behind them again, "Some pretty rough climbing ahead."

Mark nodded, "We'll make it." He checked over his shoulder before looking back to him. "Thought I was hallucinating when I saw you."

Calum grinned. "I don't doubt it."

He stumbled, Dale reached out to steady him. "So, you just on vacation in the neighborhood?" Marc asked, trying to lighten the air around them.

Dale released his arm and smiled over at Calum. "He was inside with us." Marc looked at him. "Saw him in the showers a few days ago… or I think it was a few days ago."

Calum paused and let them go ahead while he looked carefully across the terrain. He didn't know what Marilyn was doing to buy them time, but he hoped she pulled it off. Turning around, he went to check on Chad's condition, as he hadn't made a sound in several minutes. His chest was moving, so he supposed that was good enough for now.

"Cal?"

He turned to look at Dale. He looked like he was going to pass out at any second. "You okay to walk?"

Dale nodded. "From here to China if it means I'm free, damn right I am." He huffed out a breath. "That's ah…" he glanced at his neck. "quite the mark on your throat." He smirked. "You take some personal time since I saw you last?"

Gage snorted. "*The* elusive Calum is caught."

Dale shook his head. "That's what I wondered."

Marc paused and leaned on his knees for a moment. Dale paused beside him. "I'm fine, just a little dizzy." He stood up slowly again. "I look forward to meeting the woman that took you on, Cal."

Calum looked at the angry scar on his abdomen. "Were you awake when they stitched you up?"

Marc ran a hand over the scar. "Not much, in a drug haze really." He let out a shaky breath. "Had just gone ten rounds with a mystery cat in heat, so my head was fucked up before the sedative." He started walking again after a quick glance behind them. "The old doctor lady was there, but someone else with a gentle demeanor put me back together, couldn't tell you who though, as I had clouds and birds in my head at the time."

Devin glanced at his side, then gave him a nod. "That would have been his mate."

Marc's mouth dropped open. "Your mate is one of them?"

Calum nodded. "Long story." He ignored the chuckle from Gage and looked to see how much further they had to go, wondering how she was doing.

"Speaking of," Gage paused and adjusted his hold on the blanket. "think they've skinned Jake yet?" He started walking when Devin nodded. "I almost feel sorry, leaving him behind with four women to wrangle."

Devin growled, "he better not be wrangling them."

Calum froze when he saw something move out of the corner of his eye. Straightening he cursed silently. "He's not." He motioned to the top of the hill. "He's standing right there."

"What?" Gage's snapped his head up, "How the hell is he watching them if he's looking at us, *nowhere* near the cave?"

"Let's just ask him." Devin said when Jake started running toward them.

As Jake got close enough, Calum called out to him. "How the hell…"

Jake held up his hand to stop him. "Don't *ever* leave me with them again." He went straight to Marc and put his arm around him to help him walk more upright.

Calum looked up the hill. "Where are the girls?"

"In the cave." He glanced at Gage hesitantly, "Kels promised they'd stay right there before they demanded I come help."

Gage growled. "She's going to give me a heart attack one day soon, just wait and see."

Calum turned to look down the hill, to check they still weren't being tracked. It grated on his nerves, constantly having to look over his shoulder. They needed to come up with a permanent solution, and soon.

Jake was still mumbling under his breath. "When Brock came running in with Nona's medical bag and grabbing things, the girls damn near freaked out…"

"He ran from the village to there and back to us?" Gage asked.

Jake shrugged. "I guess."

"Holy shit," Gage said under his breath, "fast."

Turning back, Calum motioned to the top. "Lets just get there. I want to be in the 'no male' zone before they come looking for us." Chad lifting his hand caused them all to stop. Calum went over to him and leaned down. "What is it?"

"Scent…" Chad whispered, "tracked us."

Calum shook his head, "Don't worry about that. Marilyn and Brock said they had that covered." He looked up at Devin's curious look before straightening. "I didn't ask… figured I wouldn't want to know."

"Probably that god damned weed they sprinkled all over our cells like potpourri." Dale mused more to himself then any of them.

As they reached the top of the gulley, Calum felt relieved. "Few more minutes now." He went to go over and help with carrying Chad, when he caught sight of something out of the corner of his eye. "Promised that they'd stay in the cave, huh?"

All the men looked in the direction he was looking to see Rayne, Kelsey and Shaelan running toward them.

"Son of a…" Jake hissed

"Not your fault, Jake." Devin said, not hiding the annoyance in his tone. "There's not a man alive that can stop that force of nature, if they don't want to be stopped."

Gage growled.

Calum moved around to get to Shaelan before she saw the state Chad was in. She stopped in front of him and looked him over from boot to the top of his head, then smacked him hard in the center of his chest.

"Don't *ever* do that to me again." She hissed, then went by him to look at Chad.

"I'm sorry, maybe it's the drugs…" Dale said in a quiet tone, "but did she just hit Cal? *The* Cal that even wild bears run from?"

"Yes, she did." Marc said with a grin on his face.

Rayne came running over and went right to Shaelan. Her eyes flicked to Devin briefly. "Not a word, Devin Addison."

Calum heard Devin's teeth clacking together as he snapped his mouth shut. He was still standing where he had been, rubbing a hand over his chest where she'd smacked him.

Kelsey appeared and stopped in front of Gage and pointed a finger at him. "Bad," she hissed then looked to Shaelan. "What do you need?"

Shaelan was trying to look at Chad, without moving him, mumbling quietly to herself. "Tell Billie to get out of the tree and get some water boiling. I'm going to have to clean this up to see the extent of his injuries. Then tell her to get Nona up here as fast as she can."

Kelsey nodded, then took off back toward the cave.

"I'll go help." Rayne said and was running after her.

Shaelan looked Marc up and down, then Dale. "I'll check you two over when we get there." She told them softly before she turned to Calum. "Help them get him laying down, but not flat on his back, outside in the sun, the cave is too dark." When he nodded, she turned and ran after the other two.

"Damn." Dale whispered. "Those are your mates?"

Calum nodded.

"They're like a whole bundle of feminine force that I wouldn't want to deal with." He glanced to Gage and Devin. "Good luck to you all."

Shaking his head, Calum went ahead of them to find a good location to put Chad down. Later, when he wasn't stunned and in awe of his mate, they were going to have a chat about her safety and it being the most important thing on the planet. In fact, the population of the planet was safer as long as nothing ever happened to her.

Chapter Sixteen

When things finally settled down, Calum stood back, wrestling with his own personal demons. It had been hard to stand back and watch Shaelan touch other men, even though he knew they needed her help. Her gentle looks in his direction was the only thing that prevented him from going full berserker mode. He needed to get a better handle on this if he was going to make it, and he didn't want to be arguing with his mate every other day.

It had taken a good hour, maybe more, for Nona and Shaelan to get Chad patched up and comfortable. As strong as his new-found abhorrence to sedatives was, he knew the longer they kept Chad drugged, the easier it would be on him. Over one hundred stitches, Nona had counted, they had put into him. He was too weak and swollen for her to clear him to shift, because until the swelling went down she didn't know the full extent of his injuries. That, and she was afraid in his debilitated state he'd get stuck halfway through a shift and be stuck that way. He couldn't even imagine that. There was man and cat, no pausing in-between. Eyes, sure or some claws from time to time, but half-shift. *Damn.* As he stood there helplessly as the women tried to help Chad as best they could, Calum decided then that Jerome deserved no mercy.

Marc and Dale both had cuts and bruises all over, open sores from the cuffs and collars. Sitting on the cold floor that long hadn't done them any favors either, but Nona expected in a few days they'd be running again. Both were going to be okay, physically at least. Marc was always going to have that scar to remind him, but he supposed the mental ones were much worse. Hell, he hadn't gone through anything similar to what they had, but a man being chained like that… it left its mark, where no one could ever see.

Glancing around, he saw that Gage and Devin had finally settled down and were sitting with Marc and Dale. It was a small comfort that Dev and Gage were having just as hard a time with all of this as he was. He hadn't seen Gage pace this much since he'd realized he had a mate he couldn't have years ago.

Sighing, he went over to sit with them. Shaelan wasn't leaving Chad's side anytime soon. Her skill for healing was astonishing though, he admitted, even if it nagged at him that she may be a little too smart for her own good, and his comfort.

Sitting down, he looked at Dale's drawn appearance. "How are you feeling?"

He shrugged. "I'm good, it's nothing a half a side of beef, long run and…" He stiffened and sat straighter.

Calum turned to see what he was looking at. Billie was standing in the cave entrance.

"That's one of them." Dale said quietly. "That… that I was with."

Calum realized the trials of the day weren't over yet. "Yeah, I was going to give you a few hours to recoup before we talked about that."

He glanced to Devin who was cringing as well.

Dale snapped his head back to him "What? What do you mean?"

Calum rubbed the back of his neck and tried to think of a way to say it gently, but couldn't come up with one. "She's pregnant."

Dales face paled even more than it had been. "With...
ah..." His eyes didn't leave Calum's.

He nodded. "Yours."

Blowing out a loud breath, Dale swallowed. "Is she
mated?" He looked around quickly. "Should I be expecting
some big ox to come rip my throat open?"

"She's not," Devin assured him.

Dale looked at her once again then back to Calum, an
anger burning in his eyes. "So... so what, they just get young
women knocked up and leave them to go through it all
alone?"

Feeling like he had weights on his shoulders, Calum leaned
onto his knees and looked over at Billie. "I don't know...with
the other women, she would have help, I guess."

Dale swore. "That's inhumane." He looked at the ground
and swore again. "It was... I can't explain how... how *bad* it
was... is she okay?" His head snapped back in her direction.
"Did I..."

"She's physically fine." Gage said in a voice that held an
undertone of rage.

Dale huffed out a relieved breath. "Does she hate me?"

Calum glanced over to see Shaelan coming out of the cave
and was walking toward him. She looked tired, and upset.
"No, she knows it wasn't your fault." He answered when he
realized Dale was staring at him.

Rubbing a hand vigorously over his dark, brush cut hair,
Dale stared at the ground for a moment before looking back
to him. "Do you think she'd talk to me? I mean we are going
to be parents..."

Shaelan came over and stood by Calum. "I think with
some time, things will work out. Billie..."

Dale turned to her "Her name is Billie?"

Shaelan offered him a gentle smile, "Yes. She's kind of
crazy at times, I'd know, she's my best friend, but she's a very
loving person."

Nona cleared her throat and they all turned, not even
realizing she'd been standing there. "I know this is the last

thing on your minds right now, but Mari and I talk to the women that you fellas were… with. They've agreed to talk with you, meet you… considering what happened with Shae and Calum, they just want to be sure."

Dale groaned. "Fuck, wouldn't that be a new cruel punishment?"

Calum gave Dale a curious look.

Dale shrugged, "Meet my mate and have a baby with another woman…"

Nona chuckled, "We can hope that isn't a fact."

"Fuck hope, pray for me." Dale groaned again then looked to Nona, his eyes wide. "I'm sorry for my language…"

She waved a hand at him. "If I'd been through what you have, I'd have invented a whole volume of cuss words by now." She glanced to Marc for a moment, then to Calum. "The other two fellas were only with one woman, so…"

Marc snorted, "Small blessings where I can get them" He nodded, like he was having some sort of internal conversation. "I swear when I get back to the farm, I'm never leaving again." He growled and looked at Devin, "I can give you a description, down to the guys' shoes, the one that sent us 'hiking' up here." He growled in a hoarse way. "Had a lot of time to think about him."

Devin nodded, his jaw twitching, "the alliance will deal with him"

"I'll track the bastard myself." Calum spat out.

"So…" Dale rubbed a hand down his face, "it sounds so bad out loud, but who else was I with?" He puffed up his cheeks for a moment then exhaled, "I can vaguely see a face, but have no name and that makes me feel…"

Shaelan nodded, slowly. Calum knew she'd had that feeling too. "Natalie." She said looking to Dale. He stared off over her shoulder for a moment then nodded. Shaelan turned her head and gave Marc an inquiring look. He looked like a deer in headlights for a moment, then gave her an apprehensive nod. "Marcia."

It made it so much more real, Calum thought, putting names to it.

Shaelan tucked her hands into her pockets. "Chad was with Madison." She glanced toward the cave. "We'll tell her what's happened to him."

"And Gene?" Marc asked as he looked from Devin back to Calum.

Calum shook his head, his heart paining. "They don't release their captives and set them free."

"So, if you hadn't gotten us out…" Dale's expression went blank. He dropped his hand over his chest and looked at the ground.

Devin nodded, a grim expression on his face.

"Fuck me," Dale hissed.

"What about Gene?" Marc asked with a pained voice, "Is there a pregnant woman here carrying his…"

Nona nodded and clasped her hands against her chest. "Brooke, she knows, and is coming to grips with it."

With everything else happening, Calum had forgot to ask about all of this. It wasn't like him to not get all the details and know all the facts.

"That baby is one of ours, Cal, the clan will look out for her and the child." Dale said firmly.

He sighed, and closed his eyes for a moment. This needed to end. He opened his eyes and gave his clanmates a stern look. "We will. I'll talk to my Uncle, but I'm sure they'll bring her there and see her through this, if she consents."

"Help me get to my feet," Dale held out his hand.

Shaelan shook her head, "Dale, you should eat and rest for a…"

"I want to talk to… Billie." He said glancing in her direction.

Sighing, Shaelan touched Calum's shoulder lightly. "I'll go tell her."

Dale glared at Calum. "Help me get over there, I don't want to do this in front of everyone."

He helped him over to where Shaelan now stood with Billie. Dale moved away from him, even though he wasn't steady, wanting to be standing on his own two feet as he met the mother of his child. Calum paused in thought, how messed up was that? Shaking his head, he stepped back and put his arm around Shaelan. She glanced up at him and he realized she wasn't sure if they should stay or leave them. He'd follow her lead on that.

"Hi," Dale took a shaky step and held out his hand, "I'm Dale."

Billie looked at his hand for a second, then shook it quickly, before clasping it with her other one. "Billie." Dale swayed and she inhaled sharply. "You should sit down." She reached out, then pulled her hands back and motioned to the wall by the cave entrance.

Nodding, Dale moved over and sat down, then looked up at her. He motioned to the other side of the entrance. "Please."

Billie sat down and pulled her knees up to her chest and hugged them. "I'm glad you got out." She said her eyes flicking from him to the ground and back. "Are you okay?"

"I'll be fine." He cleared his throat a few times. "Are you okay?"

She blushed, then huffed out a breath. "Can I get back to you on that?" Looking back at her feet, she continued in a quiet voice. "It's been a… uh… rough few weeks." She glanced at Shaelan then briefly to Dale. "I find out I'm a shifter, have my… I'm going to be a mom." Her voice cracked. "I'm just processing." She nodded then looked back at Dale.

He nodded a few times. "So…"

Calum realized Shaelan was tugging on his arm to go. He glanced at her then back to Dale before following her. She smiled up at him and he hugged her to him.

"They'll be okay." She said quietly as they walked back toward where the others were sitting.

"As first meetings go, awkward is the norm around here." He kissed the top of her head.

"I'm going back to check on Chad, so Rayne and Kelsey can have a break from watching him."

He nodded. "Think he'll be alright?"

She pursed her lips for a second before answering him. "It's too soon to give any definitive answers." She offered him a sad look, then turned to go back inside.

Swearing under his breath, Calum walked over and sat down.

By dusk, Calum was craving a run. A real run on four legs, fast and long. So much anxiety, sadness, anger and just about every other emotion possible was grating on his nerves. If he didn't run soon, he was going to snap. His cat was assaulted with the emotions he was, picking up from everyone else, and at times was rubbing so hard on the inside Calum was sure if he checked he'd see worn patches on his body.

"The tension here is crushing me," Devin mumbled quietly. Turning, he looked to track his mate with his eyes. "Rayne, she's got that look again—the one that means I'm going to be adding more cabins to the campground and bringing in more people for her to mother... or we're going to be moving here indefinitely."

Gage, who was sprawled out on the ground beside him, turned his head and looked at him. "Maybe you should make her an actual mother."

Devin looked down at him, shaking his head. "I don't even know if I'd live through her going through *that*."

Gage grinned, "I don't know if I would live through a miniature version of you."

"Here's hoping they take after mom." Calum glanced around. Kelsey was standing smiling and talking on the phone. How was it she got a signal anywhere, and everyone else had to wander around and waved their phone in the air? He looked to Gage and motioned to her.

Gage lifted his head and looked at her, then sighed and lay back, rubbing his hand over his face a few times before he spoke. "She'll be talking to Blair."

"I was a bit surprised when he didn't come with you…"

Devin snorted, "We wanted someone left alive."

Calum shrugged, "Just as well I suppose. How's he dealing with Kelsey being mated, finally?"

Gage propped himself up on his elbows. "Did everyone know but me?"

Calum grinned, "Probably, you're not the most observant man."

Gage lifted his lip in a half snarl at him, then he sighed, "He'll be going to help Bruce out, once we get back." He glanced back to Kelsey, "she keeps trying to find a way to be mated *and* keep him close."

"Good luck with that. I have my own problems." He looked at Devin. "So where *are* things with Tomas?" He needed anything to take his mind off the insane things swirling around in his head. Insane, as in they could get him severely maimed or killed.

"We've gotten several out. It's going to be a long-term recovery for most of them." Devin glanced to Rayne. "The campground is now a hospice for those in trouble, recovering, scared or just worn out."

Calum couldn't think of a thing to say that could make Devin feel better about that. The fact that Devin, the same guy that had been alone for years by choice, had accepted that, was shocking. Finding his mate had changed him. He wondered if it was going to change him. Aside from not being able to focus on anything longer than two minutes before he thought of Shaelan, he hadn't noticed anything different, yet.

Gage sat up. "Noah is doing better, but I don't think that he'll ever be a normal guy."

He didn't know who Noah was, presumably someone they rescued. Calum realized he had a lot to catch up on. *That's what I get for traipsing around strange mountains.* He thought of Shaelan, *and a mate*, he'd gotten her too.

Devin nodded his head to where Shaelan sat, a book open on her knees.

Calum turned to watch her for a moment. Rubbing a hand over his chest, because he was sure his heart jolted when he looked at her. "Yeah, she's practically got the book memorized now—she's trying to figure out how to connect the names and people that are still living—together."

"What do you mean?" Gage frowned at him.

"Devin said the alliance will have names of those missing, she's going to backtrack them from birthdates to times of conception, so we can confirm the names of some of the men that never went home… She thinks people have a right to know they have a blood relative here on the mountain. Also, thinks it will give the families that have been left wondering about missing members some closure."

Devin leaned closer, lowered his voice. "She'll be looking for her father's family too?"

Calum nodded slowly. "Yeah." He rubbed a hand over his heart again, "not looking forward to that emotion-fest." Both her and her mother were going to be a whole whirlwind of feelings when that happened.

Gage got up and brushed off his jeans. "You have any missing male relatives over the years?"

Turning Calum gave him a blank look. "Why?"

Gage smirked. "Just what if…" He lifted his eyebrows and glanced to Shaelan.

Scowling at him, "I will kill you, if I have to." He said in a quiet voice, only half meaning it.

Gage and Devin both started laughing. Calum growled low.

"If you don't stop rubbing your chest and sending out waves of sappy emotion, *I'm* going to hug you," Devin complained, "go soothe your mate and get away from me."

Getting up, Calum nodded. "Fine then. I will."

Before he could get two feet, Marilyn came jogging up the hill.

"Whew! I keep running up that every day and this ass…" she patted her backside, "might be firm again." She laughed, nodding as she looked around before turning back to Calum. "I couldn't come sooner, it's like a contagious madness in the village." She pursed her lips together for a moment, then sighed, "might have something to do with the herbs I used in the stink bombs."

Gage sat down. "This, I have to hear."

Nodding, Calum motioned to the rock he'd been sitting on. "We're trying to let Chad get some rest, so we're parked out here for now, until we're ready to sleep."

"How are they?" She shook her head as she sat down. "When Brock told me about that poor man, well, let's just say Faye had to stop me from getting the fork."

Calum debated on asking, but let it go. "He's in rough shape. A lot of healing to do." He sat on the ground.

"When Nona told me he shouldn't shift…" She shook her head, "I knew how bad it was." She motioned to the cave, "the other two doing okay though?"

He nodded, then turned to watch Shaelan come over. She sat down in front of him, leaning back against him.

"I have to ask," Gage said with a smirk. "Why do you smell like a perfume factory?"

"Heh, I may never live that one down." She nodded to Shaelan, "Faye and I were *busy* today. We made stink bombs, gave them to most of the women…" she fanned her face excitedly, "let's just say when they were lit up all over the place…" she sobered, "on the sly of course, so no one could get blamed." She clapped her hands together lightly, "the whole place was puffs of smoke all over." She frowned. "We should have asked Nona for help with our selection though, half of us were hyped up like happy squirrels, and the rest wanted to lay down right where they stood and hum a lullaby." She exhaled loudly, "it's why I'm late in coming, it had to wear off." Shaking her head, she grinned, "By the time we were done, no nose there could have tracked a thing." Inhaling slowly, she gave a small laugh, "still can't smell a darn thing."

Despite the somber tone, there wasn't one person present without a smile after her story, Calum noted. He didn't want to halt the only reason they'd had to smile today, but he needed to know. "Did they find the guards?"

She gave her head a quick shake. "No and they won't either. The entire village is in on keeping them hidden." She opened her mouth looking completely animated for a moment, then looked to Shaelan. "That Brock, he's storming around with your... Leroy, his chest all puffed out, stomping around. He's such a hoot." Nodding, she grinned wide, "saying he's checking homes *personally* while Leroy stands there pacing like a rabid animal..." she chuckled, "then he stomps out and off they go to the next one." She laughed loud. "I tell you, if we get out of this alive..." Her head bobbed a few times, "I'm sending him to that place I read about." She smiled wide, "That *Hollywood Loss Angelees*, so he can be a famous actor."

Devin put his hand over his mouth, his eyes wide. Gage tilted his head to the side, smirking. No one even attempted to correct her, it would just take too long. Calum figured.

"What about mom, she can't stay with Leroy...." Shaelan asked with a shaky voice.

Calum straightened and was ready to take off to the village when Marilyn waved him off.

"She's at Nona's. Told Leroy those nasty herbs made her real sick." Scowling, she huffed out a loud breath. "That man don't care if she's ill, so he won't even care where she is." Looking around she turned to Devin. "Your alliance get here yet?"

Devin shook his head. "No. I got a message from my father and they should be here by tomorrow afternoon."

Her eyes widened. "Then what happens?"

Calum exchanged a glance with Devin and Gage briefly, he'd been meaning to talk to them earlier, but with one thing after the other happening, there just hadn't been a moment they could plan without interruption. Hell, he wasn't even sure what he was thinking, so voicing it wasn't going to be easy. "I don't think we can wait until then." Gage looked at him and frowned. Calum shrugged, "the fact that they haven't thought to look in the most obvious place this long, is surprising." If it were Calum looking for people, the first place he would have looked was the areas they weren't supposed to be in.

"I was wondering on that too." Marilyn said quietly. "I don't know where else to move you though, I've been thinking on it. I know Brock is distracting him from coming this direction a lot, but Leroy goes for runs and he's going to think of here one of these times."

Calum felt Shaelan tense, could taste her fear. He looked to see both Devin and Gage watching him carefully, as if they knew what he was going to say next. It was the only solution he could find. He was the only healthy male present the same species as Shaelan's clan. It had to stop. Stalling, one way or the other, wasn't going to change it.

Unless Devin's father came riding in on a tank, it was going to get messy before it got better. Those people didn't know him, or know what was the truth or lies regarding the alliance. They didn't even know what it meant to be in a functional clan. He exhaled slowly and looked to Devin as he spoke. "I'll challenge Leroy."

Shaelan was on her knees, in his face before he could take his next breath. "What? No." She shook her head. "You mean fight him?" She looked at the others. "Isn't that to the death?"

"In most cases." Devin answered quietly.

Her head snapped back to look at Calum. "No. You can't. He killed the true alpha…"

"That wasn't no fight." Marilyn said with disgust in her voice, "Leroy had Jerome shoot your momma's man in the back with a tranquilizer as it started." She shook her head slowly, "it was over before it begun."

Devin growled and jumped to his feet. "So, this *lunatic* didn't even take over the clan in a legal way?"

A sadness came over Marilyn. "No. Anyone that said a word about it, or against him…" She looked at her hands. "disappeared." Her voice was barely audible. "Enough get to vanishing like that and people tow the line," she glanced around at them, "you know?"

Calum felt his cat roll over his skin, the animosity very easy to pick up. He looked at Shaelan and cupped her face gently. "It's the only way to free your people." He glanced at his mark on her neck, "our people."

Kelsey came over, "What is?"

Shaelan dropped back onto her heels and looked at her, "Calum is going to fight Leroy for alpha."

Kelsey's eyes went huge, she looked to Gage, then back to Calum. "Your what?" She shook her head. "We don't even know how big this man is? Or… or…" She looked to Gage, then Devin and covered her mouth with both hands.

Calum stood up, his hands on his hips, purposely avoiding eye contact with his mate. What her clan had gone through, for *years*… it had to be stopped. He could see no other way. The only decision, as far as he was concerned, was if he was walking boldly in the front gate, or sneaking in the back door.

"You haven't seen Calum fight." Gage said in a serious tone, as he got up to go to Kelsey. "If Leroy picks cat form, he's dead before he lifts a paw and on two legs…" Gage blew out a breath, "it's not any less painful."

Devin nodded then paused to watch Dale walking over.

"Couldn't sleep, woke up needing air." He stopped and looked at everyone. "What's happened now?"

"Calum's going to fight the alpha." Shaelan sobbed as she got up and ran toward the trees behind the cave entrance.

He exhaled slowly and watched her go.

"Oh shit. Sucks to be the alpha." Dale said.

Turning, Calum looked back at Devin, who motioned with his head to follow her. Shaking his head, he went after her.

Chapter Seventeen

Shaelan hadn't gone far. Calum was thankful that she knew enough not to take off alone. He could hear her sobbing and felt like the air was harder to draw into his lungs. His cat had gone completely still. Figures, he thought, bail on me and leave me to do this without help.

Moving silently, he went over and pulled her to her feet, and tried to wrap his arms around her, but she swatted them away. "Shaelan…"

She jabbed him in chest with her finger and glared at him through the tears. "This he-man, king of the jungle stuff is ridiculous." Shaking her head, she stepped back from him and hugged her arms around her waist. "I don't care if this is how it is in the animal world." She paused and looked at the ground, "a week ago, I didn't live in the animal world with all…" her hands waved in the air, "*this.*"

He moved to go to her, his cat reappearing and almost shoving him, but the warning look she gave him told him he needed to ride it out a bit longer.

"Leroy is a cruel, sick man that has filled the lives of the whole village with violence and fear." She stomped over and smacked him on the chest. "How is fighting him by using *more* violence going to change that?" Turning away from him, she stood and looked into the night.

For whatever reason, he had always thought mates couldn't harm one another, yet she'd smacked him twice now. Before this, no one would have dared. His mate was incredible, filled with so much emotion and passion. He clenched his jaw, so he wouldn't grin at this revelation. She put her head down and started sobbing again. Moving quickly, he grabbed her and pulled her into his arms. "It's going to be okay, love."

"You can't." She looked up at him with tears running down her face once more. "You could die." She buried her face in his chest again.

He could, he knew that, but it didn't mean he was going to dwell on it. "There is no other way, that I can think of to end this." Lifting her chin so she'd look at him, "It could take weeks for the alliance to get everything under control—without going in guns blazing and innocents getting hurt." He wiped a tear from her cheek. "How many more people will pay the price with Leroy and his henchmen in that time?" Smirking, he tried to lighten the mood. "The cave isn't big enough for the whole village."

Taking a ragged breath, she shook her head. "You can't. There has to be another way."

The way she was looking at him, almost had him willing to back down, then he remembered how her mouth had looked when it was swollen. How she'd risked her own life to save his. How right in this very moment there was a man that may never recover in the cave. Gene, he couldn't think of a worse way to go, lost, alone and no one would have known if Calum hadn't gone in that direction by mistake. He ran his hand down her back gently. "I can't think of another way, love, and believe me I've been thinking about it since the moment I regained consciousness."

"What if… what if… you…"

He placed a finger gently over her lips. "Don't think like that. I can't think like that going into it." Moving his finger, he replaced it with a soft kiss. "For all we know, he may just turn tail and run when confronted by someone that isn't afraid of him."

"You're not afraid of him?" She blew out a shaky breath. "Everyone is afraid of him."

He shook his head and smirked. "I don't think they are. You're not, or you wouldn't have marched up to Nona's when you were just a kid and asked to learn how to care for every person in that village." Kissing her again, he continued. "How can I not help my mate do that?"

"I could see even then, that people needed help." She exhaled a ragged breath, "Nona was always so strong, always knew what to do… I want to be like that."

"You are."

She shook her head. "No, I'm not, or I would have a better solution than you fighting him."

He grinned. "It's who I am, I can't walk away when someone is in trouble… never could, despite Devin and Gage trying to drag me away. I got them beat on many times while we were growing up." Hugging her, he inhaled that sweet cinnamon scent. "And now fate has given me a mate that compliments who I am perfectly."

She leaned back and looked up him with a questioning look.

He shrugged, "you can patch me up afterward, whenever I have to step into a situation."

The look she gave him, told him that revelation was not a good thing. When she blew out a breath, he could feel some of the anguish leave her on it.

Her dark eyes moved over his face for a moment. "You can't just walk in the gates and call him out." Biting her lip, she paused briefly. "I think he has someone watching it all the time. It has to be a surprise, catch him and the men loyal to him off guard." She leaned into his chest and rubbed her face there.

He grinned, she may not realize it, but that was very cat like gesture. "I was thinking I'd go to Nona's tonight and already be *in* the village in the morning." Looking back up at him, she searched his face as a shudder went through him seeing the soft expression in her eyes. "Everyone can hide at Nona's." He hoped it was a small consolation that he wasn't going to try to exclude her from this, of course that didn't mean he was letting her watch, either.

Biting her bottom lip again, she shook her head. "Chad can't be moved yet, and I don't think Dale and Marc are ready to be..." she gave him an annoyed look, "physical."

He looked from her mouth back to her eyes as she kept nibbling at that lip when she talked it through. When this was over, if he was still standing, he was abducting his mate and spending a week with her, alone, without interruption. "They'll be safe here. I'll text Jesse to send someone here when they're coming back up here."

She nodded, but didn't say anything.

He pulled her closer, just in case she had any ideas about hitting him again, sensing that now would not be a good time to tell her he found it sexy as hell that she did. She looked up at him for a long, silent moment, then reached up and grasped his hair to pull his head down to hers. She kissed him with such passion, he had to remind himself they weren't alone out here as he pulled her tight against his body and molded her to him with his roaming hands.

Pulling her mouth away just as suddenly, she glared up at him. "If anything happens to you. No one responsible will survive. I will tear them apart with *my* own hands." With that she stepped out of his arms and started back down the incline. "I'll tell everyone to get ready to go."

Calum stood there and watched her go. Blowing out a long, drawn-out breath, he rubbed a hand over his chest again where it still stung from her palm. Two weeks, he needed at least two weeks alone with her... for a start. Shaking his head, he went down the incline to see Devin and Gage waiting there and looking at him.

"That went well," Devin said with sarcasm.

Inhaling sharply, Calum glanced toward the cave. "Yeah."

Gage motioned to the cave. "The girls are getting our stuff. Marilyn took off back to the village as soon as you went after Shaelan."

Nodding, Calum turned and looked out into the night. "I don't see another way…"

Devin moved to stand beside him. "We don't either." He glanced over his shoulder. "They're going to be pissed when they realize Gage and I won't be standing idly nearby."

Gage tapped Calum on the back. "We'll be there to even the odds, something tells me this Leroy won't fight a fair fight."

Rubbing the spot on his chest again, Calum sighed. "Just don't let him shoot me with a fucking tranquilizer dart."

The walk to Nona's was long, tension keeping every person there silent. Crouching down, he paused to watch Shaelan and Billie move by him to catch up to the others. Neither had been in touch with their new-found cat side long enough to have it ingrained in their movements, but they moved as silently and stealthy as the others. It was just one more thing that showed him they had grown up under all the wrong circumstances, yet learned it to survive.

Gage stopped beside him and nudged him. "Knock it off. The rage coming off you has my cat wanting blood."

Huffing out a breath, Calum tried to shake the feeling off. "Stockpile that feeling, we may need an enraged tiger before this is over." He watched Shaelan motion for Billie to keep going and then turned around and looked back at him. She hadn't said a word to him since she'd walked out of the cave carrying his pack. He honestly had no idea if that was a good or bad thing. This mating stuff was complicated enough, he could have done without all the other complications involved. Things like being held captive, escaping, and freeing a whole village from a maniac.

Shaelan looked back at Calum again. Her chest ached with the thought of what he was going to do. Every thirty seconds, since they'd started back to the village, she'd had to fight the tears. She couldn't believe he was going to do it, but knew no one could change his mind. A part of her was still stunned that she had a man, a mate that was so noble with firm principles. Then there was the other part that wished he was more like meek men she'd been raised around. Only they weren't really meek, she supposed, just terrified to speak out.

Idiot man. It was the most astonishing, selfless thing she'd ever known. A complete stranger going to fight—possibly to the death, to free her clan from Leroy. Turning, she followed the path Billie had taken. *Stupid man.* She was mad *and* proud of him. She couldn't even speak to him right now for fear she'd howl like she was dying, or scream at him for being so... wonderful and stupid.

There had to be another way. There just had to be. *Think!* The only escape she'd ever had was her mind, as long as she kept it moving, she could live with the tension and apprehension that was her life. Now that she needed it, she could barely form a single clear thought.

Stopping, she crouched lower when Billie all but lay in the grass ahead of her. She set her bag down and listened to see if she could hear anything. They were only five minutes from Nona's now, had one of Leroy's men found them?

She sensed Calum move up beside her before she saw him. He stopped and lifted his face to the sky, inhaling slowly. Frowning, Shaelan did the same to see if she could... she did smell something she'd never picked up on before. It was an animal... something familiar. Her heart skipped a beat, hoping it wasn't one of the men.

"It's Brock." Calum whispered. "Keep moving."

She huffed out a breath and grabbed her bag. Brock must be prowling to watch for others to make sure they made it to the house, she hoped. Later, when her heart wasn't in her throat she'd think about how she could find one smell among all the grass and nature around them.

As they reached the bottom of the hill to Nona's she ran up. This area she knew, it had been the only way Billie and her could escape the village to be alone when they were growing up.

Reaching the top, she saw Nona on the deck, holding the door open. She paused to let the others go in ahead of her.

Aunt Marilyn greeted everyone as they came in. "We kept the lights off," she waved to a few candles, "so no one looking up could see in."

Shaelan huffed out a relieved sigh that they'd got here without incident. Pausing, she looked at the seven people standing in her home. Aside from Billie, they didn't seem phased with all of this, and here she was an emotional wreck, and her skin felt several sizes too small for her.

Brock came in the front door wearing only a pair of jeans. She looked at his bare feet and almost laughed when she realized the casual dress that she'd grown up with wasn't because of people were easygoing, but those wandering around half naked and barefoot had been because they had shifted back to their human bodies. How had she never fit all the pieces together before? Then again, she never could have imagined that turning into animals was a thing, so of course she hadn't seen all the signs.

Brock blew out a breath. "I swear, when this is over I will have lost ten pounds from running around this much." Holding a palm over his toned stomach he rolled his eyes, "but I guess it helps my manly figure." A serious look replaced the animated one as his eyes stopped on Calum. "I can't believe your doing this." His eyes teared up, "but I'm so thankful you are." he whispered.

Shaelan had to look away from him before she started crying again. "At dawn, you need to ring the bell, Brock." She glanced quickly to Calum, then everyone else. "It brings every resident to the area in front of the meeting hall."

Nona came over and took the bag Shae was clutching tightly to her chest. "That's good, child, catch Leroy off-guard."

"We were finally able to replace Jerome's bullets with the blanks they used for target practice." Her aunt told everyone.

Shaking her head, she glanced to Brock, "don't ask how we managed it." She gave them a wide-eyed look. "Let's just say one of the women went above and beyond."

"Oh." Rayne said quietly. "I will personally take her to the spa to… *cleanse* it away."

Aunt Marilyn nodded. "I'm not too sure what that is, but sign me up too." She sighed, "it's been a long, trying life and we all could use some spa when it's done." She turned and looked to the hallway, where Shae's mother stood. "Faye gets twice as much spa as the rest of us for what's she's had to put up with all these years."

It hit her all at once, what her mother had withstood during her life with Leroy. Brushing by Nona, she went quickly to her and hugged her. Burying her face in her soft hair and inhaling the scent that was so familiar, realizing it had a completely different meaning to her now. She squeezed her to not sob and crumble to the floor in an emotional heap. She wanted to cry and say she was sorry for not understanding, and to whine because her mate may die in the morning, but instead she hugged her tight and shook from head to toe trying to keep it all in.

With a gentle touch, her mother leaned back and pushed Shae's hair aside to look at her throat and the mark left there by Calum. A relief filled her eyes. "I think," she said in her caring way, "I should meet my son-in-law."

Shae nodded, realizing in all of this she hadn't even gotten to meet Calum. Turning, she watched Gage give him a shove in their direction. She almost laughed at the expression on her his face. *Now,* he looked afraid. The prospect of meeting his mother-in-law scared him, more than his planning to fight for the position of alpha of her clan.

He came over and pulled her gently to stand in front of him, she didn't miss the smirk on her mother's face as he did.

"Calum, this is my mother, Faye Black."

It dawned on Shae, she didn't even know this man's last name. She'd marked him… among other things and she was now mated to a man and she didn't even know his last name.

He reached around her and held out his hand. "Ma'am."

"Please, Faye." Her mom stood there, holding his hand for a moment, her eyes searching his face and moving to his neck more than once. Shaelan swallowed, feeling the tension in him where he stood behind her. When her mother released his hand, she smirked again. "That's... quite the mark you managed, Shae."

Shae felt her cheeks go red, "I don't have sharp teeth... yet." She said quietly.

Giving her an understanding look, she tilted her head and looked back to Calum. "If he's not complaining, then I guess it's fine." She glanced back to Shae. "How are you feeling?" She rubbed her hands up and down her arms. "I can't even help you, I've never shifted."

She felt the tension drain from Calum immediately. He moved so he was standing beside her now.

"It's okay, m-Faye, Kelsey and Rayne are here, she'll have all the help she could ever ask for on the female side of things." He squeezed her with his arm around her waist. "I'll be with her and talk her through her first shift."

Shae understood now, how he was on the inside. He *honestly couldn't* stop himself from helping someone, even as simple as reassuring her mother. She leaned against him.

Her mother smiled at him. "Thank you. I sense her cat more, so I don't think it's going to be much longer."

Holding her breath for a moment, Shae thought how she felt about that. She was excited, but frankly, scared to death about turning into something else. She wondered if she'd have dark fur like Calum or the lighter spotted shade she'd seen on the mountains many times. Shaking her head, she blew out a breath. "I just want to get through tomorrow, then I'll take things as they come."

Both arms wrapped around her waist now, Calum leaned down and kissed the top of her head. "You'll be fine."

The expression on her mom's face changed, more serious and forlorn then she'd ever seen it. She looked to the floor for a moment then to Calum. "I don't know... I feel I should thank you for…" She hugged her waist, "for doing what I never had the strength to do." Her eyes teared up. "I thought about killing him in his sleep many times." She covered her mouth with her hand for a few seconds, "but knew that wouldn't end it. He has men that…" She shook her head, not finishing.

Calum's muscles tensed against as he straightened back up.

"I'm glad you didn't, in that it would have changed you in an irrevocable way." He told her in a quiet voice. "It will end tomorrow, one way or another. You can count on that."

All of it came back to Shae at once. Why they were here, what could happen… she turned in his arms and looked up at him.

"I'll give you two some time." Her mother said as she moved by them to go in with the others.

He shook his head, a tender expression in his eyes. "Don't talk about the what-ifs, it will only put both of us more on edge." Glancing up, he motioned with his head down the hall.

She didn't want to talk about any of it in front of the others. They may not be standing right beside them, but she knew they could hear every word. Grabbing his hand, she walked down the hall to her room and went in. Only to stop suddenly and look around. She'd forgotten she'd all but torn the place apart, and hadn't been back since. There were books and papers from her shelves all over the place, the wooden shelves were broken and tossed in a heap on the floor, her mattress was half off the bed, and clothes were strewn all over the room.

"Maid's day off?" He asked over the top of her head.

Turning, she gave him a blank look. "I forgot I had a… moment."

"I've had moments before." He stepped into the room and looked around. "You have a violent streak at times." His eyes were sparkling with humor.

"I do?" She looked at him, her eyebrows up. She wasn't the one going to fight Leroy.

Calum nodded and waved his hand around motioning to the mess, "this and you've hit me, twice."

She felt some tension drain out of her, "*that* was not hitting you." The offended look on his face made her smile, "that was getting your attention."

"You always have my attention." Shaking his head, he looked at the books all over the floor. "You read all of these?"

Moving over, she knelt and started picking them up and closing them. "Yes, and every book in the village, twice." She shrugged, "I almost lived at the library while I was at school."

"Mmm," he squatted down and picked up one of them and looked at it. "Environmental Science?" He glanced back at her before adding it to the pile. "I thought you studied medicine?"

Nodding, she pushed the stack toward the wall and started another one. "I did, do." She shrugged, "I'll read anything with words really."

Adding a few more to the pile, he stopped and looked at her. "I think, my beautiful mate, you are entirely too smart for me."

She shook her head, "I don't think so." She looked him over slowly. "I think you hide intelligence behind the brawn, so people don't see it."

He smirked, "Is that so?"

"It is." She moved the books over beside the other stack and looked around. "I really made a mess in here."

Chuckling, he sat down. "You had every right to have a *moment*." Reaching out, he played with a lock of her hair on her shoulder.

"I just… there were so many lies." She sighed softly, "Then there's all this… everything I don't know anything about." Shrugging, she watched his face, noting again that she had his full attention. "I don't like not understanding, or knowing, about something."

His eyes looked around at the papers and books still scattered on the floor with them. "You don't say."

"I don't know anything about being a shifter. Is there a book…"

He chuckled, "I don't know. Maybe somewhere there's something with information." He shrugged, "you would have to ask Devin or his father, the alliance may have rooms full of books for all I know."

"I hope so."

Rubbing his hand over his forehead, he stopped and looked at her. "I can see you reading each one if there is."

"At least twice," she said widening her eyes at him, teasing him.

"I can answer some questions if you have anything nagging at you right now." He watched her face while she thought.

She couldn't believe they were sitting here talking like this when in a few hours… everything was going to change. He was so calm. Inhaling a sharp breath, she remembered. "I do have one question." She shook her head, "I can't believe I don't know it…"

"What is it?" He eyes searched her face.

Biting her lip, she felt her cheeks flush, "I don't even know your last name."

Smirking, he rubbed the back of his neck. "Mmm, yeah the moment for proper introductions was skipped right over wasn't it?" He looked back at her. "I didn't know yours until you introduced your mother a few minutes ago."

Her face flushed, she covered it with both hands. "I still can't believe how we met," Dropping her hands, she gave him a stunned look, "How could we ever explain to anyone how we met?" She giggled, "Well, he was chained to the wall…"

He reached out and grabbed her, making her shriek, and pulled her into his lap. "We won't be sharing *that* with just anyone."

His smile told her he wasn't upset. She chuckled again. "So, do you have a last name? Or are you just *The* Calum that wild bears even run from?"

"You heard that, huh?" Hugging her tight, he laughed quietly. "I have a last name and some stories from when I was younger that are never going to go away."

"Who do I talk to so I can hear them."

"No one, ever." He sobered. "Dante. Calum Dante."

She paused and wrapped her arms around his neck and looked into those deep green eyes. "Calum Dante," she said softly. "So, with mates do they use the same last name?"

He was watching her mouth as she spoke. "They can. We have actual ceremonies as well. Mates get married like other people do. We have to live in the normal world like everyone else, with all the associated paperwork."

Biting her lip, she thought about that for a moment. "Shaelan Dante," she said softly trying it out. "I like it."

"I like all of it." He said, leaning closer to her mouth. "The brains, beauty, even the violent moments," he kissed her softly, pulling her tight against him.

Shae leaned into his kiss, craving the taste of him, almost needing it.

"Shae…Oh." Kelsey stood in the doorway, looking shocked as she surveyed the room.

"She had a moment," Calum said.

"I would say so." She smiled at them. "Nona made some food, says Shae's Calum needs to keep his strength up." Kelsey smirked at Calum.

Shaelan nodded. "That's a good idea." She glanced at the clock on her wall. "Only four hours until dawn." Exchanging looks with Kelsey, who silently acknowledged the fear and anxiety of what was to happen. She could feel his reluctance as Calum stood, bringing her to her feet as she did.

"I'd just like ten damn minutes alone with my mate." He grumbled quietly.

Kelsey grinned, "Poor man." She gave him a serious look. "After things are… resolved, tomorrow, you can hide with your mate in your cabin for weeks."

"I plan on it."

Kelsey turned and went back out.

He sighed and took her hand and starting walking out.

"You are?" They walked slow, in no hurry to go eat. She wasn't even sure if she could eat.

He nodded, "Yeah, it's small, I'm still working on it. It has power, satellite, and internet though, so it's not as rustic as it looks. I finished the hot tub…"

She tugged on his hand. "Don't tell Aunt Marilyn it has a hot tub or she'll be visiting. She's been wanting one for years."

He stopped abruptly and looked down at her, a serious expression on his face. "Will you come there with me? I know you have responsibilities here and…"

She put her hand over his mouth. "Yes. I think it's a good idea, to get to know each other and then we'll decide where we live, maybe both places part-time?"

Kissing her quickly he nodded, and pulled her close against him again. "We can do that."

Winding her arms around his neck, she gave him a soft smile. "The internet is like an endless book…"

Frowning, he studied her. "So, you're coming to use my internet?"

She bit her lip and tried not to smile. "Of course."

There was quiet snickering behind him, she looked around him so see the others watching them, trying not to laugh.

Calum growled playfully, "We'll finish *this* discussion later."

"Oh, I don't know, Cal, I think the internet is what has her interest." Gage said smirking.

Shae went to the table and sat down, while watching the interaction between the men. It was clear they had been friends a long time.

Devin laughed, "Maybe the hot tub was a good draw too."

Jake grabbed his sides, laughing so hard at the expression on Calum's face.

"Hot tub?" Aunt Marilyn came out of the kitchen carrying a tray of sandwiches. "Who has a hot tub." She set the tray down and stood with her hands on her hips.

Calum lifted his lip at his friends in a fake snarl. "Marilyn, I will build you your own private hot tub, if you keep these clowns out of my face."

Aunt Marilyn looked at him for a moment, then looked Devin and Gage up and down. "Nona, grab the fork."

Raising their hands, Devin and Gage backed up, big grins on their faces. "We'll behave." Gage said trying not to laugh.

She gave them a quick nod then sat down and looked at Calum. "I want one big enough for friends." She motioned to Nona, "we could have parties in my hot tub."

Nona laughed and sat down, motioning for the others to help themselves.

Shaelan sat there, her hands in her lap smiling, trying not to think that it all could change in a few hours. Her chair suddenly slid as Calum pulled her closer to him.

"Don't dwell on it," he said next to her ear.

Chapter Eighteen

As the early light of dawn appeared, Shaelan was pacing by the window, looking down at the rest of the village. The others were moving around quietly, she wasn't sure if they had slept, she knew she hadn't. For a few hours, she lay in Calum's arms, watching him. She didn't know how he had managed his short nap. Although he was probably more used to this sort of thing than she was. When he'd finally spoken, she'd almost fallen off the bed in surprise, not even realizing he was awake.

The village was so quiet now, no one was awake yet. She knew that was going to end shortly. Everyone would come out of their homes when the bell rang, all would be present to witness their lives changing.

She was sure it was the stress. The unknowns weighing on her that made her feel this way. Panicked, but almost depressed at the same time. So many things could happen, the outcome was not guaranteed. If Leroy backed down, was it truly over? She didn't trust that. He could only be saying that, saying anything to buy more time to come up with a new plan or angle. He could take off and then the wondering would always be there, they'd be looking over their shoulders for the rest of their lives.

If Calum did fight him and won, what then? They'd be free, but at what cost? If he killed Leroy there would be that weighing on them forever. She knew Calum had a more violent nature to him than she did, and that he'd probably exercised it in his life, but this… this could change a person deep inside. What happened if he did win, was he then the alpha of the clan? How would that work with him having to be Devin's second when he became leader of the alliance?

So many shifter and clan things she didn't know. Was it all just passed on by word of mouth or was it written down somewhere? She didn't even know that. Then, as hard as she was trying to ignore it, the thought kept coming back, what if Calum was seriously injured or worse… she wouldn't have him. *Oh god, I can't do that.* There was no way to move beyond that. Her life wouldn't have any meaning if he were gone and Leroy remained breathing.

So many emotions, her chest was tight, she was sweating too, hot one minute, then cold the next. Her entire body was tingling, her skin was too tight and she physically felt ill, all the way to her soul, if that were possible. What was she going to do?

"Hey, love," Calum came up behind her.

Shaelan jumped, she hadn't heard him coming. She turned to look and was surprised he was just wearing his jeans, nothing else. She paused to look at him, her eyes wandering over his chest slowly, taking in the sculpted muscle, then looked at her mark on his neck.

"Keep looking at me like that and we're going to have a problem." He said quietly.

Her eyes jumped up to his. "Sorry." She cleared her throat. "Why are you dressed like that?"

He moved closer to her, in a slow easy motion, like he was afraid she was going to take off, and honestly, she may just do that.

"In case I need to shift." His eyes held hers.

"Oh." Inside she'd known that, but didn't want to admit it.

He ran his hand down her arm gently, "Are you okay?"

Just him touching her almost hurt. She shook her head. "I don't think so. There's something…"

He stepped closer, still not pulling her into his chest. "I can smell your cat. Not just sense her but smell her." Leaning down, he brushed a brief kiss on her lips. "You're going to shift for the first time, soon."

She looked at her arms, like they were going to suddenly grow fur. "How soon?"

His tone was gentle, "there's no way to tell, could be an hour, could be a few more days. You could feel the way you do now, then it stops and then happens again right before. It's not the same for everyone."

Blowing out a deep breath, she glanced out the window again. "Talk about bad timing."

He chuckled, "could have been a whole lot worse."

She turned to see that heated look in his eyes. "Yes, I guess it could have." She tried to smile, but failed, even for him she couldn't. There was just too much battling through her.

"I want you to stay up here when I go down…"

"What? No." She shook her head, wanting to grab him but couldn't stand the feel of anything against her right now. There had been moments she'd even entertained the idea of stripping off her clothes to see if it would help.

He grasped her hand lightly, barely touching her. "When I go down there, I need to know you are safe and out of harm's way." The expression in his eyes was serious. "If I'm worried about watching over you, then…" he shook his head, "I can't have that distraction."

She knew he was right, but the idea of standing up here… what if he needed her?

"We don't know how close your shift is, and the tension could bring it on faster." His tone was so tender.

The very idea of shifting in front of everyone, turned her stomach inside out. "You think it could happen?"

He searched her face, "I don't know. I need the fewest possible variables when I go down there."

Her brain kicked in. What he was saying was if she was there and distracted him, he could die. She didn't want to stay behind, but she wanted him to live more. "Okay." She nodded, close to tears. "I'll stay here."

He kissed her mouth softly again.

"No, please not again." Jake's voice made them both turn.

Shae saw him standing there with his hands on his hips and shaking his head at Gage.

"No *what* not again?" Kelsey asked in a tone that said she already knew and was unimpressed. "Gage. Why are you half naked?" She turned and looked at Calum then her head snapped around to Devin as he walked out of the hallway. "What's going on?"

Rayne moved around from behind Devin. "They're leaving us here. Again."

Kelsey gave Gage a narrow-eyed look. "Shocker that is. What I want to know is why they're all ready for a fast shift."

Jake lifted his hands and backed away. "Not my plan. Obviously."

Gage sighed and then looked at his mate. "Dev and I are just going to make sure it's stays fair." He waved a hand down his half naked body. "This is just in case."

Shae stood there, hugging her arms around her waist, not sure if it was her place to speak or not, but it was her mate going down there as well. "I'm glad your staying up here with me. I don't feel well at all, and Calum says he can smell my cat."

Kelsey and Rayne both turned to her at once, sympathy on their faces.

"We'll be right here with you." Rayne said in her gentle way.

Her mother and Aunt Marilyn walked in the door and stopped to look at everyone. Shae could see the tension on their faces. Her mother stopped and looked at her.

"Shae?"

Waving a hand at her, Shae stepped as close as she dared to Calum without touching him. Being near him made her feel slightly less awful. "Apparently, my cat is working on making an appearance soon."

Her aunt's face lit up, "well you tell her, to just put the brakes on for a little bit." She looked around, "I'm too old for too much to be happening all at once."

Calum cleared his throat and looked at Nona, then her mother and aunt, "Can you ladies stay up here with her, I'd feel better if she had all of you."

They nodded, and Nona turned back to the kitchen. "I have a tea that helps, I'll get some steeping."

Calum turned back to Shaelan, as he did the bell at the hall rang out.

Everyone in the room stopped what they were doing and came over to the window. You could taste the anticipation in the air. Slowly people started to come out of their homes below.

"Jake?" Calum said in a quiet tone without turning from the window.

"Yeah?" he answered from somewhere behind Shaelan.

"If this starts to go south, you get all these women the hell out of here. Just in case."

A chill ran down Shae's spine, she turned to look up at Calum. His green eyes caressed over her face. She couldn't breath.

"Will do, Cal." Jake answered quietly.

Rayne turned to Devin, "Nothing better happen, *just in case.*" The emotions in her voice clear.

Calum turned back to look out the window again, there were a lot of people standing in front of the hall now.

"Cal doesn't lose," Gage was saying quietly to Kelsey.

Exhaling slowly, Calum turned to look at Shaelan and tipped her chin up so she was looking at him. "I have too much to come back up here for." He said.

She wasn't sure if it was to her or the others, but she couldn't stop looking at him to check. "You better come back up here."

He nodded, and kissed her mouth softly.

She watched him walk out of the house and could barely draw air into her body as she did. She watched the three men go down the stairs, her whole body was shaking. It was all she could do to stand there and not run after him. The other women stood beside her and the emotions she picked up from them was the same. The three men walked down the steps slowly, looking like honed warriors, the way they moved. Shae turned to looked at Nona and she didn't know why, but she didn't look as worried as the rest. She had to hold on to the thought that her mentor was always right.

Halfway down the stairs, Calum spotted Brock standing in the middle of the crowd, playing the fake Brock. He was looking around as if he was trying to figure out who had rung the bell, even though it had been him.

"I didn't realize how many people were here." Gage said, surprised.

Calum had to agree with that, there had to be at least fifty people, that he could see so far and others were still walking in that direction. He didn't see any children. Hopefully there was some plan in place that young children went somewhere else and not to the hall when the bell rang.

"See anyone that looks like a maniacal lunatic yet?" Devin asked with a growl in his voice.

Just as Calum went to answer, the crowd parted and three men walked between them. "Anyone of those three work for you?" He zeroed in on the one walking beside the man clearly leading. He didn't know how he knew, but he knew it was Jerome. "The one on the left doesn't get away."

"That who did that to Chad?" Gage asked.

Calum growled low. "He's carrying the gun, so I'm going to say yes."

"Then he shot Gene as well. We've got him." Devin said so low that his words were barely a whisper.

When they reached the bottom of the stairs and started walking toward the crowd, it parted for them as it had for the other men, the only difference Calum could see was the faces they walked by didn't show fear. In the eyes watching the three strangers was hope, hope that they were going to end their nightmare.

Calum stopped walking, keeping twenty feet between them, Leroy and his goons. He noticed Brock slowly vanishing into the crowd. Not many knew he wasn't the complete asshole he pretended to be, so it was a wise move on his part to remove himself from the equation.

The man standing in the center of the three, snarled at him. "The green eyed one returns."

Calum growled low as a response. He watched Leroy look him up and down, noting his state of dress and then the cocky expression turned to an apprehensive look. The man was a coward, he thought, and that pissed him off even more.

Looking around at the people standing there, Leroy waved his hands around. "Are you all just going to stand there and let strangers take over your village?"

There were a few sneering remarks and retorts that weren't in his favor as the people slowly moved, standing more to the side nearest Calum. That left Leroy and his men standing alone.

He felt someone come up beside him. "I tried." Jake said out of breath, "but when the clothes started coming off and they called me Jacob, I got out of there."

"What?" Devin looked around.

"Shit," Gage hissed.

Calum looked away from the man he was going to kill long enough to glance at Jake, he held up his hands.

"They're pissed. *All* of them…" he held up his hands again.

Before Calum's rage-clouded mind could process what he was saying, he heard a warning growl from behind him.

Turning, he saw a blonde she-wolf prowling toward them. On her left was an orange tiger, ears back and teeth bared.

His heart and cat jolted in unison when a blacker-than-night female jaguar flanked Rayne's other side. Her eyes were on him with each step she took and he couldn't have looked away if he tried. She was the most beautiful thing he'd ever seen and later, much later, he'd berate himself for not being there for her first change. His cat alerted him as soon as he could sense hers, Calum should have known it would be today.

Kelsey bounded over to Gage and rubbed up against his leg, before she moved past him to go stand between him and the alpha of the village. She emitted a low warning growl and crouched down like she was going to pounce.

Rayne didn't pause to formally greet her mate, as she leapt past where they stood to stand near Kelsey. The growls coming out of her, if they had been directed at Calum would have made even him back off and be somewhere else.

Shaelan paused as she reached Calum and he could only nod to the questioning look in her pale feline eyes. It was her right to end this, her way. She nudged his knee with her shoulder as she moved by him. He turned, feeling nothing but awe at how graceful she was in this form. It had taken him months to master his balance in cat form to look that sleek.

"Should she be doing this on her first shift?" Devin asked quietly.

Calum watched her walk out in front of the other two women, with long nimble strides. "Are *you* going to tell her she can't?"

"Fuck no. I like breathing." He whispered.

"This is Shaelan's to end, but he dies if he so much as touches a hair on her." Calum snarled. He started to close the distance between them and then stopped so fast Jake walked into him. Nona and Aunt Marilyn came out of the crowd, walking toward Shaelan. From the other side her mother and Billie emerged, and a few other women. From behind them, a few jaguars with various coat colors came stalking forward slowly. All females.

"Fuck me," Gage hissed quietly, "his ass is toast."

"Is that a serving fork in Marilyn's hand?" Devin inquired in a hushed voice.

Calum made a note to find out later, he wasn't taking his eyes off Leroy as he started to walk toward Shaelan again. He knew she needed to do this for her people, for herself and her mother, but he sure as hell was going to be beside her when she did.

A large black male cat came charging out of the group, and in a few long strides Brock reached Shaelan and actually did the equivalent of a hip bump on his way by her. He headed right toward Jerome without hesitation. He knew why he was going right for him, but just as long as he saved a few hits for Calum, he didn't care.

Jerome pulled his gun from its holster and aimed but Brock pounced and knocked him up against a tree, the gun hit the ground without being fired. The two guards came out of the crowd and put a collar around Jerome's neck while Brock leaned his two large paws on his chest holding him in place. They clipped the electrified club to it and held him. Calum would be having a chat with them later about letting him flip the switch on it a few times, *while* it was still attached.

Nona nodded once to them, then turned to look at Leroy. He was down to one lackey with him now, or none, Calum thought as he was getting down on his knees, with his hands raised in the air in surrender. As least his brain worked. Now.

"Shae's mate was going to challenge you to be alpha." Nona said loud enough all could hear as she stopped to the right of where Shaelan paced. "To protect herself, to free us…" Nona shook her head.

"Then what?" Leroy demanded. "Follow that alliance and a stupid wolf?"

Rayne turned to face him, and emitted a growl so ferocious that all the hair on Calum's arms stood.

"Not too smart, is he?" Gage commented.

Devin shook his head as he took a few steps closer to the women.

Shaelan's mother went right over and stood beside her daughter. "Her mate was doing what was right. That's what love should be in a clan." She glanced at her daughter prancing beside her. "You are not the rightful Alpha of this clan."

Leroy's face went red with rage. "Who's going to be alpha? A true blood bitch that can't shift or her half breed daughter…"

Calum growled a long, low warning. Shaelan answered him with a soft yowl, before she bound toward Leroy so fast, no one could have seen it coming. With a leap, she knocked him down to the ground and held him there, her teeth clamped around his throat and one paw on his chest pinning him to the ground. She continued to growl without releasing him.

"Dad kind of wants him alive," Devin said moving up beside him, "we can't find out who has been working with him if he's nothing but chewed up fleshy remains."

Grunting and annoyed because he knew he was right, Calum moved to get to him before he was stupid enough to piss off Shaelan any more. He was almost there, when her mother pulled out a dart gun and shot him with a tranquilizer. Twice.

By the time Calum reached him, the man was unconscious.

Shaelan released him and sat down looking at him for a moment. She turned and looked at Calum, then took off running in the direction of the stairs. He was stunned by her speed for a second and then realized nothing about her was normal, or like any other shifter he'd ever met.

"I think your mate just became alpha of the clan … or her mother … it's tough call." Gage said as he smiled down at Kelsey.

"I think for our own personal safety we'll let them decide who is alpha." Calum said with a smirk and watched as Shaelan bounded up the stairs to Nona's.

"Wise words." Devin agreed.

Nona elbowed Calum, "you should go make sure she has no problems shifting back." She shook her head, "never seen anyone just do it in a blink the first time."

He jolted, completely forgetting again that this had been her first shift. Hell, he hadn't been able to co-ordinate four paws to run like that until his at least his second, and here she was half was to the top of the stairs. "*Shit.*" He took off running in her direction.

Chapter Nineteen

Calum ran into the house to see Shaelan laying there on her side, naked and shaking. She was probably in shock. He cursed silently for not being with her again. "Shae…"

She rolled over onto her back and was laughing quietly. "*That* was amazing." She smiled at him, then rolled and started crawling to him slowly. Stalking him as if she were still in her cat form.

Calum swallowed, his mouth suddenly dry and just watched. He couldn't have communicated with his legs to get them to move to her, even if there had been a dire need that they moved.

"I think I like being a cat," she said in a soft whisper as she continued toward him.

He hoped she didn't want him to actually answer, because he was having problems remembering how to speak. Dropping to his knees, he watched the slow, elegant movement of her graceful body. Never in his life had he been rendered speechless by such exquisiteness.

She stopped a few feet from him. "Cat got your tongue?" She smiled.

Huffing out a breath, he nodded with a slow motion. "And any other part she wants."

Stopping, she knelt when they were close enough to feel the heat from each others' bodies, but weren't actually touching. She smiled again and his cat stilled at the same time his breath hitched in his throat when he saw the sharp incisors in her mouth.

"I think I need to fix my mark… now that I can." She moved slowly and climbed onto his lap and licked over her mark gently.

His body shuddered with need, so hot and fast he fought to breathe, grabbing her waist, he pulled her tight against him. If anyone interrupted them, he was killing them without pause. Her bare flesh pressing against his upper body made him growl softly.

She wrapped her legs around him and squeezed. "Mmm, I like your animal side."

Grasping the back of her head, he pulled it back and looked into her eyes that were already heavy with lust. He kissed her mouth, forcing hers to open for him. When she did, he stabbed his tongue in and felt the sharp edges of her teeth. Growling again, he stood in one motion and started heading for the hallway.

Breaking the kiss, she licked down his jaw and over her mark again. With a soft growl that sounded like she said mine, she bit into his neck over her other mark and his knees buckled. Hitting the wall with his shoulders, he locked his legs so they wouldn't land on the floor. He held her head where it was, reveling in the feel of her claiming him.

Reaching with his other hand, he boosted her up higher, then tugged at his jeans to undo them. She used her legs to push them out of the way, as eager as he was to be joined in all ways. Before he could brace himself, she lowered herself onto him, her tight muscles squeezing his throbbing shaft as she did. He smacked his head against the wall when he stiffened and gasped, it felt that good.

Turning, he supported their weight with one hand on the wall and grasped her ass to help her ride him. When she moaned deep in her throat, she released her bite and licked over her mark before grabbing his hair and pulling his mouth to hers.

Stumbling with his jeans half down, he headed toward her room, and flung the door open. He saw her dresser and leaned against the edge of it, lowering her back onto it. Whatever had been on it crashed to the floor, but she still kept kissing him like she was trying to consume him and he had no plans to hinder her.

Bracing a hand on the surface, he pulled his head back and looked down her body to where they were joined. Straightening, he slid out of her a few inches, then thrust into her. She moaned as their bodies connected, drawing his attention back up her body. Grasping her knee, he pulled her leg higher on his waist and began thrusting into her, going deeper. She reached up and pulled his head down toward her breast where her hand was rubbing over his mark on the soft flesh.

Shaelan was on fire, it was as if her cat, now fully realized had taken over and was in need of feeling his. She couldn't explain it, didn't want to, all she knew was if he didn't stop being so gentle and careful with her she was going to scream. She needed to feel his teeth pierce her flesh now that she fully understood the emotions that went with it.

Grasping his hair tightly, she pulled his head toward her breast. "Calum…" she moaned as their bodies connected again making her hunger for him stronger. She didn't know how to voice what she wanted, she could barely focus to guide his movement.

His mouth closed over her aching nipple and she arched her back and moaned again. Hooking her heels behind his back, she encouraged him to move faster. Her hands released her head and she slid them over any part of his bare flesh should could reach. When he bit into her breast over his other mark, she felt the claws in her fingers dig into his shoulders.

He growled low and began thrusting with a force that would have sent her falling to the floor if she hadn't been holding on. A sound as deep as her cats' cry came out of her throat and heat went straight to her core.

Her mind was a blur, all she knew was she needed more. As if sensing it, he pulled his teeth from her breast and moved to the other one. When his teeth sunk into it, she screamed and her body exploded in an orgasm so powerful, she was only able to gasp for air and ride it out.

Calum pulled from her in a sudden movement and leaned down over her to lick up her thigh and over her sensitive pulsing flesh. With a grunt, he moved his mouth to her the bottom of her leg, right where it met her buttocks and bit into her again. Shae's boy convulsed and began to climb again.

She couldn't even find the strength to move at this point, then found herself being lifted and gently tossed to the bed face down. With a growl from behind her, he was pulling her hips up and drove into her wet folds again. Her body exploded with so many sensations at once, she could only moan.

His mouth found his mark on her neck and as his teeth sunk in, her body shattered in another orgasm that was so close to pain there was no way to differentiate. Calum lifted his mouth and stiffened over her as his heat flooded into her, making her quiver once again.

Unable to hold her limp body up any longer, she slid to lay flat on the bed, his weight falling on top of her as she did. The sound of the bed frame breaking echoed in the silence of their heavy breathing.

"Earth moved." He panted beside her ear.

She would have laughed, but still couldn't catch her breath. "Bed broke." She whispered.

"That too," he gasped.

She didn't know how long they lay there like that, she didn't care, her whole body was buzzing and it was unlike any feeling she'd ever had. When he shifted his weight off her, he pulled her with him so they were laying face to face. Later, when she recovered she'd laugh at how it must have looked to be on the mattress, tilting on a broken frame. She was pretty sure it was slowly sliding to one side, and them with it. "I think I need a new bed."

He grinned, with his eyes closed, "love, you need a whole new room. This one is wrecked."

Chuckling, she leaned her head against his chest and listened to the pounding of his heart. "I've been a little busy to worry about housekeeping."

Calum snorted. "I don't care if it's a disaster, as long as you're in it… I'm there."

Remembering her claws, she propped up on her elbow and lifted his arm. Down the side of his ribs were tiny punctures from her where her fingers dug in. "We're going to be scarred from head to toe." She said then gnawed on her bottom lip.

Opening his eyes, he looked at her. "ones I'll wear with pride."

She glanced down to her breast. "I need to talk to Nona about those." She looked up at him again, "do you think they'll damage them?" He gave her a curious look. "For breast feeding… I love children." She felt her face blush.

Propping his arm under his head, his eyes moved down over her breasts in a slow appreciative way. "Is it perverted that I'm turned on by the thought of our child at your breast?"

She laughed. "I don't think so." Kissing his mouth softly, she smiled, "I think it's endearing."

His green eyes caressed over her face. "I'm a bit worried about when your heat hits, love…" he smirked, "we may need oxygen masks and IV's to live through it."

Her eyes went wide. "I can't even comprehend it being…" her cheeks flushed, "possible to be more… need between us."

His lips brushed over hers, "I look forward to the challenge." Turning, he looked around the room, "I think we should probably go check on the aftermath of what happened before you distracted me."

"I didn't distract you..."

He sorted, "You did, but I'm not complaining. You can stalk me looking that hot, anytime you want." He winked, "I'll even let you tie me up."

She blushed, "I've already had you chained up, is tying up as appealing?"

Calum's eyes moved over her slowly, "I think anything with you would fall into that too hot to handle category." He grinned, "but I'm willing to try. I almost fainted from the lack of blood to my brain when you came stalking toward me as a sexy, gorgeous black cat."

She stiffened, having forgotten entirely that she'd taken down Leroy. Scrambling off the bed, she looked around in the scattered clothes to find something she could put on. She stopped and studied him as he watched her. "Thank you, by the way."

He smirked, "Oh... anytime."

She shook her head, "not for," she waved to the bed, "that. I meant for letting me end it my way."

He sat up. "It was your right, and I will have your back, *always.*"

Grabbing the first thing she recognized, she pulled on the black skirt, then paused and looked from it to him.

He growled low, "I remember that skirt." Easing up off the bed, he leaned down and kissed his mark on her breast. "Don't wear anything under it, just in case."

Her cheeks flushed again. Turning she watched him pull on his jeans, as muscles flexed from his movement, she smiled to herself. Just in case was a good idea.

Chapter Twenty

They paused at the top of the stairs and looked down. Calum noted that the two guards were standing over Leroy where he still lay on the ground, mostly so no one would come up and stab him. He didn't see Jerome or the smart one that surrendered, so with any luck they were chained to a wall in one of the cells they had put too many men in. Faye was surrounded by people, hugging and talking to them as they came up to her. Probably congratulating her on being free of Leroy's clutches.

Turning, he saw Nona and Marilyn were with Devin and Rayne. He wasn't looking pleased, which wasn't unusual, but his mate was standing there wrapped in only a blanket, so that may be the reason. He looked around for Gage and then spotted the three white vans parked by the entrance of the village. The alliance had arrived, and Gage was mostly likely there filling the men in on what had happened.

"How do you acknowledge the clan alpha?" Shaelan asked him quietly.

He looked down at her for a moment and recognized the look that said her mind was going at top speed again. It dawned on him once again that this clan had a lot to learn about the way things were normally. "You kneel before them.

It's how you submit to an alpha or superior when in two leg form."

Her eyes searched his for a moment. "I think this clan needs healing and a gentle touch right now. More than someone physically powerful."

Nodding, he hugged her into his shoulder. "The alpha isn't always the most powerful, but they are usually the most respected."

Turning, she looked back down at the people below. Nodding her head slowly, she grasped his hand started walking down the stairs, pulling him along with her.

She didn't speak again and he wasn't going to interrupt her thoughts to ask questions. Weaving among the people, she acknowledged each that spoke to her, but kept moving. It took him a few minutes to see who she was trying to reach. Her mother.

Faye stood on the steps to the hall, a look of complete understanding and contentment on her face. He supposed out of all the people here, she would have gone through the most, having to live with Leroy all these years, and yet she was completely steady in the wake of today's events.

When they reached her, he expected Shaelan to let go of his hand and hug her mother. Instead she stopped a few feet from her and dropped down to one knee and lowered her head.

"Shae?" Her mother came over. "What are you doing? I mean I know *what* your doing, but why?" There was nervousness in her voice.

Grinning, Calum realized what his clever mate was up to. This clan needed the gentle demeanor of her mother to heal the years of abuse. Turning, he slowly got down on one knee beside her and lowered his head in submission.

Lifting her head, Shae looked at her mother. "This clan needs you to recover, not a strong hand, just a loving one."

Her mother's eyes teared up for a moment, but she nodded abruptly and then placed her hand on her daughter's head.

Calum smiled when she put her hand on his for a brief moment. When he pulled his mate to her feet, there were several people kneeling before her now. Backing away, he pulled her back against him and tucked him under her shoulder.

Going over to stand with Devin and Rayne, he stopped before reaching them when he heard the conversation.

"I want one of those do-dads, so I can see the babies growing." Nona told Devin.

"I believe she means an ultrasound," Rayne told him quietly.

Devin rubbed the back of his neck and looked around. "We'll get your power supply more stable and I'm sure the alliance can get you equipment you need."

Marilyn nodded, "I need me one of those microwaves, oh, oh and a jacuzzi." She paused and looked to Rayne, "is that the same as a hot tub, because Calum is already making me one of those." She squealed, "and a car. I think I could drive. How hard could it be?"

Brock came running up, wearing a sheet like a toga and grabbed Marilyn's hand. "Come, let's kneel before our new alpha."

They looked to where he pointed to see Faye surrounded by the rest of the community.

"Hot damn." Marilyn said excitedly. "Hold my fork." She handed Devin a large serving fork.

Calum covered his mouth so he wouldn't laugh out loud. After they went to join their clanmates, he went over.

"They think I'm the alliance's damn order desk or something." Devin mumbled to Rayne.

Hugging him, she laughed, "it's all very new and unknown to them."

Devin nodded to Shaelan, "Wise choice on the alpha."

She snuggled against Calum's chest. "It's always been someone in our family, or so I was told." She looked up at him, her eyes searching his for a moment. "Maybe some day

I'll have a son or daughter that can take over, but for now my mother will nurture this clan back to a healthy state."

Calum swallowed and refused to look anywhere but her mesmerizing eyes. He blew out a breath. "Can we at least have a day together without mayhem before that happens?"

She blushed and nodded her head. "I didn't mean right now."

Devin started laughing until Rayne whispered something in his ear.

With a grin to Calum and Shaelan she turned to go to the stairs, probably to get some clothes.

Devin looked at him. "I'm not ready to…" he looked to watch Rayne for a moment. "She wants…" He growled, "shit." Then ran after her. "Rayne, hun…"

"I didn't ask earlier, it's okay that I want children, eventually?"

Her soft tone had him looking down to her again. "Yeah. I just never thought you'd even want to discuss it… yet." Glancing around he noticed the children had come out from wherever they'd been. "With everything that happened here, I wasn't sure." He finished quickly before he could say something that would mar this perfect day.

Smiling, she glanced around quickly then looked up at him with her eyes sparkling, "well, you were captured for that reason, so its only right that you…"

Growling he picked her up and squeezed her. "That is never to be mentioned in public, again."

She hugged her arms around him, still giggling and then nodded her head.

"Calum," He turned to see Gage and Devin's father coming toward them.

"Ready to meet our king?"

Her face sobered immediately. "Yes." She released him as he lowered her back to her feet and turned slowly to watch them walk over. She backed up so her back was against his chest.

He could feel the nervous anticipation going through her and looked to the man approaching them. He'd grown up around him, so to Calum he was Devin's father, the same man that had helped raise him, and chastise him when the three of them would get into trouble. Calum could look him eye to eye on most things. To him he was an older, more pleasant version of Devin, but to Shaelan, he guessed he was a larger than life representation of this new world she was now in.

When he stopped in front of them, Shaelan dropped to one knee and lowered her head.

Devin's father gave her a wide-eyed look, then glanced to Calum, his eyes moving to his neck, one brow lifting at how his throat must look at this point. Then he did something that surprised Calum and from the look on Gage's face, him as well. He dropped to one knee before her and lifted Shaelan's chin with a touch.

"There will be no kneeling to me this day. I should be kneeling before you, asking forgiveness for my predecessors not doing something about this and helping your clan a long time ago." Taking her hand, he stood and pulled her to her feet. Then stepped back a respectable distance so not to disturb the mating protocol. He smiled down at her. "If you could introduce me to your new alpha, I would appreciate that. We have many things to discuss."

Shaelan glanced to Calum, shock plain on her face. Turning back, she nodded and motioned for him to lead.

He paused and looked back at Calum, "Chad is being moved, and when we can get a chopper in to transport him out. Gene's family is on their way as is Chad's clan." He heaved a heavy sigh. "There are many living blood ties in this village to those at the grave. I think it's best we proceed with the utmost care, and allow each person involved to pay their respects."

Calum nodded. "I agree." He glanced to where the guards were standing watch over Leroy to see a few men from the alliance picking him up. "I think those that put the men in that grave should begin penance and dig as many graves as there are bodies."

Devin's father smirked, "a feasible plan."

He stood beside Gage and watched Shaelan move through the group, pausing to speak to people and introduce their new leader.

"So…" Gage leaned and made a point at looking at Calum's throat. "We going to have to get you some turtlenecks or something?" He smirked, "so you can be seen in public from time to time?"

Calum sneered at him jokingly, "How often do you see me out in public?"

Gage nodded. "Good point." He tapped him on the back when he spotted Kelsey coming back down the stairs. "Next time you decide to go off and find a lost clan, maybe bring backup with you at the start?"

Calum laughed as he looked to locate his mate. "I'll keep that in mind." He stood there alone after Gage went to Kelsey, just looking around at everything going on. The alliance men were dragging Leroy's limp body toward the yard. Brock and Marilyn were excited about something, if the hand waving and expressions were any indication. Nona was walking toward him.

She stopped and stood beside him, her hands clasped together and looked over the commotion. "I knew you were strong enough to let her be her."

He smiled down at her. "I'm glad one of us did." He tracked his lovely mate with his eyes as she spoke to some children, her face animated and hands moving as she did. "Any words of wisdom to keep up with her?"

Nona chuckled. "Not a one. I spent years trying." She patted him on the arm. "I think you'll do just fine. Your both passionate people, it will be quite the adventure."

That didn't reassure him in the least. He glanced back to Faye, she was completely surrounded by her clan. "Faye is what this clan needs."

She nodded, a thoughtful expression on her face. "She may not be able to shift, but she knows the pain and trials of what it means to be who we are."

He thought she was talking about Leroy and surviving him for so many years, but a sadness came over her.

"Will do some good to have a ceremony for those poor fellas' bones you found." She tsked softly, "I don't know how many others knew, but I'm certain Shae's real daddy was Faye's true mate."

He gave her a surprised look.

"Oh, she loved the man she was with, but she was never the same after going into that yard to get Shaelan. Part of her was missing when the fella was gone." Sighing, she nodded again, "Faye will steer this clan the right way." Turning, she headed to the stairs.

Calum watched her for a moment. He couldn't even fathom losing Shaelan now. How had Faye managed all these years he had no idea. Hell, between Nona and Faye both losing their mates… they made him look like a meek kitten.

He turned back to watch Shaelan walking toward him, she had the grace of her cat, even on two legs and he'd be lying if he said he didn't find it sexy as hell. She smiled and he couldn't help but smile back at her, wondering how soon they could pack a bag and leave for the privacy of his cabin. He knew it may be selfish, but in his mind, they had both earned some quiet time alone. Of course, she wouldn't require a lot of clothes during their time there. He frowned and wondered how he was going to prevent her from bringing a case of books as well.

"You look like your plotting something, Calum Dante." She said quietly as she reached him.

"I could be." He pulled her into his arms and hugged her.

"You can tell me all about it while we walk." She rubbed her face against his chest.

"Where are we walking to?" He inhaled her sweet cinnamon fragrance and felt his cat brush against him with a contentment he'd never felt before.

She looked up and gave him a duh expression. "To your car. Unless you are carrying me to your cabin."

Grinning, he picked her up into his arms and held her close. "If that's what it takes, I will."

She giggled. "I don't doubt you could." She rested her hand on his shoulder for a moment then licked over the bite in his skin.

He growled, "doing that is going to make it a very long trip." He turned to go up the stairs and pondered briefly whether he should tell her no books allowed this trip. Deciding it would be safer to just distract her from her books after they were there, he kept walking. His mate was going to be a handful, but it was the first challenge in his life he looked forward to.

KEEP READING FOR AN EXCERPT OF

Salvation

By

Jacqueline Paige

Chapter One

He watched the child in silence, not that he could be heard even if he wanted. If his math was correct, she was three years old now. Stepping into the room and away from the window, he watched her small body shake as she pressed an ear against the door. He couldn't see her face with the fall of wavy black hair covering it. But he knew the face under her messed hair was round and angelic.

From the other side of the door she was carefully leaning against, he could hear the yelling...again. Her parents spent most of their time screaming at each other and breaking things. He'd sat with the child many times in the last year while the adults in her world showed her all the wrong ways to live.

It worried him that she no longer cried; no longer curled her tiny body into the corner and tried to make herself invisible. At least the quarrelling adults had never brought it to her; he didn't know if he could stand to see her hurt in any way. He closed his eyes and cursed himself; what could he even do to help if they did?

A loud crash brought him back to the moment; he opened his eyes to see the girl remove her ear from the door. Her face was visible now and it pulled at his heart to see tears rolling down her round cheeks. It made her dark brown eyes seem blurry and vague. She hugged her tiny arms around her middle, trying to comfort herself. A small part of him wanted to take her in his arms and shelter her from the sadness, not that he knew how to hold a child.

She took two steps back from the door but still watching, as if she was afraid it was going to fly open. She sniffled once and raised her face, then looked right at him. Did she actually see him? He was tempted to look behind to see if there was something there that would catch her attention, but he was afraid to look away and go back to being invisible to all.

She blinked and cleared the tears from her eyes yet continued to look right at him. With her chin up she used her sleeve to wipe across her face, then raised her chin with a determination he knew all too well. Her eyes appeared as if they were looking right into his, causing his heart, if he truly still had one, to jolt inside of his body.

Finally, she turned from him, went to the little table in the corner, and sat on the small chair. She opened a book, took colored sticks from a messy carton, and scribbled in angry motions over the outline of the picture in front of her.

Sighing, he closed his eyes. She would be fine. He really did need to stop coming here.

He had tried to stay away, as he knew he should, and had been able to watch from a distance. But the child lay on the bed with her face hidden, shaking and distraught. He didn't know what he could do, but he liked to believe his presence would be sensed and she would somehow be comforted.

Glancing away from her, he noticed papers crumpled up on the floor. He couldn't pick them up to look at them, but he could read part of one. *"Happy 7th birthday."* She was seven already? Had not only a few months passed since she was that tiny cherub-faced child? He frowned. How had he lost track of four entire years? What did he have to keep track of except time? All he *had* was time, endless expanses of time.

Shaking his head, he stepped closer to the bed. If only he could offer a calming touch to let her know she wasn't alone.

But in truth, she was; he could hear the screaming outside of the walls of her room, and knew that she was very much alone in this world.

She rolled onto her back, clutching something to her chest. With an angry swipe she wiped across her face and took a long shaky breath. He leaned down to see her better and was surprised to see how she had grown since he last let himself get this close. Gone was the childish softness. In its place, the beginning of a more mature form was now visible. He sighed and stepped back; this small one was going to be a world of trouble for some man in the years to come.

Looking back he found her eyes looking right at him, as only she had ever done. He stepped back in shock. He told himself she was just staring into space and it happened to be in his direction, but her eyes moved over his body in a slow, measured way. If he spoke would she hear him? He clenched his jaw; hadn't he spent years trying to be heard by others? He wouldn't waste one more ounce of energy on that ever again.

When she stood up, he almost stepped back again, afraid she'd go right through him and make him feel undetectable. Instead, she stopped in front of him to look up at his face. Inside his head he smiled at her, but the movement did not show on his face. She couldn't really see him; he must be creating this from years of desire. She turned and walked to a shelf in the corner. He hesitantly took a few steps to follow her.

He was astounded when she turned and motioned to a ship sitting on the top shelf. He looked at her for a moment and then moved his eyes to the ship. He smiled; it was a small model of a galleon. While it looked quite like a real one, very majestic and formed well enough, he frowned. Why would she want him to see that? Why would a young girl of seven even want a scale model ship? He looked back to see she had calmed and wasn't the distressed child she'd been just moments ago. He noticed the tilt of her chin and recognized that determined glint in her eyes. He smiled at her and hoped by some fanciful miracle that maybe he was partially responsible for this.

So he was a completely spineless man, he thought as he entered her room yet again. He had not lost track of time and knew she was twelve years older now. He had only allowed himself to come this close while she slept over the last few years though, for he was uncertain of what her ability to see him actually meant. She stormed past him, opened her door, and screamed obscenities that he'd only ever heard from older, weathered males. She shocked him, made him wonder whether he should really be here. The door slammed, and he turned to see her take a leap and flounce onto the bed.

She had definitely lost that helpless, angelic look. Her dark eyes turned to him and he had no choice but to stand there and watch her look at him. She bounced off the bed, straight up as if she were pulled by a rope, and walked past him to the shelves along the wall.

He turned slowly. Gone were the childish toys and trinkets. There were no more coloring sticks in this one's life. His eyes moved over the top of the shelf. She had, over the last several years, added to her galleon, and it now held a detailed frigate and shebec model. If he were the size of a mouse, he could have lived on them, they were that detailed. She had associated him with the ships, and he supposed she was observant to have done so.

With a hesitant movement he raised his eyes away from the ships he'd last seen in their real and true form to look back at her. She smiled at him, or possibly it was a snarl; it wasn't easy to distinguish, but the point was she could really, truly see him and he was once more left to wonder what it meant. He heard a door slam downstairs and watched her turn quickly to the window.

Stepping closer so he could see, her mother was leaving, and with her was a man. Even though he had never seen this man before, he knew it was the sort of man any woman was better not getting close to.

Hearing her heavy sigh he turned. She had walked back over to the bed and was putting tiny drops with wires attached to them in her ears. He'd noticed most children of her age walked around with wires coming from their ears. Somehow he doubted it was to lessen the sound of cannon fire. He watched her for a moment longer, decided she was well enough for now, and left without further hesitation.

The sound of sob haunted him once again, without intending it, he found himself inside her room. In the last four years he'd managed to stay away, but in an odd moment of weakness, had spent a few brief moments here, just to assure himself she was well enough. The room had undergone enormous change; it now assaulted his senses to be in it. It was a mix of bright and dark, contrasting with each other in ways that it made him dizzy. Gone were the pretty pinks of childhood; in their place was black with blood-red splatters.

He stopped beside the shelf and wanted for one moment to touch the ships. Two more spectacular replicas displayed on the top shelf. A caravel, which, he thought with a smirk, looked as pieced-together in this size as he had always thought they were in the real versions. The man-o-war filled him with longing, just as the real thing had once done. There wasn't anything that could compete with the force of it, the sheer threat its appearance on the horizon had wrought. Bringing himself from memories of a past long gone, he turned to find her sprawled half on, half off the bed. She was talking low into a phone; yes, he knew what a phone was— now.

"I hope he falls and breaks both of his legs and has to spend the rest of the year hobbling around on crutches! He's such a loser; I don't know why I even bothered." She sniffled.

Pausing, he raised his eyebrows and tried to understand what she talking about. A male was no doubt involved; he was not so long gone that he didn't recognize the tone that every female adopted when a male had done wrong. What he didn't understand was the word *loser;* had there been a race? He shook his head and decided he needed to observe more television in his wanderings. It had been his only way to discover a world outside of his confinement. The only link that let him feel as if he were still part of the human race, not a lonely drifter who felt no peace. Of course, the first time he saw the wondrous thing they called a television, he was intrigued by such a puzzling contraption.

"Yeah, okay, later!"

Turning, he watched her hang up the phone and hop off the bed. He knew his eyes bulged when she stood up and walked over to close the door. He felt like he'd just been broadsided! What was she wearing? He seriously doubted she should even leave the building. Her shoulders were bare, as was her midriff, and his throat practically seized shut when he realized she was no longer a child in any sort of way. She had breasts! When had she gotten those? His eyes traveled down to see bare womanly legs beneath a short skirt. If he actually had such a thing as saliva left in his body, it would have dried right up inside his mouth.

She walked over and touched the man-o-war ship with a feminine hand, and he suddenly felt like an extremely old man. Turning with her hand still on the ship, she looked directly at him, and he froze, not knowing how to react. She was past sixteen years now and more than womanly, but he felt saddened to realize that she had never been allowed much of a childhood.

His eyes traveled the length of her again, noting that she was just a little more than a hand's span shorter than his own height, but it was her eyes that swallowed him. Her dark hair hung to her shoulders, untamed waves of thick silk. Her deep brown eyes had been highlighted with coloured powders, and the result completely robbed him of air, or would have if he still breathed. A child of this age should not know how to look at a man the way she was looking at him.

He watched without movement as her hand ran over a sketch of a face propped behind the ships, he would swear it was a likeness of his own face—himself in a looking glass, the way he remembered looking. He moved a hand to touch the scar that ran from his temple to cross his cheekbone. The sketch was of him, including the scar. He glanced back at her and had so many questions, but none he would ever ask. She could see him, but how? And why?

Inclining his head to her, he turned to leave before he could change his mind, making a silent vow he would not return again.

~

Miranda got out of her faded, rust-covered car and slammed the door. "Great!" She looked down the dirt road only to kick the tire as she walked to open the hood. "You couldn't die where there are actual people or traffic, could you? It had to be in this scenic, stupid, middle-of-absolute-nothing spot!" She propped the hood open and leaned on the front of the car, looking in. "Nothing's smoking, sizzling, or hissing...which means I am so screwed! I can't even fiddle with anything to make you start again, you stupid piece of—" She took a deep breath and tried to calm down. With a sigh she turned around, feeling defeated. "Okay, Randy, you just need a little reflection time here to come up with a new game plan." She walked across the shallow ditch, and headed toward a large tree. "No need to stand in the sun and bake your brain while you do."

Dropping to the ground, she sat with her back against the tree. "This has not been one of my better days." An orange butterfly fluttered down to sit on the top of some weeds a few feet from the tree. She watched it for a moment. "It started out bad enough. Can you believe he dumped me? I mean, seriously, he was hardly the catch of a lifetime or anything, but to leave me a message, breaking up with me on the phone? That is so low!"

The butterfly's wings flitted a few times, making her feel as if it were responding to her dilemma. "Apparently, I'm too blunt, and that bothers him." She snorted and shoved her heavy hair back from her face. "I just tell it like it is. It's not my fault most people prefer to be lied to." The butterfly moved to another plant a few feet away.

Randy sighed. "I should have taken that as a sign and just stayed home, called in and played dead, or something... Going in to work in the mood I was in was such a huge mistake." She beamed at the frantic fluttering from the creature. "But you won't tell anyone I screwed myself right out of a job, right?" She shrugged. "The job sucked anyway. I should have left there a long time ago. I mean, really, I was hired to work in the art department...which for some silly reason I thought might have something to do with art...but, nooo, was I wrong or what? I spent all my time being the flunky and running this here and that there... I don't think I was even allowed to contribute to more than a handful of projects the whole time I was there"—she huffed out a breath—"and the boss...what a chauvinistic asshole!"

The butterfly seemed to pause in its movement, and Randy nodded. "Yeah, you're right. Telling the boss man that I was not his personal gopher was probably not the best way to go about it." She pulled her knees up and rested her chin on them. "I'm single and unemployed all in one day. Oh, and let's not forget that stupid piece of crap sitting over there." She looked at her car on the road. Looking back, she watched the insect flutter up and hover for a moment at her eye level before it flew off in the direction of the car. "Yeah, I better see if it will start...not that I have anywhere to be, but I'd rather sulk at home than in the middle nowhere." She got up and brushed off her pants.

She tried looking under the hood again. "Maybe you just needed a break, huh?" she said to the car. "I'm going to try to start you now, and if you can just be nice and get me home, I promise I'll call someone to fix you up." She patted the car gently before climbing in behind the steering wheel. "Impress me," she whispered as she turned the key.

Three times she tried and although it made noise like it wanted to start, it didn't quite seem to have the energy to complete the task. "Well, at least you're not completely dead.

I'll just give you a few more minutes to get it together." She got back out of the car and leaned against the side, peering down at the motor. "I should have taken shop in school instead of art," she mumbled to herself.

Sighing, she closed the hood with a loud bang. She glanced up at the sky to see dark clouds rolling in fast on the breeze, covering the sun. "Oh, that's just what I need to complete my—" The rain began so quickly she had to close her mouth to stop from swallowing it. It pelted her, soaking her before she could get to the door of her car.

Hopping in quickly, she slammed the door shut and brushed wet hair out of her face. "Perfect!" It was hitting the windshield so hard she couldn't even see the road. She wiped her wet hands down her drenched pants a few times before she realized it was useless; they weren't going to dry. "I have seriously pissed off the world today, haven't I?"

Waving her hands around she tried to dry them before she dug into her purse for her phone. She held it in her hand and squeezed her eyes shut as she opened it. Opening them slowly she almost laughed. No signal. "I'm shocked," she mumbled without emotion as she tossed the phone over her shoulder into the backseat. The rain ended as fast as it had begun.

Grasping the steering wheel, she slowly lowered her forehead to rest on it. A strange, yet familiar feeling prickled across the back of her neck. She didn't raise her head, just smiled into the steering wheel. "You could do something to help."

She lifted her head slowly, afraid to move too fast, and turned to look beside her. She watched the image of the man she'd been seeing for years become clearer. If she focused hard enough, he almost appeared to be real. Many times over the years she thought she was seeing things, possibly ghosts, but it was only ever him.

He gaped at her, his shock more than obvious. "How...you can see me? Truly?"

Randy sat there wanting to reach out and hug him. Hallucinations didn't talk—did they? His voice was rough and deep, and she'd never been happier to hear someone speak. "I more or less sense you most of the time, but if I focus hard enough I can see you." She looked at the scar across his left cheek. "You're very clear today."

He frowned. "And you can hear me?"

Randy tried not to grin. "I'm answering you, aren't I?"

"That's impossible..."

"And yet, here we are talking and being all visible-like." She looked at him, from his long ebony hair down to his black worn boots. "I have a lot of questions, mostly pertaining to whether I'm sane, but right now...I don't suppose you know anything about cars?"

Dark eyebrows shot up, he opened his mouth and then closed it for a moment "I have never actually been inside one until this moment."

"Ah. I figured as much." She reached around and grasped the key. "If this happens to start, I'll be driving like a speed demon to get home ASAP, so will you be able to chill right there and come with me or am I gonna watch you poof away again?" Serious pale blue eyes looked over every inch of her face.

"I don't think I comprehend the meaning of what you just said." He said it softly, still frowning.

Randy laughed. "Sorry. I want you to come to my house with me, is that possible?"

He opened his mouth then closed it for a moment, a serious look in his eyes. "I am not certain I will remain with your car when it's moving, but I will come to your home later on if I cannot."

She bobbed her head a few times, smiling. "Cool." She let out a quick breath. "Cross your fingers."

Frowning again he looked down at his hands. "For what purpose?"

Randy chuckled. "Never mind!" She turned the key, it groaned a few times, a bit faster than before. She tromped on the gas and the car roared to life. Without looking beside her, she threw it into drive and slammed her foot on the gas, trying to get home as fast as she could just in case it died again.

"I believe I will meet with you at your home. I do not like being in this thing while it is moving," he murmured between clenched teeth.

Randy glanced beside her and swore her ghost was slightly green and suffering from motion sickness. "Okay... Hey, what's your name?" She looked back at the road and gunned the gas pedal again.

Closing his eyes briefly, he opened them again quickly and swallowed. "Jareth Blackwood." He inclined his head to her. "Until later."

She glanced over to see him gone already. "Jareth," Randy whispered. Her ghost had a voice and a name; maybe today wasn't such a sucky day after all.

KEEP READING FOR AN EXCERPT OF

The Huntress

Alterealm Series

Book 1

By J. Risk

Chapter One

I didn't even get both eyes opened and focused before I knew something was wrong. Where was the color? I was only seeing sepia? Everything was brown. Blinking rapidly, I tried to readjust my eyes to see if there was any other hue. It didn't change a thing and for the life of me I couldn't figure out why.

Sitting there, I tried to decipher what was going on and why I was sitting on the ground. Looking down I ran my hand over the dried dusty surface. Why was I on the ground? Craning my neck as far as I could in all directions, I looked around. Okay, where was the pavement and cement? The buildings and streets I called my natural turf?

The why's flying around in my brain suddenly decided the top question, was what the *hell* was going on?

Squeezing my eyes shut, I struggled to recall the last thing I remembered doing. I was hunting down a bounty—a nice one with a large dollar sign attached to her. I had tracked her ass down and…

I confronted her? Yes, I was minutes away from calling Frank and telling him to get out his shiny pen and sign my check.

So what happened between then and now? Not to sound repetitive, which is something that drives me nuts, but *what* the hell was going on?

Startled, I started to check for bullet holes or the deep crevices that knives leave behind in flesh. That had to be it, I'd taken a beating and this was that in between place you sit when your near death's door, but not quite ready to see what lies on the other side.

Finding no critical injury, I slumped forward and rubbed my head. There was some rational explanation for this, there had to be. Had I been drugged? It could be some crazy hallucination. Any minute now I was going to either wake up in my bed at home or some hospital with a cheery nurse leaning over me, reassuring me we are going to be *just* fine. I only had to wait it out a little longer and all would be normal.

To kill time until I woke up, I looked around some more. Wherever this was it looked like a burnt-out world. Not the charred kind of burn, but depleted and completely used up sort.

Vacant.

Sitting still wasn't really a strong trait of mine, so I figured I'd get up and take a look around, there had to be something to see around here. If my body was actually somewhere else for safekeeping, what harm could come to me, right?

I staggered like I'd never stood before, struggling to get my balance. Whatever was going on with me, my equilibrium was totally shot. Standing there swaying like grass in the breeze, I turned carefully trying to see if there was anything around me except rust tinted dirt and nothingness.

My heart stumbled around in my chest when I spotted someone coming in my direction. Yes! I wasn't the only one in this soulless place.

The closer it got to me made me the more I questioned my original conclusion. I didn't know, exactly, but it was not some*one* it was a some*thing*. No one label could describe it. Standing over six feet, it had the shape of a man dressed in jeans and a large, very out of fashion gingham snap up shirt. When I reached the face, I can only describe it as part wrinkle puppy dog with floppy skin crossed with Freddy and Jason after the slash scenes.

It stopped in front of me and instinct had me reach around behind me under my jean jacket for my raptor claw knife, which I put on as regular as underwear when dressing; and that would be everyday, by the way. Relief washed over me when I felt the small circular handle. At least while waiting to survive I got to bring my toys with me.

Big brown eyes assessed me slowly and I wanted to make the call that it was harmless, but yeah, having tracked down anything from a sicko killer to a card shark in the last three years, I knew better than to fall for sappy looks.

"Are you a magishian? You juisht appeared."

A male voice, even though he spoke with a heavy lisp that randomly inserted *ish* into his words. Then again if I had saggy lips like he did, I'd be happy to talk at all. I sized him up for a few more seconds, trying to gauge whether he was really in front of me, or if I was having some sort of psychotic episode. Was a magician good or bad? I decided the play dumb, being blonde did have *some* advantages. "A magician?"

Those brown eyes developed a nervous quiver. Magician equaled bad. "No…"

He looked relieved. "Oh good. I didn't want to have to bash you over the head."

I grasped my raptor tightly and shrugged. "Yeah, me either."

The sky brightened and began to glow a rust orange color. When I asked for some color, I'd hoped for something out of the orange family.

"We better go, they'll be coming soon."

"They?" I glanced around quickly, not wanting to take my eyes off him for long.

He nodded and pranced on the spot, the nervous movement had me on high alert. "The daywalkers." He whispered.

Daywalkers? Did I even want to know? I didn't think so, but this bizarre nightmare wasn't going to be complete if I didn't ask.

Looking me over a few times, his eyes widened under the pressure of his drooping forehead; *that* was quite the expression. "You're not one of them, are you?"

I walked in the day, night and even at dusk, but I wasn't going to tell him that. I decided honesty might work, if not violence was always a good backup. Judging by his expression daywalker ranked on the bad list with magician. "I—I don't know what you'd call me."

Those sappy eyes looked me up and down a few times trying to figure me out. "You better come with me. It's not safe to leave you wandering around." He looked behind him and then motioned behind me and started walking.

I knew in my gut it was a mistake, but as I had no other real options… I didn't know where I was or what was going on and so far he knew more than I did. "Where are we going?"

Pausing he glanced over his shoulder and then lumbered along again. "I'll take you to Troy, he'll know what to do."

My eyes were starting to strain as the sky brightened. "This Troy, he's in charge?"

He stopped so suddenly I almost ploughed right into his back. When he turned and looked at me, his eyes weren't a sad brown any more but were leaning more towards red. It had to be from the strange color of the sunrise. "You're not from Alterealm are you?"

"Is that where we are?"

He nodded.

"Nope."

That nervous jitter of his seemed to return all at one. "How did you get here?"

A reasonable question that I had nothing to offer that resembled an answer. "I don't know that either."

His red eyes darted to the sky. "We have to go."

Turning, he began jogging toward, well, nothing that I could see. Not wanting to find out what he was afraid of, I ran along behind him. All I could think was this Troy person, if he was a person, better have some answers.

He stopped again and dropped down onto his knees. Was he hurt? Surely that short jaunt hadn't winded him that much. He began tapping his hand on the ground. What was he doing? Looking all around us, I kept watch for anything really, not wanting to meet these daywalkers in the slightest. Just when I'd had about enough of his short break, he grasped something in the sand and pulled a door in the ground open.

"We're going to have to use the shortcut. We don't have time to get to the main gates."
Looking down into a hole with a ladder, I glanced around again and despite every muscle in my body telling me to run and get the hell out of here, I started down the metal rungs into a deep hole that would take me, hopefully back to friggin' reality.

About Jacqueline Paige

Jacqueline Paige lives in Ontario in a small town that's part of the popular Georgian Triangle area.

She began her writing career in 2006 and since her first published works in 2009 she hasn't stopped. Jacqueline describes her writing as *all things paranormal*, which she has proven is her niche with stories of witches, ghosts, psychics and shifters now on the shelves.

When Jacqueline isn't lost in her writing, she spends time with her five children, most of whom are finally able to look after her instead of the other way around. Together they do random road trips, that usually end up with them lost, shopping trips where they push every button in the toy aisle, hiking when there's enough time to escape and bizarre things like creating new daring recipes in the kitchen. She's a grandmother to eight (so far) and looks forward to corrupting many more in the years to come.

Jacqueline also writes under the pseudonym of J. Risk

Jacqueline loves to hear from her readers, you can find her at

http://jacquelinepaige.com

Author note:

Did you enjoy reading one of my books?

If so, PLEASE help spread the word on social media. You can help by sharing on Facebook, tweet about it, post something on Instagram, Pinterest. Posting a review on your favorite book sites go a long way to help authors. With your help in keeping my books "out there", I can continue writing to keep those stories coming.

Writing and promoting can be very time consuming. I love talking to readers, but the hours spent on keeping so many social media outlets current can become overwhelming and time for writing pays the price. If you can take a few minutes to help, that would be awesome. Thank you!

www.ingramcontent.com/pod-product-compliance
Lightning Source LLC
Chambersburg PA
CBHW021146110726
47900CB00002B/453